Picture This

Camden Grove Series: Book Two

Tessa Kinkade

88 Plumes Press

Picture This

Copyright © 2023 by Tessa Kinkade

88 Plumes Press

All rights reserved.

ISBN Paperback: 978-1-958994-05-4 (paperback)

ISBN eBook: 978-1-958994-04-7 (ebook)

Editor: Danielle Dimond

Cover Design: The Write Design and Pretty Indie Cover Design www.prettyindie.com

For Eli
because you get it.

Also By

Tessa Kinkade

Camden Grove Series

The Perfect Shot
Waiting for You

Chapter One

Ava

All Ava Fenn needed was a place to forget and be forgotten. She just wanted to start over. When she pulled into the drive of her newly purchased home, she hoped she'd made the right decision.

Is starting over just my version of running away?

That question had gripped her thoughts every day since before summer.

She put the car in park, rested her hands on the steering wheel, and peered up at the bungalow in front of her. The tapered columns framed a spacious porch, and she decided at a glance that the trellis, layered in a lush tapestry of pink climbing roses, offered just the kind of privacy she'd need on those lazy summer afternoons when she swayed in the porch swing in its shade.

She also scanned the street and could see the knob of the cul-de-sac, where a couple of kids rode bikes in circles at the keyhole. With a deep breath, she stepped out of the car and yanked the SOLD sign from its perch in the front yard.

At least she had one friend here. That would be enough. Carly Kirkpatrick had been the one to convince Ava that Camden Grove would be a safe, quiet place to call home. She'd also been the glue holding Ava together through the whole fiasco that had been her life in the last few months—the disaster she still worried hadn't seen its end.

With key in hand, Ava opened her front door. Boxes stacked in every corner greeted her as she stepped into the entry. While packing back in Nashville, she'd bought color-coded stickers to go on each container and requested that the movers put them in specific rooms according to the color legend she handed them after signing the forms.

Color-blind movers.

After she set her purse on the floor, Ava peeled off her shoes and threw her jacket on top of a covered chair. They had put that in the right room at least.

The four-hour drive to Camden Grove had been tiresome, but she hoped the distance would be enough. When she looked at the boxes, the thought of unpacking exhausted her even more. She grabbed a water bottle from her purse and took a long, slow sip. Her phone jingled with the annoying ringtone she associated with the Nashville office. She made a mental note to change it and never to use that ringtone again.

Cradling the phone with her shoulder, she peeled back the tape on a packing box. "Hi, Paige, what's going on?"

"Hey Dr. Fenn, some mail came for you. Should I forward it to your new address, or will you be back in town?"

"New address is good. I'm hoping I'll have no reason to come back." Ava paused. "Look, Paige, I didn't have a chance to talk to you before I left. I wanted to tell you how much I appreciated working with you. I just . . . well, this has all been such a mess."

"I'm really sorry," the secretary lowered her voice. "Things shouldn't be this way, Dr. Fenn." Before Ava responded, Paige whispered, "I knew from the beginning you weren't involved with Dr. Simmons. I-I mean with any kind of fraud. Well . . . I should probably go."

Ava straightened her posture and clutched the phone. The muscles in her shoulders tensed with the mention of his name. "Thanks, Paige." She ended the call and put the phone on the coffee table.

Short as it was, the conversation left her head swimming with the need for that porch swing. No doubt, her life in Nashville had taught her two valuable lessons: one, don't place faith in someone just because he shows personal interest; and two, she should steer her own ship if she wanted to stay out of troubled waters. She hoped that Camden Grove would be the best place to dock that ship. Either way, she had no other choice.

As she focused on unpacking, Ava regretted not taking time to cull her old stuff when she'd left Nashville. She'd promised herself that after getting settled, she'd simplify and reduce. Those words had become her mantra.

When the phone rang a second time that evening, the living room had turned into a heap of black lawn bags full of papers, trinkets, and keepsakes no longer worth keeping. Climbing over the mess, Ava located her phone and saw the tawny, attractive image of her wavy-haired best friend smiling back at her.

"Hey." The tension in her voice hadn't dissipated much since the earlier call.

"Why, hello, Dr. Fenn," Carly said, her tone a cross between bubbly and badgering. "Did you not see it was me calling? You sound so serious."

"Sorry. Guess I'm a little touchy." Ava could tell Carly was on the move. "Where you headed? I can hear you in the car."

"Just pulling onto your street. Put on some shoes. We're going out for ice cream."

Ava pushed a box out of her way and looked out the window. "How'd you know I needed some Rocky Road?"

"You're not only serious, but you're also predictable. I'm guessing you're unpacking, dredging up all the old stuff your psyche needs to purge. That's what my therapist says old stuff does to you."

"You don't have a therapist."

"I know, but it's fashionable to say such things nowadays. Open your door for me. I'm almost there."

Ava had been friends with Carly since college when the housing office assigned them as roommates. They'd come from similar working-class backgrounds but with different ambitions and vastly contrasting ideas about how to manage campus life.

Carly spent most of her academic time in the photojournalism department and the rest trying to find the perfect specimens to photograph. That often found her on the practice fields at the University of Tennessee, which later landed her the top spot for the school newspaper's sports department.

For Ava, undergrad was her first plunge into workaholism. After a car accident claimed her parents, she allowed her class load to consume her—a combination of morning labs, afternoon tutoring, and evening study groups all providing the escape she needed.

Carly wouldn't allow her to fall into the well of self-pity and overwork, though. They complemented each other well and became even closer friends.

Staying in touch through med school hadn't been as easy, but they always connected during downtime, catching up on Carly's latest news assignment or the grossest of Ava's current medical studies. Residency had been much the same. But after Ava started practicing with Corbin Simmons, Carly made no secret she didn't like her friend's new gig or love interest. Her goal had always been to get Ava to move to Alabama, and she insisted that something was off-center about Corbin.

When Ava called her last month at the point of a nervous breakdown in the middle of the scandal, Carly took charge and helped her focus on starting over. In the end, she kept her emotionally afloat.

From the living room window, Ava watched an SUV pull into the drive. The magnetic sign on the driver's side door read *Then Comes Marriage Photography* in a flowery script. Photography was the passion Carly had pursued when her photojournalism dreams hadn't panned out. The local newspaper she worked at and planned to purchase had gone belly-up before she could afford a takeover, and as relationships went, Carly wasn't without her own battle scars. Only recently had she begun to step back into the dating scene.

As her friend approached the front door, Ava could see her auburn waves bouncing in rhythm with her step. Something about having an ally to take you for ice cream at dinner time made life seem a little more tolerable.

"New business name?" Ava stepped out onto the porch, purse in hand, and nodded toward Carly's car door.

"Yeah, clever, right? Jex is helping me rebrand, but I'll have to tell you about that later."

"About this new guy or the rebranding? I've still got to get the details on him, you know."

"Yeah, I know. C'mon, we need something rich, sweet, and refreshing first."

"Sounds like we're already talking about him."

"Well." Carly's lips curled at the mention. "I'll just say this. He's all the above. Now, let's get moving."

Dawson's Creamery stood, a quaint staple along the more modern side of Camden Grove's colonial-style courthouse. It sat between a family-operated drug store and a chic Southern boutique, the windows of which were bursting with the newest styles in linen.

Carly ordered a confetti scoop in a cup and parked herself in a corner booth. When Ava scooted into the bench across from her, holding a generous serving of Mint Chocolate Chip in a waffle cone, Carly's eyes came alive. "What's with you and the minty-ness, and where's my best friend? I thought Rocky Road was your flavor for life."

Ava took a defiant round-the-cone lick of her ice cream. "You're looking at someone who's ready for change. My life's been a rocky road for a long time now. I need a new flavor. Did I tell you I'm scrapping a lot of my old stuff? Simplifying and reducing. My new buzz words. And besides, the mint chocolate chip just sounded good."

"How introspective of you. Here I got you a new place, you're setting up a new office, becoming one of those zealots who have an empty house with two shirts in the closet, *and* you're rockin' a new ice cream flavor? This, my friend, is a bit much, don't you think?"

"What? Are you paying for my house now?"

"Hardly." Carly sucked on her loaded spoon. "But I do claim a reasonable percentage of responsibility for getting you in that little beauty at such a steal." A smug grin appeared over the top of her ice cream cup. "It pays to have a friend whose dad is in foreclosure banking. Wouldn't you agree?"

"Mmm." Ava stared at the cone. "This is delicious. Don't think I've ever tried mint before."

"Since you're all about the new, I have an idea. How about you help me with a little project to throw some business my way."

"Does this have anything to do with that Chicago trip last month and this new guy, Jex, with all the photography ideas? By the way, you've been a totally different person since you got back. I'm half afraid to ask what's up your sleeve."

"Different person, huh?"

"Yeah, it's like you got your old college sass back, times ten."

In the last month, Carly had shared a few of the new developments in her personal life, but with all the chaos of her own, Ava hadn't taken much time to get the details. It was good to see her friend perked up.

"Hm." Carly shrugged. "Imagine that."

"So?"

"So what?"

"Does it have something to do with Chicago and the new guy?" Ava prodded.

"Maybe." Carly buried her coy tone in a big bite of ice cream. With a swallow, she continued. "But, I'll fill you in on him later. Right now, I need your help."

"Sorry, I'm far from being on the hunt for a wedding photographer."

Carly waved her off. "That'll come eventually. But it's not a wedding shoot I want."

Ava continued to work on her cone.

"You remember Jessie, right?" Carly had partnered with Jessie Galloway to take on the role as an engagement photographer while Carly's specialty was capturing the big day.

"We met once."

"Yeah, well, she's had a lot going on with her mom lately. She's just gotten Mrs. Galloway settled in some kind of Alzheimer's assisted living place over in Hartley. And, among other things, because the *First Comes Love* photographer has been out of commission, our *Then Comes Marriage* photoshoots are taking a loss." She waved her spoon in circles between them. "You know, people like to line up our services together. Anyway, to drum up business, I need to feed the engagement schedule, and to feed the engagement schedule, I learned in Chicago—"

"From Jex?" Ava cocked her head.

"Yes, from Jex—that I need to think outside the box. Knock a few fresh ideas around. Basically, I want to try a little experiment to see if a new concept Jex and I have been working on would be feasible to generate some ads. Make sense?"

"Sorry, no engagement on the horizon for me, either, but if I hear of anybody—"

"No, that's just it. Let me explain."

"Before you get started, I've never been a good godmother to your brainchildren, and honestly, despite the fact that I've been completely negligent of our friendship, I've got a lot on my hands right now getting back on my own feet."

"That's why this is perfect! It would only be for a day. A Saturday, maybe. We just want to do this test run and I think we can get some great results. You know how I like to have all my ducks in a row before I go full-scale with anything."

Ava cut her eyes at Carly.

"At least let me tell you about it."

"I'm sure you're going to anyway."

"Exactly!" Carly settled into her seat. "Okay, so I just need you for a couple of hours at most. You'd get rid of your lab coat and come dressed in some cute little jeans and maybe one of those peasant tops—that would look adorable on you. Oh, and you could bring a dress. Something summery and feminine."

Ava swallowed a cold bite. "Now that we've got my wardrobe picked out. What am I supposed to be posing for?"

"Ready for this? You are going to be doing a *stranger* thing."

"When it comes to hanging out with you, I've already done stranger things than most, but I'm not sure I catch your drift."

"No, it's not you doing something strange. You kind of go on a . . . blind-date photoshoot. You know, with a stranger." She took the last bite of ice cream and licked the edge of the cup.

"Wait, are you saying I get all dressed up to take photos with a blind date?" Ava dropped her hand. The bottom of the waffle cone crunched against the table. "That's beyond strange, Carly. That's dumb." Her forehead wrinkled in confusion. "And what do we do? Just stand there and look awkward while somebody snaps a picture? That's the most ridiculous thing I've ever heard. I think your brainchild just suffered an aneurysm."

"Come on, give me a minute. I think it could be fun. We'd vet potential partners, and . . . think of it, a spontaneous afternoon, then it's no strings attached. It's even better than a blind date because you have an excuse to bow out. You know, you were just helping out a friend, everybody has a fun afternoon, and then, you get to leave."

"No, you're really just trying to get me to go on a date. This isn't me helping you with your business. It's you trying to fix me up and calling it a favor."

"Seriously, you *would* be helping me with my business . . . aside from any other possibilities, and take it from me, potential exists." Before Ava could respond, Carly continued, "Don't shut me off yet. Just think about it. We would set up boundaries, but you'd be posed in different settings, holding hands, hugging, looking into each other's eyes. Just think of it as your being a model for an engagement shoot."

"But I'm not engaged. I'm not a model. And I'm not interested."

Carly sighed, her words dragging through a vocal sludge. "Honestly, Ava. Go with me on this."

"For what purpose?"

"To help a friend in need . . . and maybe to see if any sparks fly," she quickly added.

"I once thought there was such a thing, but the only *honest*, elemental sparks I've had in the last ten years have been trying to get through chem classes in med school. I'm sure you can find somebody else with a taste for the kind of chemistry you're talking about."

"That's exactly why you'd be perfect. No expectations. No practice. Total spontaneity. It makes for fantastic candids."

Exasperation set in. "I don't think so. I don't need this in my life right now, Carly. You should find another friend."

"Everybody else is married. Besides, that's not the draw for a shoot like this. It's to see if, when you're put in an intimate situation with somebody you don't know, you find the fireworks. And if those fireworks are caught on camera, then that's the bonus for me."

Ava finished her waffle cone. "The answer"—she crumpled a napkin into a tight ball— "is no."

Carly's tone changed to pleading. "Come on, Ava. I helped you get a house for a fraction of what it's worth so you could put the extra funds toward the old newspaper office." Carly scooted up on the bench. "Won't you come do this as a favor for your best friend? We can scrap it all if it doesn't turn out."

Carly didn't often pull the guilt card, but Ava hated when she did. "And what will you do if it does turn out?"

"I'll get you on my calendar for some wedding shots in the near future?"

Ava's eyes widened. "That's not what I mean. If the photos were to look decent, I wouldn't be comfortable with your using them in ads. I came here to establish a reputable practice in Camden Grove. How would my patients respond if they've seen me in some cozy little picture with a guy I don't even know? That doesn't exactly scream professionalism."

"Already thought about that. We could shoot in the next town over—Hartley's booming with possibilities. In fact, I'm vying to get in the door with the Generations Bridal Boutique there. They have a sought-after wedding planner on staff, and she's in my sights. The only thing I'd possibly use your shoot for is to network with them at the next regional bridal fair. Show them some samples. This could be a big break for our business." Carly put on a droopy face. "I need this, Ava. Come on. Help me out."

Ava sat brooding in silence.

"Please?" Carly's voice rose an octave.

"I get all the veto power if this is a wash."

"All the power."

"And you can't pin me in a corner anymore about your helping me get the house or office."

"Never again."

"And my second scoop of ice cream is on you."

"Mint Chocolate Chip?"

"Blue Cotton Candy." Ava threw the wadded napkin on the table.

Carly rose from the bench. "You're getting more exotic every second."

Ava rolled her eyes. "Looks like."

Chapter Two

Logan

The construction office for Modern Design and Building sat on the dusty side of town along the last row of structures deemed the Industrial Park. Logan Carter had built his business, like most of the projects he'd completed, from the ground up. Holding his own in the ranks of builders for the Camden Grove and Hartley areas, he managed the workload much the way he handled life in general, from under the hard hat.

His workhorse approach served as the best replacement he could find for forging more personal things, like relationships. He'd wasted way too much time in that arena the second Eliza Montgomery stepped into his life eight years ago. But at least he had Toby. A six-year-old ray of sunshine was the only good thing that had come out of his train wreck of a marriage.

When the office door sprang open, he barely looked up. Pouring over the plans for a contract he'd been trying to win took priority over the visit from his twin brother.

"Hey man, you get much closer to those prints, and your nose'll be blue."

Logan eased back in his chair to face his mirror image, only in a suit and tie. "On lunch break?"

"Nope. Taking the afternoon off." Wyatt Carter plopped down in the chair across the desk from Logan, his jacket now unbuttoned and tie loosened.

"What brings you to the Grove? You land an account or something? Off early to celebrate?"

"Just wanted to come see my brother."

"You can look in the mirror and call me next time. Save you the drive."

"Nope. You seen yourself lately? I'm more handsome, so it wouldn't be the same."

Logan had long ago stopped rolling his eyes at the stupid things his brother said. Instead, he turned his attention back to his work. "Lydia okay?"

"Yeah, she's great. We've got a trip planned next week. Going to the mountains for a few days. I was wondering if you and Toby could come stay at the house and take care of Milo for me." Logan and Toby were the go-to sitters for their golden retriever with hypothyroid issues and a propensity for chewing socks.

"Guess we could do that. Just clear off a spot for me in your office. I've got a ton of work to do to get these plans ready. And you could also stock the fridge."

Wyatt nodded and pulled at his ear.

"So, what else are you doing here besides asking me to keep your chunky mutt alive?"

"He's sensitive about that, so don't go making fun of him." He cocked his head. "And what makes you think I want something else?"

"You just pulled at your ear. Mom always knew you were lying or stalling if you pulled at your ear."

Wyatt ignored Logan's question and ran a hand through his hair instead. "It'll do you some good to come to Hartley, watch Milo, and get out of Camden Grove for a while. Maybe get a breath of fresh air."

"Don't start."

"On what?" Wyatt shrugged.

"On why I should be dating and getting my life back together. Who put you up to it? Lydia?"

"She's worried about you too. You're sitting in this office all hours. Toby always has a great time through the summer with Mom and Dad, but you need to take a break, man, have some fun with him. The work'll be here when you get back."

"Now you're trying to tell me how to raise my boy?"

"You know better, and don't get all uptight. You've got the best kid around, but I think he's been missing you lately."

"Because you're suddenly the authority on six-year-olds."

"Because that's what he told Lydia when Mom and Dad brought him over last weekend."

Logan bowed his head and pinched the bridge of his nose. "That's what he said?"

Wyatt nodded. "Yep."

"I've been working late hours this last week, trying to keep a business afloat so he can have a good future."

"And that's a great thing. Just don't forget that he needs a good present, too, and that happens to involve you."

The silence lasted until Wyatt stood and crossed to the coffee pot on a corner table. "You thought about going out lately?"

"You mean on a date? First, you tell me I'm not spending enough time with my son. Then, you tell me I should take time away from him to go on a date. Make up your mind, brother. It can't be both ways."

"That could be good for you *and* Toby if you had some fun with another adult." Wyatt poured a cup. "Just throwing out some thoughts. Your frame of mind is beginning to show."

Logan crossed his arms and frowned. "What's that supposed to mean?"

"Just saying"—Wyatt took a long sip— "you look like a lumberjack with that beard. And how long has it been since you bought a new pair of jeans?"

"Look, I've got work." Logan nodded toward the blueprints. "You can leave me your house key. We'll take care of Milo while you're gone. Let me know when you want us to be there."

"Are you trying to hustle me out of here?"

"I'm trying to get some work done so I'll have time to spend with Toby."

Wyatt scanned the spread of sheets on Logan's desk. "Is that the Brashear building you're working on?"

"For weeks now."

"I know. Big scale changes for them. Our office was hired to beef up their ad campaigns and social media presence." He tapped a finger on the stack of papers. "You know, I could probably get you the in with Mr. Brashear."

"Nope. Don't need your help."

"Of course, you do. All this business needs is one huge project, and you'd have more contracts than you can handle."

"I've got more contracts than I can handle right now. Most of them are just not paying." Logan rubbed his stubbled jaw.

"You've wanted to add employees, but it takes revenue. And revenue comes from people who have the money waiting. Like Brashear. More money would give you more time with Toby." Wyatt pulled out his phone. "Here, listen to this."

He dialed and put it on speaker.

"Brashear Technologies, Sandra speaking."

"Sandra. Wyatt Carter here. How ya doing?"

"I'm well, thanks." A voice with a deep Southern drawl replied.

"Say, Sandra. I had a meeting scheduled with Mr. Brashear for next Friday at 3 p.m. We were finishing up a few of the layouts for the new campaign. But I'm having to go out of town next week and was wondering if I could push that meeting up to Tuesday?"

"Let me see." She paused. "Yes, it looks like he has a brief opening Tuesday at 10 a.m."

"Perfect. Oh, and Sandra, could we keep the Friday appointment open for Logan Carter? He's developing some blueprints for Mr. Brashear's new facility. I happen to be here with him now and was hoping to lock in that appointment for him."

"Brothers watching out for each other, I see," Sandra's saccharin voice purred. "Why, yes. I think I could do that."

"You're an angel." Wyatt winked at Logan. "Tell that good husband of yours I'm jealous."

The phone call ended, and Logan sat shaking his head. "How do you pull off such things?"

"I know her birthday. I know her favorite chocolates. And I send her flowers every time we score a campaign. Charisma goes a long way, brother. You should try it sometime."

"I guess you're waiting for me to say thanks, then."

Wyatt began to pick at a fingernail. "You should."

"So, you show up and ask me to take care of the dog, schedule an appointment to share blueprints with this man I've been trying to meet with for a month, and make me feel like I owe you something else. What is it? What else do you want?"

"We may have too much of the twin vibe going. I can't have you in my head."

"I've been in your head for years. It's a scary place."

"Well, since you asked. You remember Lydia's sister, Jessie?"

"Stop while you're ahead."

"Just shut up. You don't have to comply with what I'm asking. Just listen." He started again. "Lydia wanted me to talk to you about Jessie."

"I'm not going on a date with Jessie."

Wyatt sighed. "That's not it. She's trying to fill up her photography calendar and needs some help. Since she and Lydia had to put their mom in assisted living last month, her business has suffered, so she and her business partner are searching for a couple of people to do a photoshoot for some advertising. She wants a rugged type." He eyed his brother up and down. "And you, man, fit the bill if I've ever seen a bill fitter."

"Rough around the edges, maybe. But photogenic? I don't think so."

"You look like me. You're definitely photogenic." Wyatt smiled a dimpled grin. "You just need to spiff up a little."

"I don't do suits, and I don't do shoots."

"No, a suit's not what she wants. All you've got to do is trim the beard and buy a good pair of jeans. Maybe throw on a button-up shirt that doesn't look like it's been dipped in concrete."

Logan sat still for a moment. "Why don't you find somebody else? I'm apparently on a tighter deadline now that you've got this appointment for me."

"Lydia asked if I could get you to do it for Jessie. She thinks you'd be perfect."

"Ah, the truth comes out. You're under pressure from home and hearth."

"As they say, happy wife, happy life. And besides, now you owe me. Tell you what, I'll make you a deal. You get this contract? Then you do the shoot for Jessie. You're happy because you got the contract, and my wife's happy because Jessie's happy. We're all just one big ol' happy family. Right?"

"And if I don't get the contract?"

"I'm on the couch for a week because I didn't come through."

Logan smirked. "That's almost worth a good sabotage job."

"Just shake on it, man." Wyatt flashed another carbon copy of Logan's perfect smile and grabbed his brother's hand. "We'll be leaving for the mountains Tuesday evening. Milo'll be glad to see you and Toby."

"Yeah. Get outta here. I've got work to do."

"I'm going. I'm going." He opened the door to leave. "Oh hey, you might want to get those new jeans soon." Then, he ducked out in a hurry just before a paper wad bounced off the closing door.

Chapter Three

Ava

The small office building Ava purchased in the town's business district had been sitting empty for a while. Though Carly liked to remind her she'd gotten it at a good price, the cost of the renovations required to convert it to a doctor's office was racking up.

After her first walk-through in late spring, she'd discovered why the sale price had been within her spartan budget. The previous owners of the old newspaper office must have liked brown carpet, walls with yellow smoke stains, and dingy windows. No wonder the bank jumped at the chance of letting it go, and Ava didn't have much choice except to buy something cheap. Once she closed on the property, she began making calls to contractors to arrange the needed updates.

Now, a week after arriving in Camden Grove, Ava entered the front door of the building, hoping for a near-magical transformation. Instead, she found two dust-covered contractors huddled against the floor installing tile in the far half of the small waiting room. They looked up as she came inside.

"G'mornin', miss. Something we can help you with?" The oldest of the two men stood.

Ava scanned the room. "I'm, uh, Dr. Fenn. I was just coming to see the progress." Her hopes that she could open within a month settled in a heap right along with all the old grout dust. She needed a solid grand opening before school started, with parents lining up vaccinations and sports physicals. It was the best time besides flu season she could put out a shingle. But, looking around, she didn't know how it could all come together. "Do you think this can be ready by my contract deadline?"

"There's a lot of work to do, yet. If you walk through, you'll see that may be a lofty goal. A lot more than floor work has to be done in the back."

Ava stepped past the reception area. From room to room, panic began to bubble up in her throat. They were nowhere near ready for an opening. The drywall wasn't even up in two of the rooms, and electrical wires hung out of the studs like drooping bouquets. Not to mention the flooring, cabinets, and exam tables needed installing.

When she came back to the entry, the men were back at work, stooped again in the far corner of the room.

"Excuse me. Are you supposed to be working on the drywall and electrical too?"

The older man on the floor pulled up the back of his pants as he stood again. "No, ma'am. That's not our crew."

"What do you mean?"

"We're the tile contractors. You'll need to call the main man to find out when he's getting all that done."

She sighed. "When will you be finished with this room?"

The man shrugged his shoulders. "Probably in the next week or two. We've got another job to finish on the south side of town. We were just waiting on some materials, so we came here to work a few hours."

Ava put her hand to her head. "But I need this job done. I can't have the office half-finished on opening day."

"We'll do what we can. Shouldn't be a problem for us." He nodded toward the back rooms. "But past the lobby, you're looking at a lot of work in a little time. Don't know about that getting done by your deadline."

Ava stormed into the office space. That was the trouble with hiring people over the phone. Getting any kind of commitment was a rarity if you weren't face-to-face—sometimes even if you were—and chasing down contractors to finish their work was the last thing she needed.

As she scrolled through her phone to find the number of the man she'd hired, the screen lit up with Carly's face.

Ava huffed into the phone as she answered it.

"Hey, Doc, you sound mad."

"I've got a grand opening in a within month, and nothing is ready."

"Relax, it'll come together. In the meantime, let me brighten your day." Carly's voice rose to singsong. "I've got a surprise."

Ava manifested the enthusiasm of a slug. "What?"

"That photoshoot. I've got it all set up. Jessie's doing the pictures, and she's picked out a great match for you."

"Carly, I—"

"Don't you dare try to back out now. I've been counting on this, and so has Jessie. Besides, it'll be fun. Spontaneity, remember? Have you picked out your clothes yet?"

"When have I had the time? I'm playing construction manager these days."

"Go shopping. You have until Saturday. I'm sending you an address. It's at the Old Mill at Fordham Creek on the other side of Hartley. You should be there by four. Show up in the casual outfit and take the summer dress with you. There's an old barn there you can change in."

"Seriously?"

Carly sounded offended. "Yes, I'm serious. Now, plan for some fun. I can't wait to see the pictures."

"Wait, you said something about a match."

"Yeah, Jessie picked him out. Sounds like you two are totally compatible. He's a workaholic—you're a workaholic. He's not interested in relationships—you're not interested in relationships."

Ava breathed a little easier. "Perfect. Just so he and you and everybody knows this is a favor and not a real date."

"Definitely. But I'll tell you this: Jessie says he's pretty hot."

"Don't. Just don't, Carly." She could almost hear her friend smiling on the other end.

"Okay. Okay. Just be there Saturday."

"And where will you be?"

"I'm meeting Jex in Atlanta. He flew in from Chicago on business, so I'm driving over for the day. Doing some venue planning with a couple I've got on the calendar, so I can't be on-site with you. It's probably best, though. You might hold back if I'm there."

"Lucky for me."

"I'll call you Saturday night on my way home, see what kind of fire I've set." The phone clicked as Ava stood looking at the drooping electrical wires.

After shoving Carly's photoshoot to the back burner, Ava scrolled through her phone again and called the contractor she'd hired weeks back. On the fifth ring, his voice mail picked up. When the tone sounded, Ava's words spewed like steam from a pressure cooker. "This is Dr. Fenn. I hired you to do a remodel job at the old newspaper office, and I'm standing here right now in a heap of rubble. I'm supposed to open my door for business in less than a month. I have two men here putting down tile only because they're waiting on another job. Wires are springing out of the walls like fountains in a fishpond. I have no furniture or cabinets installed. And, I have naked studs everywhere. Are you planning to do something about this mess? Please call me as soon as possible."

When Ava ended the call, she rubbed the back of her neck and then realized the regrettable part of what she'd just spouted into some man's voice mail. "Naked studs?" she whispered as she palmed her head.

Chapter Four

Logan

Tuesday evening, Logan left the construction office and pulled into his parents' drive just at the finish of dinner. Toby came running to the truck and jumped into his dad's arms.

"Hey, Peanut Butter. How's it going?" Logan ruffled the boy's straight blond hair as they walked toward the house. "You have a good day with Nana and Pops?"

"We washed Nana's car and made cookies and ate watermelon and watched cartoons."

"You've been busy, then."

"Wish you could've been here."

A twinge of guilt settled in the bottom of Logan's stomach. "Yeah, well, we've got to get your things and go to Uncle Wyatt and Aunt Lydia's house. We're taking care of Milo for the next few days. He's probably ready to play."

The boy's eyes lit up. "I can't wait to see Milo."

"Thought you might like that." Logan opened the door to the house.

"Like what?" Logan's mother, wearing an apron and perpetual smile, came to the door drying her hands with a kitchen towel.

"We're taking care of Milo, Nana."

"Oh, you better get your things, then. You might want to take some of those cookies we made. They're in a bag on the bar along with a dinner plate for your daddy." She turned to Logan. "You want to sit down and eat here?"

He shook his head. "Nah, thanks, though. We need to go. I've still got work to do."

"You work too much," the rough bass voice of his father rang through the entry as he came around the corner.

"I know, Dad. You tell me every time I see you."

The man's forehead wrinkled in waves. "So, when you gonna change that?"

"I've got bills to pay and a son to raise. I can't be on a constant vacation."

"No, but you *can* slow down." He nodded toward Toby running into the kitchen. "He won't be young forever, and you could run yourself in the ground if you're not careful."

"Maybe I take after you." Logan squeezed his dad's shoulder. "Haven't seen you slowing down lately."

His mom cut in, pointing her finger at him. "You're still taking time off for Toby's party next weekend, right?"

"Of course. I wouldn't miss his birthday. Thanks for putting a little something together for him."

"We're glad he wanted to have it here, aren't we, dear?" She turned to her husband.

The older man nodded. "He's the life in our day."

"Toby's been awfully thirsty today. Your dad took him outside to wash the car, so he was out in the heat for a while. He drank a lot when we came in, so I think he's hydrated. After that and eating watermelon for dessert a while ago, you may want to make sure he uses the bathroom before he goes to bed."

Logan always left with a laundry list of instructions from his mother based on their daily activities. Summer at the grandparents was never dull for Toby, nor did it lack in orders for Logan at the end of each day. He could've recited from heart most of those directives, but as he watched his mother help Toby with his backpack, Logan couldn't help but appreciate that his son had the influence of a good woman in his life.

Wyatt and Lydia owned a home on a ten-acre plot with a lake bordering one side and trees on the other. The long drive, shrouded under the arms of old pines, opened onto a meadow where the cabin stood. Wyatt had always said his house would be a retreat, and he had stayed true to his dream.

As they arrived, Logan parked the truck and loaded his arms with a cylinder of blueprints and the dinner plate and cookies his mother sent, while Toby pulled his backpack from the truck. Milo, the plump golden retriever, greeted them at the door with a soggy gift of one of Wyatt's old socks.

"Good boy, Milo." Logan tossed the sock on the couch. "But you've got to get a better-smelling chew toy."

Toby set his backpack at the door and began a low-key wrestling match on the floor with Milo.

After unloading his arms, Logan opened a bag of dog chews left on the table beside a note from Wyatt.

"Here, Milo. Looks like you need a treat."

The dog jumped up from his play session and wobbled across the room as Logan skimmed the note and Toby got a bottle of water from the fridge:

Chews are for Milo only after he's gone outside and done business.
Saturday, 4 p.m., Old Mill at Fordham Creek for photos.
Buy clothes and trim up beforehand.
The sexy twin, W

"Just remember, Milo, your master is really the evil twin." Logan gave the dog another treat and opened the back door to let him out. He asked Toby. "You want to go toss the ball for Milo a little while?"

"Sure. Are they still making him exercise?"

"Yep, Aunt Lydia says he's gotta lose ten pounds." Logan whispered, "They just want him to think he's having fun."

The boy shrugged and took off out the door.

"Don't stay out for long. We need to clean up and get to bed early tonight," Logan called after him.

Toby played with Milo until the evening heat diffused into a summer haze and dew blanketed the grass. Logan ate the warmed-over dinner plate while he watched Toby and Milo from the back porch. The boy's laughter and the dog's barking echoed across the yard. The lightning bugs made flashing constellations against the dusk, and, for the first time in a long time, Logan sat and did nothing.

The next morning, Logan was up by sunrise and parked at the kitchen table with Milo under his feet. He sketched for a couple of hours while Toby slept. When his phone rang, he was pouring the last cup of morning coffee into a travel mug.

"Hey, chief. You wake up with Milo in bed beside you this morning?" Wyatt sounded his usual chipper self.

"Nope. His behind is usually parked at the side of my head, but he hung with Toby last night."

"You should feel so lucky. You get my note on the table?"

"I got it." The thought of the photoshoot crossed his mind. "But we haven't closed the deal yet. I've still got to meet Brashear on Friday. I may not get the contract."

"You'll get it, and even if you don't, you'd better show up at the Old Mill so I have some warm, cozy nights with Lydia while I'm here in the mountains. I'll have to owe you one."

"Just like you to modify on the fly. You learn to do that in college?"

"I'm trying to keep the wedded bliss, man. You'll understand that someday when you give it another shot."

"Count me out."

"That's exactly where my money is after . . ."

"After what?"

"Nothing. Gotta go. Lydia's heading out the door in one of those little tennis skirts. Just make sure to give Milo a snack for pooping outside, and don't forget to buy some clothes."

The phone clicked. Logan wondered what Wyatt was up to. *Clothes shopping? Good grief.* Milo nosed Logan's hand, the cue to let him out. "You've got a doggie door. Why don't you use it, old boy?"

Milo stared at him with an innocent expression.

"Go on. I don't have all day. Too many things to do." The dog waddled outside, unenthused.

"Toby?" Logan started gathering his things as he called up the stairs, "Come on, buddy. I need to get to work."

A moment later, the boy appeared at the kitchen table in drenched pajamas. "Dad?" He looked down at his pants.

"Ah, Tobe." Logan checked his frustration when he saw the boy's face. "C'mon sport, we'll rinse off and change. We just need to do it fast. I've got some calls to make."

He set everything back on the table and ran Toby upstairs to the tub. As Logan turned on the water and began to help peel off the wet clothes, Toby's eyes glistened. "I'm sorry Dad. I didn't mean to."

"Hey, now." Logan knelt and held his son by the shoulders. "Don't you worry about this. Everybody has accidents sometimes."

"Yeah, but if I hadn't wet the bed, you'd be able to go to work."

Logan's heart sank. He pulled the boy to his chest and held him for a long moment. "You know what? Work isn't everything." He paused. "What do you say we do some fishing today?"

The little boy wiped his eyes. "Really? You mean it?"

"Tell you what, let me make some phone calls while you get cleaned up, and we'll make a morning of it at the lake. Uncle Wyatt's bound to have some rods around here somewhere."

Logan set a fresh change of clothes in the bathroom while he tried not to think of all the jobs he was leaving undone. The remodel gig downtown in Camden Grove was at the top of the pile. The sassy message he'd gotten from the lady doctor the day before had left him with a whole list of jobs to sub if he didn't do them himself, not the least of which was addressing the *naked studs* she was so flustered about. He'd let things slide on that job since he'd been so tied up working on plans for the Brashear building, and she'd be chewing his ear some more if he didn't get back on track soon.

Back in the kitchen, he scrolled through his phone after letting Milo back inside. When he landed on the number he wanted, he tapped call and watched the dog wobble up the stairs toward Toby.

"Dakota. It's Logan. I've got a job I need you to do."

On the other end, he heard the rapping of a hammer. "Sure. Man, I'm finishing a up a residential right now but should be able to help you in a couple weeks."

Logan ran a hand through his hair. "No way to squeeze me in any earlier? It's an office remodel for that new doctor coming to Camden Grove, and I'm sitting in hot water. It's partially done. Wires are run. Just some finish work left."

"What's your time frame?"

"Yesterday."

"I can stop by and take a look."

Logan smiled. "Saturday?"

After they settled on a meeting time, Logan tossed Milo a treat and breathed a momentary sigh of relief.

Dakota Renshaw was one of the handful of people Logan trusted enough to subcontract for him—trusted enough to call a friend. Having come to town fresh out of prison the same week Toby was born, Dakota had seen Logan framing out Wiggs's Barbeque Place, stopped, and asked for a job. Had Logan not been knee-deep in deadlines and needing some time off to help Eliza with a new baby, he might've passed on the request. An ex-con wasn't exactly his first choice for a new hire. Dakota had been upfront about his circumstances, though, and something about that kind of honesty and the fact that he didn't wear his prison time like a badge, pulled at Logan enough to give the man a chance. It turned out to be one of the best business decisions he'd ever made. The man's work potential far outweighed his past, and his friendship had proven even more valuable.

In fact, Logan's good turn came back around only a couple of years later when Eliza left. Wyatt was away in Atlanta, and Logan's parents turned to Dakota, asked him to stay close to their son, because they knew he was bad off. Lots of deep conversations and few all-nighters later, Logan started picking up the pieces of his life, focusing on Toby and his construction business.

Shaking the memory from his thoughts, Logan took a long drink from his mug, and began assessing the next week. If he could push the doctor back a few days, and if Friday's meeting with Brashear went well, he would catch the couple of breaks he needed to keep his promises and see some progress.

Chapter Five

Ava

The following Saturday afternoon, an overcast sky hinted at rain, but Carly had always said lighting on those kinds of days worked best for pictures. No squinting from the sun and a much softer look even without filters. When Ava arrived at the Old Mill, the museum traffic had cleared, and the curator had posted the Closed sign and locked up.

Fordham Creek Mill had once been a booming business for the town of Hartley before it declined to a decaying piece of historical architecture. Built in the 1930s, it had all but become a heap of ruins when the archeology department paired with the architecture division of the local college and proposed a restoration to put the grist mill back in working order.

In its second life, it became a functioning machine again, open for museum tours at posted times throughout the year. The updated facilities often served as the venue for weddings, reunions, and several Christmas events when it was decorated to the hilt with white lights and mistletoe around the holidays.

Though Carly had mentioned the place before as a favorite spot for photoshoots, Ava had never imagined how beautiful the old water wheel was. She could see from the upper side of the lot, as she parked her car, its slow-spinning buckets pouring and dipping.

Carly had told Ava to look for a blue Civic and that Jessie would be the athletic-built redhead with the big camera. As she stepped from her car, Ava spotted Jessie coming around the side of the museum toward the parking lot. "Dr. Fenn? Are you Dr. Fenn?"

"Please, call me Ava. You must be Jessie."

"Tried and true." She nodded toward the building. "I just came from the museum, and they're letting us use their outdoor bathrooms for changing instead of you having to skinny down in the barn."

Ava laughed nervously. "That's a relief."

"Let's go ahead and get you inside. Your date should be pulling up anytime."

The word made her cringe a little. "Um, 'date'?"

Jessie motioned for Ava to follow her. "Carly said you'd probably be a little nervous. Don't worry. I can already tell you'll be a natural."

Ava glanced toward the road. They rounded the corner of a modern building made to appear old, and Jessie opened an outer door to a large bathroom.

"Right in here. There are hangers on the back of the door. You can put your dress there. And, by the way, you look adorable in that outfit." She winked. "This'll be so much fun."

Ava had settled on the camp shirt and jeans Carly had suggested. "Do you think it'll take very long? The shoot, I mean?" She rubbed her stomach to calm the nerves.

"Not long, but you may get so caught up that time will just fly by." She turned to the door. "Now, before I go get our guy, I should tell you his name's Logan, and he is definitely easy on the eyes. Oh, and speaking of eyes, I've got a blindfold I want you to wear for the reveal." She pulled a red bandanna from her back pocket and handed it to Ava.

"Wait. What?"

"It's all a part of the shoot. You'll both be blindfolded, and I'll bring you to stand in front of each other. When I give the green light, you'll take the blindfolds off and fall completely in love. Now, I'll be back in a minute to get you."

"Hey, what do you mean—?"

Jessie had already pivoted and slid through the door.

By the time Ava hung her dress on the hook, she'd begun to fume. Carly's photoshoot had become a turkey shoot, and she was the turkey. She sat on a stool in the corner and jerked her phone from her purse.

On the fifth ring, Carly answered. "I know what you're going to say, but just stop. You've been alone now for too long."

"Too long? I've not been single for a full two months and you think I should jump back on the bandwagon? This coming from the woman who went an entire year shunning any mention of a man?"

"Yes, I know, but I was wrong. I was *so* wrong. Anyway, we're not talking about me. You can't help that the only guy you ever cared about turned out to be a criminal jerk no more than I could help the fact that my first love was a rotten philanderer right under my nose. The fact is you can take control of what happens next. It's time to move on, Ava. I'm just trying to help you get started."

"Carly Kirkpatrick, I can't believe you set me up."

"Like I told you from the beginning, no strings attached. I just wanted to put a few stars in your eyes again. This guy may *not* be a match for you, but even if he's not, you don't need to waste time like I did. The truth is if anyone deserves to be happy, it's you."

Ava didn't cave to Carly's compliment. "If you were here right now, I would—"

"Wait 'til you see Logan, then finish that thought."

"Oh, you're insufferable, and I'm not wearing a blindfold."

"Make some good pictures for me, love. And wear the blindfold." The phone went dead.

Chapter Six

Logan

On the way to the Old Mill, Logan re-ran in his head the meeting with Mr. Brashear the day before. The plans he'd worked on for weeks would require only a few adjustments. He would finalize those with Brashear and the board and then start on the job next week. Things really couldn't have gone much more smoothly. And to beat all, he had his brother to thank.

Before the meeting with Brashear, Logan had considered bowing out of doing the shoot. Hadn't Wyatt said there would be a couple of people there to help with photos? At least one other person could possibly step in for him. But, after everything went so well with Brashear, a little guilt set in, and going back on the deal didn't seem right.

Maybe Jessie could take just a couple of shots and call it good. He needed to get back to Camden Grove anyway. The work he'd gotten behind on from the day of fishing with Toby and the extra hours with the Brashear project had stalled him enough that he'd be scrambling to get everything covered as it was. And he still had the feisty doctor to appease.

At least his parents had offered to watch Toby for the weekend. He'd been so excited about the spontaneous fishing trip that he'd called his Pops and Nana on the way home that day to tell them of the bluegill he'd caught. That report had earned Logan at least a minimal break from his parents' nudges to take time off. He'd have to use the extra hours to catch up on work.

As he drove into the Old Mill parking lot, he recognized Lydia's red-headed sister mounting a camera to a tripod beside a Civic he thought was hers. The only other car in the lot was a white Prius. After parking his truck, he took a deep breath and put on a smile.

"I'm so glad you made it. You're right on time." Jessie folded the legs of the tripod and leaned it against the car.

Logan nodded. "It's been a long time. I think the last I saw you was at Wyatt and Lydia's wedding. You and your sister look more alike all the time."

"People say that a lot, but you would know how that feels, having a twin." As they walked from the lot, Jessie chattered about locations to shoot, and Logan followed her. Then, she fully settled into photographer mode with her first request. "I want you to come with me down to the water." She pointed to the massive rotating wheel. "You and I'll set up down here, and then I'll bring her out. Her name's Ava."

Jessie kept walking, but Logan stopped. By the time she realized he wasn't following, she was ahead a good ten paces. "What's wrong?"

"You said you'll bring her out . . . and her name's Ava?"

"Right, that's the way we set up a stranger shoot." She eyed the confusion on Logan's face. "Oh no, Wyatt didn't tell you, did he?" Jessie set the tripod on the ground. "Well, all the more of a surprise, I guess."

"Can you explain to me what Wyatt failed to tell me?" Logan squinted his eyes.

Jessie tilted her head. "Well, in this session, we're bringing two people together who haven't met each other before." She drew up her shoulders. "It's kind of a blind date. Except you treat it like an engagement session with hand-holding and touching and maybe even kissing, like an engaged couple would do."

"Where on earth did this idea come from?"

"It's a new trend." Jessie's words came more quickly. "It's actually been a big hit and generated a lot of chat on social media and in photography circles."

He started shaking his head. "I didn't sign up for this."

Jessie's disappointment showed. "I get it." She sighed. "But . . . but what if you just went along for the reveal, and we played it by ear from there?"

"The reveal?"

"Yes, I take you to the site and blindfold you, and then I bring her to you, and you both remove blindfolds at the same time. Big reveal. Surprise." Jessie sang her last words.

Logan cut his eyes at her. "I don't—"

"You'd be doing me a huge favor," she pleaded, her hands clasped in front of her. "If this goes well, I might be able to at least show a couple of people the samples and drum up some business. I could really use the help." She paused and dropped her hands. "What do you say? We're already here."

Logan bowed his head and thought of what Wyatt had said about Jessie's business taking a hit lately. He knew what it meant to need support. Since Eliza left, his parents had helped take care of Toby, his brother and Lydia had helped him work through divorce that seemed unthinkable, and Dakota had helped him finish jobs he'd already contracted but would have never completed alone. For a moment, Logan stood with folded arms and considered his options. "If I give the sign, we're done."

She sliced her finger across her neck. "Finito, the second you call it."

Another few seconds passed. Then, "Where do you want me?"

Jessie clapped her hands together and probably would have jumped up and down if she hadn't had a camera hanging from her neck. "Right this way." At the foot of the small bank, not far from the water's edge, she led Logan to a flat boulder. "You sit right here." She handed him a blue bandanna. "In five minutes, I want you to put this over your eyes, and I'll lead her down here to you."

Logan reluctantly took the blindfold and a deep breath. "Okay." Before Jessie turned to go back up the hill, he stopped her. "Hey, if I crack my knuckles, that's the sign."

Jessie nodded with wide eyes. "Gotcha. Cracking knuckles." Then she pivoted and headed back up the bank.

Maybe, if he were lucky, Jessie would see nothing through the lens worth photographing, and they could make this quick work. Until then, he was apparently at the mercy of a woman or two—a place that, after Eliza, he'd counted on never being again.

Chapter Seven

Ava

Had Jessie not been so excited, Ava would have put up more of a fuss about the blindfold. Somehow, she always softened when someone was happy. That's how Dr. Corbin Simmons had lured her. Perpetually optimistic and always smiling, he was as bewitching as a panther but had the morals of an alley cat—memories that caused her to bristle at her own naiveté.

Before thoughts of the past consumed her, she redirected her thoughts and wondered for the twelfth time why she'd let Carly talk her into such nonsense. When Jessie returned to lead her toward the water's edge, the butterflies in Ava's stomach whipped up a small twister.

"Okay, we're all set."

As Jessie led her by the hand, Ava eased down the embankment with the blindfold on. She was glad that at least she'd opted for a comfortable pair of flats.

"Watch your step." Jessie guided her. "He's just a little farther."

"Is he already blindfolded, too?"

"Um-hm, all set. This is going to be so delicious."

Ava would have rolled her eyes had she not been destitute of vision and worried about falling on her face. She gained better traction once the ground leveled under her feet. As she drew closer to the stranger, her thoughts began to swim. *What if he's shorter?* She couldn't do short. *What if he has halitosis?* She shuddered. *What if he's a lot younger?* She didn't do cougar, either.

The closer they got, the wilder her thoughts became. *Good grief, what if he's crazy?* Why was she even thinking of all these things? It wasn't like they were going out for a burger afterward. She'd give him no details. None. *Keep it simple. Yeah, simplify and reduce.* Ava felt better with her mantra rolling in her head. If she were lucky, this wouldn't last long, and Carly said he'd know the boundaries.

"You're setting up ground rules, right?"

"Oh, definitely. Almost there. Then, you'll both get the do's and don'ts, and we'll get to the big moment."

A few more steps and Jessie stopped. The flutter in Ava's stomach worsened.

"Okay." Jessie sounded out of breath. "You're standing right in front of each other, but don't take off the blindfolds yet. We've got to talk first. Let me just step over to my camera and get my notepad. I wrote down a few things to tell you."

Ava touched her covered eyes. Jessie hadn't tightened the bandanna too firmly for fear that she'd smudge Ava's makeup. A good thing. At least she could get a peek at the guy's shoes. She once read a study that proved you could tell with ninety-percent accuracy a man's personality traits just by looking at his shoes.

Maybe she could know whether to bolt for the parking lot before the guy even shed his blindfold. Birkenstocks with dirty toenails would definitely do her in.

Ava raised her eyebrows to lift the fabric and peeked toward the ground. Looked like he had on a new pair of jeans. Too crisp to be worn in. At least he wasn't a total slob. But new jeans? Was he out to impress? At least they weren't ironed, so he wasn't obsessive-compulsive.

She stretched her mouth to lengthen her face. The blindfold shifted, a little looser now, her view a little clearer. Hiking boots. He was an outdoorsman. They were worn in a little, not kid-on-the-first-day-of-school new. So, he might actually hike. No flashy colors—brown, with a nice little stripe down the side—so he was probably pretty conventional. Size eleven, maybe twelve. Not outrageously huge, which meant he was tall but not monstrous.

"All right. Let's get started." Jessie cleared her voice. "Number one, I'll be shooting non-stop before you ever take off your blindfolds so we can capture every second. Number two, I want the whole experience to be as candid as possible. Just visit and have fun. Number three, I may pose you a few different ways in the beginning, but then you see what feels natural. Number four, you don't have to do anything you're uncomfortable with—"

"Wait." Logan stopped her. "So, we'll be touching each other." Ava's ears perked up. The first sounds from him were a little sandpapery, his voice almost familiar, maybe like one of the residents she'd worked with back in Nashville or someone she'd met at the dry cleaners.

"That's right," Jessie clarified. "Just like you'd known each other for a long time."

"Um, but not a really long time, right?" Ava tried to make her point without sounding nervous.

"Exactly." Jessie continued, "Number five, you don't have to kiss, but I will tell you, that's the ultimate in a session like this. Just something to keep in mind."

"Um, I think we'll just keep it simple." Ava nearly squeaked.

"Yeah, I'm good with that."

Was that relief in his voice?

"No worries." Jessie jumped in. "I'm not pushing anything, just opening the door. And number six, just pretend I'm not here. That'll make this shoot the best."

From the rustling of the grass, Jessie shuffled back toward her tripod. "Okay, are we ready?"

No one said anything.

Jessie's voice rang out, "Strip!"

"What?" both Logan and Ava called out.

"The blindfolds." Jessie giggled. "Take off the blindfolds."

They both laughed a little, then loosened their bandannas.

Chapter Eight

Logan

When Logan had heard Jessie coming down the path with the girl, his jaw tensed, and he squeezed and loosened his fists, a nervous habit he'd picked up since the day he came home and found the note on the table. Hard to believe that had been three years ago.

When it all happened, he called his mother first, terrified that Eliza had taken Toby with her. Then, he waited for Eliza to come back with the conviction that it'd all been some crazy misunderstanding, and he'd take her back without hesitation, without question.

When she didn't come home, he called her sister, the only person who knew her better than probably even he did. Molly had been the one to tell him that Eliza always wanted to live in California, that she didn't want him or Toby anymore. The divorce papers came a month later.

Logan tightened his fist again. Maybe Wyatt was right. Maybe it was time to get his mind on something besides work. He hadn't dated a single woman since the breakup. Even though commitment wasn't in his cards, as far as he was concerned, he had to admit that shying away from women wasn't setting any kind of example for Toby. The muscles in his hand loosened.

Logan's attention shifted when he heard Jessie's voice getting closer.

"Watch your step, now. He's just a little farther."

"Is he already blindfolded, too?" He could hear the woman. She had a soft voice, lower than Jessie's—subtle, reserved.

"Um-hm, all set. This is going to be so delicious."

Logan tightened his fist.

"You're going to set up ground rules, right?"

The woman sounded as nervous as he was. He loosened his fist and stood from the rock where Jessie had placed him. He wondered if he should start cracking his knuckles now.

"Okay. You're standing right in front of each other, but don't take off the blindfolds, yet."

The whole time Jessie went on with her set of numbered rules, he thought about how to get out of this if it turned into a sideshow and if Jessie didn't take his knuckle popping hint. His fists tightened and loosened like a pumping heart. Before he could manage a plan, he caught the scent of something sweet, maybe it was rose . . . or honeysuckle . . . or maybe it was jasmine. Just a hint. Jasmine. His fists loosened. Then he heard Jessie say something about poses.

"Wait." He cleared his throat. "So, we'll be touching each other."

"That's right." Jessie sounded so chipper. "Just like you'd known each other for a long time."

He could hear the woman in front of him shift in the dry grass. "Um, but not a really long time, right?"

"Exactly." Jessie sounded hesitant. "Number five, you don't have to kiss—"

Kiss? What in the name of—?

"Um, I think we'll just keep it simple." The girl's voice broke.

"Yeah, I'm good with that." Thank goodness she said something before he did.

Jessie's voice faded. She was getting in place. His fists tightened, and his mind raced to the same tempo as his heartbeat.

"Okay, are we ready?"

Deep breath. Fists hard as rocks.

"Strip!"

"What?" He heard the woman's voice ring a pitch higher than his own.

"The blindfolds." She giggled. "Take off the blindfolds."

Another deep breath, and then a laugh escaped from somewhere.

He loosened his fists and reached for the bandanna.

Chapter Nine

Ava

W hen the blindfold slipped from her face, she steeled herself before looking up. As her eyes made contact with his, the tension in her jaw went slack. Carly said the guy was handsome, but she wasn't prepared for him to be . . . well . . . like *this*.

Her blind imaginings of him had been pretty accurate. He stood a few inches taller than she was with a lean build—the kind she'd seen on the billboards in Nashville advertising the local gyms. His dark hair, cut to a close fade, had a natural wave and blended at his high cheekbones into a freshly manicured beard—more than a five o'clock shadow but less than full-scale whiskers.

When she finally realized she was staring, she blinked and glanced away. His eyes, the color of steel, had registered something, though she was afraid to guess whether it was surprise or disappointment. His squared jaw visibly tightened as he wrapped his hand in the bandanna.

With his gaze fixed on her, she glanced at him again, searched for something readable in his response.

Jessie's voice faded into existence, and they both turned away. "Ava, meet Logan. Logan, Ava."

Another second ticked off, and then she heard him breathe. "Ava, it's . . . uh, nice to meet you." He smiled and held out his hand.

She returned a slighter smile, though out of courtesy or consolation she didn't yet know. When their hands touched, her breathing morphed into a nervous laugh. "Nice to meet you too." She nodded.

Jessie's shutter went into high gear as she began to move back and employ her zoom.

Logan held Ava's hand but didn't move it about in a handshake. "You look really nice."

"Ooh, I love the hands." Jessie kept snapping. "Don't let go."

His hand was warm. Ava willed her fluttering stomach to settle. "Thank you." She sighed and glanced down. "You do too. No Birkenstocks."

His lips broadened into a smirk. "Is that good? Bad?'

"Oh, no." She brushed off her comment with a wave of her free hand. "I just meant . . . I like it."

He bowed his head. "I'm not sure how to do this. You may have to lead me."

When he raised his eyes to her, Ava tried not to look into them for long.

Jessie kept snapping pictures. "You guys are naturals. I may not even have to edit. Logan, would you mind taking both of Ava's hands, please?" Jessie's voice faded again as Ava's fingers met his, not as they had at first in a handshake, but slowly, more intimately lacing together.

Logan cleared his voice. "I don't think I've seen you around before?"

While she had to admit, Carly was right—spontaneity had the potential to kindle all kinds of feelings—Ava resolved to share little. Keep it simple. "No, I guess we've never run into each other."

His hands tightened around hers.

"Are you nervous?"

He looked down, realized he was squeezing, and loosened his grip. "Oh, I'm sorry. Yes, quite a bit. I'm not the best at blind dates. Any dates, for that matter."

Ava smiled. "No apologies. I understand, more than you know."

"So, who twisted your arm into doing a shoot like this with a stranger like me?"

Ava nodded toward Jessie. "Our photographer's business partner, Carly, is my best friend from college. I owe her a big favor." Ava pulled her hand away and looped her thumb into her jeans pocket. "That sounded like I meant it was a chore to be here . . . to help her out. I'm glad to be here—you know, glad to help a friend." She could feel her face turning various shades of kill-me-now. "What about you?"

"I owe a favor too. I've got a twin brother who knows how to work me, but you're right, it's not such a chore."

Two like *him?*

Jessie didn't give Ava much time to let that thought sink in. "Okay, let's get to the water." She picked up her tripod. "I can already tell these photos are going to be amazing."

Chapter Ten

Logan

The wheel against the old mill that Jessie wanted as a backdrop must have been thirty feet wide. Water cascaded from its buckets in a sluggish, methodical flow. The low-set falls just below shimmered across the ford into the shallows with the same rhythm. Rolling off the rocks in hypnotic ribbons, the rushing sounds of water were mesmerizing enough to take the edge off the afternoon. A wide reservoir, dotted with steppingstones from one side of the creek to the other, made beautiful scenery for a shoot.

Jessie and Ava walked in front of Logan, moving closer to the falling water. As he followed them, Logan wondered what Ava's impression had been. When he'd first opened his eyes, his heart caught in his throat. He told himself it was more because of the nerves than anything, but she definitely caught his attention.

Even though things were a little awkward at first, he convinced himself that a one-hour photoshoot didn't mean he was committing to anything. He should just loosen up, try to engage in conversation, enjoy the scenery. No ties, no worries, no heartache . . . but she was attractive. Not like Eliza. Eliza was new beautiful, with her department store makeup and long lashes. She'd spent their money on fashions too expensive for the budget, kept a standing manicure appointment, and highlighted her hair.

Ava had the look of an easy-going beauty—classic more than flashy, natural with high cheekbones and quiet eyes, and long, dark hair that fell just past her shoulders in waves. Her lips were full but not set in a perpetual pout like Eliza's had been. He wondered if her temperament matched.

"Logan, if you'll set up the tripod here, I want to get the water behind you two and the wheel to the right." Jessie scanned the landscape. "Oh, yeah, that'll be gorgeous."

After following Jessie's request, he shoved his hands in his pockets to keep from pumping his fists. He tried not to be obvious as he glanced at Ava. She still looked nervous.

"Okay, I want you two to get comfortable. Remember, I'll do some pose prompts, but otherwise, I'm not here." Jessie drew up her shoulders and rubbed her hands together in excitement. "Come stand just at the water's edge and hold hands first."

When Jessie positioned them, they were so close he could smell jasmine again. "Are you okay with this?" he asked.

"I, um . . . well, it's not something I do every day, so if I'm honest, it's a little awkward. How about you?"

"Yeah," he lied and told the truth all in the same breath. He rubbed his hands against his jeans, then held them, palms up in front of her.

As she put her hands in his, he heard the camera start clicking. "I'm not squeezing your hand again, am I?"

"No," she smiled. Her voice relaxed. "I think we can do this."

For reasons he couldn't pinpoint, those few words broke a little bit of the ice as the camera clicked in rapid-fire.

Chapter Eleven

Ava

When the words crossed her lips, she was trying to convince herself that *she* could do this more than console him. Maybe a few words were all it took to loosen everything up. Either way, that water wheel wasn't the only thing turning on the creek bank. Emotions she'd forgotten existed began to slowly spin up from beneath the surface where she'd pushed them down after all that had happened with Corbin. Feelings that allowed her to feel . . . excited in the presence of a man. She couldn't allow them free reign, though. Could she?

Jessie made delighted noises on the other side of the camera. Then her face peeked over the lens. "Alright, Ava, I want you to hold Logan's wrist. And Logan, with that same hand, you'll touch her face. Don't worry, this is just posing. Nothing serious going on here. Just loosen up and go with it."

Loosen up and go with it. Loosen up. His hand rose to her face, paused, then slid into its place, like it had been formed to touch her all along.

Go with it.

His fingers barely grazed her jawline, sliding softly beneath her ear and resting on her neck. His thumb moved slowly along her cheekbone, and she almost closed her eyes at the warmth of it. Almost sank into his touch.

Go with it.

She touched his wrist, encircled her fingers around the narrowest part, feelings deep inside urging her to pull him closer. When she dared take a glimpse into his eyes, he held her gaze there, left her trying to uncover whether he wanted to be touched as much as she did. It was almost unbearable. She drew in a deep breath and summoned something irrelevant to say. "So, tell me about yourself. Have you lived here in Hartley for long?"

His voice was deep and soft, but he seemed almost relieved at the question. "Oh, I don't live in Hartley. I live with my son in the next town over. My family owns a farm over there—has for a few generations, so we're pretty settled in this part of the world."

"You have a son? How old?" Strangely, she took comfort in that little morsel. It gave her a valid excuse to reassemble her wall while trying not to soak up his touch. A workaholic single dad with no plans for commitment sounded like a safe bet for somebody like her to avoid a relationship with.

"Yeah, Toby. He's turning seven in a few days."

"Fun age." Some of her favorite patients were kids. She could focus on that.

"Do you have family here?" He must have inadvertently stroked her cheek. Every millimeter he touched tingled.

"Oh, no. Just me." *Keep talking, Ava. Keep the conversation going.* "And the farm? Tell me about that." She forced herself not to breathe heavily, tried not to show that it was hard.

"Oh, these are golden," Jessie interrupted. "Now, come on over here, you two."

He pulled his hand away, and she noticed him tighten his fists before shoving them in his pockets. The spot on her cheek still tingled.

At some point, Jessie had thrown out a blanket and staged the creek bank with a picnic basket and goblets. She pointed at them now. "I want you to sit here facing each other." Logan took a spot on the blanket, and Ava sat at the corner diagonal to his, at first directly in front of one another.

"Now, scoot a little closer together," Jessie directed.

When they didn't get close enough to suit, Jessie began to situate them. Finally, instead of being directly in front of each other, they sat with their left hips almost touching, close enough that she could see flecks of green in the blue of his eyes. *Focus, Ava.*

Jessie stepped back to her camera.

"So, the farm?" Ava broke the silence.

"Yeah, the farm," he continued. "During the Depression, my mother's grandparents had a little stash of money put away in places besides banks and the stock market. They bought the farm, raised livestock and crops, and gardened for as long as they were living. My mother inherited the land a few years back." He bent his legs and rested his elbows on his knees. "Toby and I have a cabin on the wooded side of the property."

"Sounds like a nice place." Ava stretched her legs. Thoughts of having a tight-knit family had died with her parents.

"What about you? Where'd you grow up?"

She hesitated. "Small-town, USA."

He grinned as if he read the reason behind her reluctance. "That's smart. Not telling a guy you've never met too much. I'd be the same way in your shoes."

Ava felt oddly comforted by his acknowledgment, even though he didn't know exactly why she'd maneuvered away from talking about herself. It was a response Corbin would have never entertained. He would have found a way to sell her on answering him.

"Okay," Jessie prompted from behind the camera. "Ava, let's have you put your arm on the ground on the other side of Logan, so you'll be leaning closer to him. Logan, you do the same thing except leaning toward Ava."

They moved at the same time until they settled dangerously close.

"I guess I'm overly cautious about sharing details."

"Don't feel like you've got to answer just because I asked. I'm just trying to keep the conversation going." He smirked. "This all feels kind of like when I was a kid at the doctor's office, making polite conversation while being asked to turn my head and cough."

A laugh escaped before she could catch it. "Haven't quite been on your side of that experience, but I'd imagine that's pretty accurate."

They both broke into a laugh.

When they stopped, Ava paused, then thought there couldn't be much harm in telling him *something* about herself. She didn't have to go into recent history.

"I grew up in Kentucky. My dad was a math teacher, and my mom worked at the bank. They passed away a few years back, so it's just me now."

"I'm sorry to hear that." His expression softened. "No siblings?"

"No siblings."

"What brought you to this part of the country?"

"I thought it would be a good place to settle for a while." It wasn't a total lie. When Carly first started trying to convince her to look at real estate in the little town of Camden Grove, it had a certain appeal. A true Southern place, the pictures she'd seen on the realtor's website showed ancient trees hovering above the streets like protective grandmothers and rural roads lined with hanging cloaks of kudzu.

"It's got its charm."

He shifted a little, close enough for her to smell the woody scent of his cologne. *It* does *have its charm*, she thought.

"What do you do for work?"

She stiffened. "I'm, uh, in between jobs right now. Hoping to start a new one soon."

Jessie's camera clicked incessantly in the background.

Ava combed her mind for new questions, the proximity between them closing. "Do you have other siblings besides the twin brother?"

He propped his hand on his bent knee as if he were relaxed. "I don't think my mother wanted any more after having my brother and me. I think we still have a habit of causing her hair to stand on end occasionally." When he smiled, deep dimples creased his cheeks beneath the stubble.

"You and your brother were troublemakers, then." The scent of his cologne tantalized her, and thinking about what to say next became even harder.

"He was the troublemaker. I just got dragged along most of the time."

"And what did you two get into?"

He tilted his head to the side and chuckled, his hair almost brushing her cheek. "One time when we were about twelve, my mom went to the store and left us at home alone. We'd heard about the local fair having a greased pig contest." He shrugged. "My brother had the bright idea that we could win that contest, but we'd need some practice. When Mom got back home, we'd used every stick of butter in the fridge to grease up our beagle hound until he looked like a canine suppository. We were chasing him, and she was chasing us. Only she had a fly swatter."

A laugh erupted from both of them as the awkwardness between them slipped away. "Poor dog."

"No, he was loving getting chased. It was my brother and me who deserved the sympathy. We ran for our lives when Mom got home. I think she may have gotten in one good swat, then made us bathe the dog probably seven or eight times to get all the butter off." He shook his head. "We never did enter that contest."

After a few more shots on the blanket, Jessie asked if they'd wade into the water. It seemed like a safe trade—water for a little more distance between them. Logan slipped off his shoes, rolled up his pants legs, and stepped into the water first, jumping across a few stones to the middle of the creek. Ava put her shoes beside his and followed as the stream gushed and trickled around their feet. In the middle, he offered his hand to help her from one rock to another.

When she jumped, he swayed against the rushing stream. She almost slipped, but his hand gripped her waist and pulled her close as she landed. With both hands clinging to his arms, she could feel the corded muscle beneath his shirt.

"Got your balance?" His grip loosened.

Then, something came over her—a feeling she hadn't known in years. As a teenager, she used to love the water. She spent hours in the summer at a local lake with the other kids in her class, playing Marco Polo, building bonfires, and learning to kiss a boy. That feeling, that streak of mischief, bubbled inside her.

"I do, but you don't." Without warning, Ava pushed Logan off the rock he stood on. He landed with an impressive splash waist-deep in the churning water. A belly laugh rolled up from her core.

When the shock wore off, a broad, devilish smile creased the dimples of his cheeks. Without a word, he slowly wiped droplets of water from his forehead with both hands. Then, with the speed of a striking snake, he whipped her legs out from under her. She hit the water at his waist, sending a splash across the creek.

She came up gasping, then laughing, then gasping more. "I can't believe you did that. I can't believe *I* did that."

"Then you'll really be shocked at this." He dived under the water, grabbing her from beneath and pulling her into his arms.

When they emerged, they were so close that his stubble brushed against her face. They both rose to a standing position, too close to make an unwise move.

She could feel his heartbeat throbbing against her as water trickled from his face and trailed into his beard. With her eyes, Ava traced the lines of his lips wet with creek water.

A craving welled up in her to feel the warmth and softness of a man's lips against hers. This man's lips. For a split second, she justified. What could it hurt? She would probably never see him again.

The same impulsiveness that had caused her to push him into the water now urged her on, brought her precariously close enough to feel his deep breathing against her skin.

That's when she heard Jessie behind her camera.

"Yes, yes, yes!"

And with that, the spell was broken. The reality of how close she was to kissing him pulled her back, reeled her into the truth that she didn't need more complexity in her life. *Simplify and reduce. Simplify and reduce.*

She spoke first. "I should probably go."

Logan loosened his grip. "Yeah . . . I-I need to go too. I've got to meet somebody later on."

At his words, Ava's heart began to close up again. Of course. He needed to meet someone. What was she thinking, being playful? Where had that come from? She turned, slipped from his grasp, and began wading back to the creek bank.

Jessie met them coming out of the water. "That was fantastic! You two gave me more than a kiss. You gave me fun and magic and . . . These photos are gonna be perfect."

Ava turned to Jessie. "Could we use your blanket to dry off? I think that's all we have time for."

"You bet. I can't wait to see what we got today. I'll load up the camera stuff if you don't mind bringing the picnic props. And Logan, once you get dried off, could you bring up my tripod?"

"Yeah, sure." Logan nodded without looking in Ava's direction.

Nearly giddy, Jessie spun around and started up the bank.

When Ava turned back around, Logan had stripped off his shirt and was ringing it out. She tried, unsuccessfully, to glance away. Now he really did look like the billboards in Nashville. "I . . . um." She pointed back toward the building.

When he bent over to retrieve Jessie's blanket, he handed it to Ava. His broad shoulders, knotted with muscles were impossible not to notice.

"I should apologize."

She stuttered, "F-for what?"

"Because I may be a little intense when it comes to paybacks. Comes from growing up with that twin brother."

Breathless, she brushed a wet strand of hair from her eyes. "No. That's okay. I'm, uh, fine. Anyway, I kind of started it." She held out a hand. "It was nice to meet you, Logan. I should get going."

He took her hand and held it steady. "Hey," he started to say something.

Ava needed to stop him. "I should tell you, in case you're wondering. I really didn't expect anything from today. In fact, I wasn't interested in a real date kind of thing. I was just doing this to help Carly and Jessie."

"Yeah," Logan let go of her hand and dropped his gaze. "Me, too. I mean, that's what I was going to say. I wanted to make sure we were on the same page. Maybe I'll see you around sometime."

"Sure, yeah. Take care." Ava wrapped the blanket around her shoulders and quickly made her way back up the bank, afraid to look back.

After stripping out of her clothes and changing into the summer dress she'd left in the bathroom, she gathered the wet clothes and crossed the parking lot. Jessie stood at her trunk packing up her car, but Logan was already gone.

Jessie put a hand on Ava's arm. "You have no idea how crazy good you two were together."

Ava draped the wet clothes on the car door. "Well, maybe you can use something from today."

"Something? I'll be hard-pressed to weed them down to a portfolio set. I've got dozens of good shots, and you guys didn't even kiss." Jessie closed her trunk. "Anyway, thank you tons. I can't wait to show Carly. I'm sure she'll share them with you once we finish editing. That'll take a few days."

"Yeah, if you have anything usable at all in that camera, I'm sure I'll hear about it. She likes to say, 'I told you so.'"

Jessie gestured at Ava's dress. "I'm glad you at least had a change of clothes. Logan didn't bring any with him and flew out of here like a wet weekend." She sighed. "Not that anyone would complain. Just a minute of that man shirtless is enough to cause heart palpitations. I might've needed a cool dip in that creek myself if he'd stayed any longer."

Jessie left with a giggle and a wave as Ava wrung out her clothes and threw them on the floorboard. As she watched Jessie's car disappear past the Old Mill exit, she sat for a moment wondering exactly what had happened in the last hour.

Chapter Twelve

Logan

As Logan drove back to Camden Grove, thoughts from the afternoon coursed through his mind. The woman he'd just met—Ava—and the scent of jasmine, the feel of her skin under his fingers. For so long, he'd refused to think about touching a woman, about what happened to his heart when he touched a woman. Those thoughts were too risky.

But now, since pulling away from the Old Mill, it was like someone had flicked some switch on his brain. He couldn't get her out of his mind.

She seemed genuine. No signs of the flirtatious head games Eliza used to play. But maybe he was fooling himself by even thinking about her being any different. Why was he thinking about her at all? Ridiculous. The photoshoot was different—fun even—but he needed to refocus on all the projects that were looming over his head.

As he pulled into the Grove, he forced work back into his mind.

He'd scheduled a walk-through at the doctor's office so Dakota could get an idea about what to take on and how to manage it before the sassy doc had a coronary about naked studs again. He smiled every time he thought about the uptight voice message.

Back at the cabin, he stripped out of his wet clothes and stepped into the shower to wash off the creek water. Thoughts of Ava drifted in and out of his mind again. Talking to her had been easier than he imagined, more comfortable than he'd ever admit to Wyatt. And then, when they'd played in the water, he felt a little bit like a kid again. Like when his stomach flipped the first time he held hands with a girl or realized how good it felt to kiss one. He'd come so close today to pushing the memory aside and claiming the real thing that it almost hurt.

He could hear his brother now, all smug, prodding him about his "blind date." Jessie probably didn't get out of the parking lot before her hot little hands were speed dialing Lydia. But what, really, could she say about the shoot? That they sat on a blanket and talked? That they'd fallen in the creek and gotten wet? All the same kinds of things could've happened if they'd wrangled somebody else into doing the shoot—nothing special about getting him and Ava together.

Because his work clothes were dirty and his one new pair of jeans were now soaked, he had to dig a pair of shorts and a polo from the closet—something he hadn't worn all summer.

Lacing up his tennis shoes, he glanced at the time, and realized he had only a few minutes to get back to town to meet Dakota. He'd already texted his friend most of the specifics. Just a quick walk-through to set eyes on the site should be sufficient. At least, that's what he hoped. After skipping lunch, he was starving and some of Wiggs's barbecue was calling his name. Maybe he'd grab a bite with Dakota before going to pick up Toby.

As Logan pulled into the lot, his friend sat waiting outside the doctor's office, propped against a sleek pewter-colored Harley, the man's summer ride on most of the sunny days Logan saw him.

After parking the truck, Logan grabbed from his console the key for the building.

"Hey, man," Dakota said with a nod. "You look like you're ready to play a game of golf or something."

Logan smirked. "I've never played golf in my life."

"Your mom get that for you so you'd have some dating clothes?" Dakota had been well aware of the his family's nudges for him to get back on that horse.

"You're not on my case, too, are you?"

"No, man, you know I'm nobody to push that button."

Logan knew the undertow of his friend's comment. He was pretty sure Dakota hadn't dated since his release from prison. "Yeah, well, I feel like the poster child for The Club of Unfortunate Bachelors. Wanna join since neither of us is sporting a wedding ring or a gal on our arms?"

Logan unlocked the office, and Dakota shook his head. "No time for clubbin'. I've got this friend who's trying to put me to work."

"Work's a lot safer than a woman anyway." Logan patted his friend on the shoulder as they stepped inside.

From the entry, through the waiting room, and further into the office, Logan inspected the floors. "Looks like the tile guys left before finishing."

"Yeah." Dakota followed. "There's still a week's work in the front alone."

"Come on back here, and I'll show you the 'naked studs'."

"Don't go getting fresh on me, man."

They both laughed as they walked down the hall.

Chapter Thirteen

Ava

After getting back from the photoshoot, Ava couldn't shake the thoughts of Logan rolling through her mind. She'd been so close to him. From the beginning, she'd nixed Carly's idea of doing the shoot, but now, within an afternoon, she couldn't get his image out of her head. The green flecks of color in his eyes. The water dripping from his hair. The ripples in his stomach when he pulled off his wet shirt. Thoughts of him made her insides flutter. For the love of Pete, she'd almost kissed him. What was she thinking? She took a deep breath, pulled her hair out of its messy bun, and went to clean up.

After a cool shower, she changed into a cotton-print summer dress and went to the refrigerator to calm her rumbling stomach. The nearly empty fridge and sparse pantry offered nothing that excited her. A trip to the store was definitely in order.

As she eased into town, she detoured around orange cones and ropes draped across the south end of Main Street from sidewalk to sidewalk. Carly had mentioned the block parties that were so popular in Camden Grove.

People in camp chairs sat along the roped-off area, listening to a street band playing on the back of a flatbed trailer. The little town, alive with walking vendors and craft tables, hosted couples dancing to a quick-paced country tune plucked from a banjo and steel guitar on the back of the flatbed.

As she approached the barricaded street, a yellow-vested officer directed traffic to turn either right or left off the main drag. Ava turned right. She'd make a couple of blocks and then pick up Main again headed toward the market.

At the second turn, she could see her office just past the lot of a local hardware store. A truck and a motorcycle were parked in front. Maybe this was her chance to meet her so-called contractor face-to-face. He still hadn't returned her call, and by the looks of the office, he had more than a month's work to finish before she could open for business.

With a short detour, Ava parked within a stone's throw of the motorcycle, got out of her car, and marched to the entry of her clinic.

As she opened the front office door, she could hear laughter coming from the back. Laughter. When they had work to do? She started to barge in at first but then had the urge to quietly see what was so funny. Their muffled voices cleared as she eased the door closed and stepped further inside.

"'I've got naked studs everywhere.' That's what she yelled into my voice mail when she called to let me know how much I was slacking."

Ava's eyes went wide. *The nerve!* She slipped past the receptionist's window and into the hallway.

"I thought doctors were used to seeing those kinds of things." It was another man's voice this time.

"Not the kind holding up wires springing forth 'like fountains in a fishpond.'" The first man snickered. "She said that, too."

They both laughed.

Did he snort? Was that a snort?

"Sounds like she was pretty hot under the collar."

Darn straight she was hot! No return calls. No work. No promise it would be done by opening day. She's furious! Ava stepped further down the hallway toward the voices.

"'Fraid she'll have to keep her hat on. I can only do so much. I don't carry miracles in my toolbox."

Keep my hat on? Ava's face twisted in anger.

"She give you a due date?"

Without the patience to wait a second longer, Ava rounded the corner. "Four weeks!" She interrupted, fury spewing as she stepped up behind them. "I'm supposed to open in four weeks."

When the two men whirled around, both of their jaws dropped like doors on heavy hinges. Then Ava's face mirrored theirs.

At first, she couldn't speak because she couldn't believe her eyes. It was him! The man she'd just spent an hour on a picnic blanket with, splashing in the water with, and almost kissing! "Wh—what are you doing here?"

The man she didn't know looked at Logan. Logan looked at Ava. Ava looked wildly at them both.

"Uh, I'm the contractor. And you're here because . . .?"

"Because I'm the hot doctor. I mean, hot-under-the-collar doctor." Ava folded her arms, and huffed, trying to recover herself. "I'm Ava. Ava Fenn."

Chapter Fourteen

Logan

Confusion, then recognition, spread across Logan's face. "I thought you were between jobs."

Once Ava recouped enough to speak, she snapped back. "I am. I'm waiting on you to get a place ready for me to work."

"Am I missing something here?" Dakota brushed his nose with the back of his hand. He looked like he was trying to conceal a smirk.

"Something like that." Logan wasn't ready for a drawn-out explanation of how he'd met Ava just hours earlier. "Hey man, I think we've got an idea of what needs to be done here, so can I catch up with you later?"

"Yeah, sure." Dakota pointed himself toward the door. "I'll just get out of your way." He slipped around Ava and gave Logan a wide-eyed glance from behind her.

She kept her eyes glued to him. "You and your friend apparently thought that what I had to say was funny."

Logan tried to gather his thoughts. "Uh, no. Well, yes—no. I mean, just the way you said—"

"I know how I said what I said, and it sounds like you got a kick out of making fun at my expense."

Logan suppressed a grin as she propped her hands on her hips.

"I've advertised this office opening its doors in one month, and you haven't kept your end of the deal. Where does that leave me, besides banking on those miracles that obviously don't exist in your toolbox?"

"I'm here because I'm trying to get things lined up to finish."

"Your friend didn't sound too optimistic."

"Did you eavesdrop on all of our conversation?"

Ava refused an answer but instead adjusted her crossed arms and continued to stare.

"Look, I've had a few delays—"

"And that's supposed to make me feel better? How does it look when a professional comes into town to open a new place, advertises the open date, and then has to say, 'Sorry, I can't come through because my office isn't ready for your hernia exam'?" Ava shook her head. "I was counting on you doing your job. And it would be a bonus if you didn't make a joke of my concerns."

He struggled to keep a straight face. "Not trying to make a joke. I was just amused at your wording."

Ava snapped again. "Do I need to find someone else to straighten up this mess, or are you good for keeping your word?"

Her question stung, and his jaw tightened. "I keep my word, Dr. Fenn."

If he'd had done anything in his life, he'd kept his word. He'd had enough of broken promises for a lifetime, enough to know he would never be on the giving end of them.

"Well, that remains to be seen." She turned to go but then came back. "Oh, and are you planning to answer my phone calls? I'd like to know that when I'm trying to get in touch, you'll at least communicate with me."

He ran a hand through his hair but didn't speak. When he looked at her again, the tension between them set his nerves on edge. He recognized it the minute she entered the room. It was the kind that wouldn't let you rest until things were settled.

She cocked her head as if expecting an answer.

Finally, he took a deep breath and released it in a long sigh. "I apologize for making fun of you, and I'm sorry I didn't answer your call." He raised his eyebrows. "I was waiting until I talked to Dakota." He nodded toward the door. "He's the guy who just left. He does work for me sometimes, and I wanted to see if he could take care of the electrical job."

Ava's hands dropped.

"I've got the tile men coming back in a couple of days. Drywall will go up as soon as the electric and plumbing are done, and you have cabinets and furniture coming in two weeks."

Her voice softened when she said, "So, is it likely to be done by my deadline?"

"I've never in my career promised and not delivered. Not yet." He bent over to pick up some wiring debris the last electricians left behind, mostly to give him a reason to look away from Ava. Since being with her at the creek, she'd changed into a dress that hugged her in all the right places and revealed enough of her long, toned legs to deserve a second or third glance.

"I guess we'll see, then." She turned and left the room, the echo of her steps bouncing off the bare-studded walls.

His neck tensed up at her leaving without a goodbye.

Before she rounded the end of the hall, he peeped around the door facing and called, "Hey."

She turned on a dime, her lips tightening in a line.

"Look, if my mother were here, she would feel like I owed you more than an apology. She'd want me to make things right."

"Should I be touched that you're trying to make amends because of pre-sewn maternal guilt complex?"

"What I mean to say is . . . when I'm in the wrong, I can hear her telling me to leave things better than I found them, especially if she knew I was the one to cause a problem." He tossed the trash wire into the hall wastebasket and stepped closer to Ava. His head dropped. "Anyway, the jabs with Dakota a few minutes ago? That was just a couple of guys trying to fill conversation, not paying attention that it was at somebody else's expense."

Her shoulders relaxed, and she rocked from heel to toe, the dress swaying just above her knees.

He narrowed his eyes. "You know, this is kind of strange."

Ava didn't speak.

"We just met this afternoon, and here we are again. Kind of odd." He raised his hands. "I know I've already suggested that I'm not really the blind-date type. Not in the market, but . . . I skipped lunch today, and I'm really kind of starved. Would you like to grab a bite with me? My treat?"

Ava started to shake her head, then glanced at a bare stud in front of her. She held back a grin. "I suppose I didn't make the best impression with that message I left."

He sighed. "You like barbecue?"

"Well enough."

He folded his arms. "I've got a friend who owns a little place a few blocks away where they have a great dinner menu." He raised his eyebrows. "It'll make your mouth water."

Ava waited. "As long as you tell your electrician friend that I've never referred to any patient I've examined as a stud. Naked or otherwise."

He tossed his head back and laughed. "Deal."

Chapter Fifteen

Ava

As they stepped out of the office, Ava's mood mellowed from snarky to appeased. In the parking lot, she started toward her car intending to meet Logan at the restaurant, but when he followed her around the front of his truck and opened his passenger door, she realized that he intended for her to ride with him . . . like a real date.

"You can come with me if you want. I'll bring you back to your car afterward."

Something inside her quickened at the prospect of riding with him, then softened at the thought of his being chivalrous enough to open the door for her. Corbin would never have so much as blinked at such a gesture, much less performed it. She'd never needed a man to cater to her, but the thought was kind of nice.

"Okay."

As she slipped inside and watched him round the truck, she couldn't help but take in the view. That made her tingle a little too.

They maintained casual conversation for the few blocks to the restaurant. It stood not far off the main drag. Red shutters against the gray metal of the exterior made a homey but fitting setting for a barbecue dinner.

Once they parked, Ava didn't wait for him to come around and open the door for her again. It seemed too presumptuous. Instead, she joined him at the front of the truck, and they walked in together.

Inside the double barn-style doors of the restaurant, a motherly-looking waitress dressed in a checkered apron stood at a long counter, taking orders from a line of patrons.

When they got close to the counter, Ava stole a glance at Logan. He seemed at ease. Maybe going for a friendly dinner wasn't so bad after all. At the very least, her stomach would thank her.

The dining area, farther inside, hosted an arrangement of red picnic tables with checkered plastic tablecloths and rolls of paper towels on knobbed stands. Squeeze bottles of extra barbecue sauce sat at haphazard intervals as a teenage worker circled the room, collecting the empty ones. The walls, made of slatted, rough timbers, held rows of business cards like a fixed garland against its rustic surface. From an old-fashioned jukebox in a far corner, Elvis sang a tune in the background.

"If you like barbecue, you'll never find another place like this one." He pointed beyond the counter. "See that guy in the back, cooking?"

Ava craned her neck.

Logan waved. A large, muscled man, with an apron to match the order waitress's, offered a cheeky grin, waved a set of tongs in the air, and wagged his eyebrows at Logan. "That's Wiggs. He's the owner of the place and the best meat smoker this side of heaven, as far as I can tell. His friends call him Wiggles."

Ava gave a short chuckle. "Wiggles?"

They stepped up to the counter. "A story for another time."

"Hey, Logan," the waitress smiled. "The usual?"

"You know it, Janine." He turned to Ava. "And whatever the lady here wants."

Once Ava placed her order and they got their tray of food, Logan led the way to a setting far enough from the music for them to talk without raising their voices. Above the table hung a craftsman's lamp made of a double-tree yoke and mason jars, lighting the table enough to make the experience of barbecue dining strangely intimate.

After he doused his plate of pulled pork with extra sauce from one of the squeeze bottles, Logan opened the conversation. "So, now that I know you're a doctor and that you're just opening up a practice in Camden Grove, how recently did you move to town?"

Ava was a little more conservative with the sauce. "A couple of weeks ago."

"Today, at the shoot, you never mentioned you were a doctor."

She shrugged her shoulders. "I almost did when you made the 'turn and cough' comment. Would it have been any different if I had?"

"No, I guess not."

"I just didn't see the need."

He arched an eyebrow. "Um-hm."

"What's that mean? 'Um-hm'?" She unrolled a paper towel from the stand and spread it on her lap.

He pointed his fork. "I think you were just as unsettled by that shoot today as I was, got pulled into it just as much as I did. You've already shared your concerns with me—pretty boldly, as I remember—about appearing professional. So, I'm wondering if you didn't feel like this side gig appeared a little less . . . suitable . . . than, say, volunteer work at the Children's Hospital."

She didn't answer.

"I'm right."

Ava shrugged. "My friend Carly has a little more relaxed definition of professionalism than I do, I guess."

"If it's any consolation, I was a fish out of water just like you were."

Ava took a big bite, closed her eyes, and couldn't hide the pleasure of Wiggs's barbecue.

"Good?" Logan asked.

"Mm. I was starving." She licked her fork clean of the sauce.

"So, if you feel a little less like I'm a stranger now that I work for you and we're eating together, where'd you move from? And what brought you to Camden Grove?"

She spooned at her potato salad. "I came from Nashville. Carly told me a while back that the closest doctor was in Hartley, so I did some research and decided this would be a good landing spot for me."

"You still seem a little hesitant when you say that."

She shifted and took another bite, a bit unsettled by how easily he could read her.

He continued. "You like it here so far?"

"It's a nice town . . . for a little while, though it's a far cry from Nashville."

Logan pulled the paper from his straw and poked it in his drink. "What does Nashville have that little Camden Grove doesn't?"

"Well, let's see. A movie theater, a nightlife, a Music Row, a Titan's stadium, a Grand Ole Opry, and a candy store where they sell warm pralines."

"That's an impressive list. You liked being in the middle of all that busy stuff?"

"Always plenty to do, that's for sure."

He stopped eating and eyed her. "So, why'd you move?"

"It was a business decision, that's all."

He wiped his mouth. "Did you have a practice of your own in Nashville?"

"I was in with another doctor."

"I guess being solo has more advantages, then." His fork hovered above the plate. "So, tell me the biggest pros."

"Well, I would know more about what goes on in the office and have a say over those things." She took a drink. "When you're in with other doctors, the lines get a little grayer."

"And you like black and white?"

"I definitely like black and white."

"Did you get burned at your old office?"

"That's kind of a personal question, don't you think?"

"Yes, but I think you did."

Ava stopped eating. "Why do you say that?"

"Because you left a city you obviously love and came to a place nearly the polar opposite. You have no family here, and if you hadn't been burned, you would have answered directly instead of asking me a question in response."

"Aren't you the detective?"

"Another question." He smiled.

"Maybe I wanted to live a simpler life."

"Maybe?" He smiled and took a sip. "Welcome to the place of your dreams, then. But you said 'a little while.'"

"Hm?"

"You said this would be a nice town to settle in 'for a little while.' Don't you plan on staying?"

"I could never stay in a small town forever. I just wanted to see if I could build a practice and sell after a year or two. I'm too much of a city girl to stay for long." She cocked her head. "So, we've talked enough about me. What's your story?"

"I've been in Camden Grove all my life. Went to college in Hartley, married, had a kid, got divorced. Not looking to go down that road again. I lead a pretty simple life."

Before Ava could respond, a bass voice rumbled from across the room, "Logan Carter, you didn't tell me you found somebody you could eat some barbecue with." The man Logan had pointed out earlier, decked in the checkered apron, sidled up beside their table.

"Hey, Wiggles. Meet Dr. Ava Fenn. She's just moved into town. Opening up a practice at the old newspaper office."

"Well, that makes sense now. She knows nothing about you, does she?" Wiggs winked at Ava, extended his large hand, and kissed hers. "Welcome to the Grove. We're glad to get a doctor here."

"Thank you." Ava raised an eyebrow at his gesture. Did all the men in Camden Grove open doors and kiss women's hands?

Maybe she could get used to this place. "It's nice to meet you, too, and your barbecue is delicious. But I don't think I've ever met anybody called Wiggles. Pretty unusual name."

"Logan hasn't told you about our annual luau, then."

She looked across the table expectantly.

"Wiggles, here, grew up in Hawaii. When he moved to the Grove, he opened this place and started hosting a community luau every year. If you noticed the town square cordoned off this afternoon, they do that here a lot on the weekends. Wiggles's luau takes place there most years."

"Anyway, the name Wiggles came about because he gets all the women worked up with his fire knife show and male hula routine. After the first luau, he was forever after renamed."

The brawny man nodded. "I keep telling Logan he should try it. It's very sexy. He wouldn't be single for long."

"That hasn't pulled you out of bachelorhood."

"No, but my prospects are narrowing. I keep my eye on the eligibles in town. And, when I find the one, my friend, it'll be aloha to the singles scene."

Logan tore a paper towel from the stand and wiped his mouth. It sounded like sandpaper across his whiskers.

"So, there you have it. Camden Grove's claim to fame is Wiggles's luau. Much better entertainment than the Grand Ole Opry or a Titans game, I promise you." Logan winked.

"And it all came about because of the man sitting right in front of you, Doc. I opened this place after my guy Logan built it."

"Really? You built this place?"

"It was my passion project a few years back. I needed the work, and Wiggs gave me a shot at constructing something I'd never done before."

"Oh, you're talking lustful now." Wiggles grinned. "I didn't know I was your *passion* project."

Across the dining area, the entry door opened, and Wiggs waved at another couple coming inside. "I'll leave you two to your dinner. Glad to have you in the Grove, Doc." He turned to Logan. "I'm having a couple of the guys over for some 8-ball next Tuesday night after closing. See you there?"

"I'm pretty swamped right now. Maybe another time."

"Alright then. Another night."

Logan's phone rang as Wiggs crossed the room and bear-hugged an incoming patron.

When he fished it out of his pocket, Ava caught a glimpse of the face of an older woman lighting up his screen.

"Hey, Mom." He took a quick sip of his drink. "What's wrong? . . . Did he eat anything different?"

Ava finished her last bite and took notice of Logan's sober expression.

"Okay, I'll be right there. Tell him I'm on my way." After ending the call, he began to gather everything onto the tray. "I'm sorry. I have to go."

"Is something wrong?"

"It's my son, Toby. Mom's worried about him. He's not feeling well. She thinks it may be appendicitis, but she always resorts to that explanation first. My brother's appendix almost burst when we were kids." He opened his wallet and threw down a tip. "Sorry to cut things short. I can still take you back to your car."

"Was he hurting in his right side?"

"She didn't say. But I don't think so or, knowing Mom, she would've already called the ambulance."

"Where do they live?"

"On the south side, out Highway 231 three miles or so. Why?"

She bit her lower lip. "I was pretty testy earlier, and I feel kind of bad." Then she bit the bullet. "Why don't you let me make up for it? I'd be happy to come with you and check on your son if you'd like. If it is his appendix, I can probably tell pretty quickly. We can backtrack and get my car later." She paused. "My place is on the way before you get to Highway 231. If we can make a quick stop, I'll get a couple of things to do an exam."

Ava noticed he hesitated, even held his breath a little. Then, he exhaled. "That would actually be great."

Chapter Sixteen

Logan

At first, Logan started to say no. All he needed was for his mom and dad to get the wrong idea about him and the doctor. But what if Toby did need medical attention? When he weighed his thoughts again, he found himself accepting Ava's offer, no matter how reluctant he was.

Her house sat in one of the quiet cul-de-sacs on the edge of town. He and Wyatt had spent quite a few nights after ball games and practices at a friend's house in this neighborhood, so pulling into the subdivision brought back good memories of a time before life got so complicated.

When she directed him to pull into the drive of the very house he'd frequented as a kid, he smiled. "You bought the Cannon place?"

"Um, I don't know. Did I?"

"Jeremiah Cannon. He was one of my best friends in middle school. My brother and I used to spend hours over here at his house." He chuckled. "This was the place I got my first cut that required stitches, told my first bold-faced lie to an adult, and learned where babies came from, all in the same day."

"Well, that's an impressive pre-pubescent rap sheet. Do share."

He laughed. "One afternoon, after ball practice, we came home with Frog, and—"

"Wait. Frog?"

"That's what we called Jeremiah, you know, a bullfrog?"

"Ah, okay." She smirked. "And he was a good friend of yours."

"Exactly. Anyway, Frog's mom was studying to be a nurse, and all her anatomy books were spread out on the coffee table in the living room when we came in. She must have been tackling the reproductive system that day. So, being inquisitive boys, and since she was nowhere to be seen, the three of us started casually glancing through the pages of, um . . . reproductive science."

Ava raised her eyebrows.

"Before we knew we were caught, she showed up over our shoulders, wrapped in her bathrobe, towel-drying her hair. When she asked what we were doing, all three of us jumped so hard that I bumped against Wyatt, bounced off Frog's shoulder, and tripped back against the mantle. I cut my head wide open, all while promising Mrs. Cannon that we didn't see anything we weren't supposed to." He chuckled as he thought about the memory. "Guess I was lucky she had a towel handy, or else I'm sure I would've bled all over her living room carpet."

"Was she upset?"

"Oh, no. After she and Frog followed Mom, Wyatt, and me to Hartley for stitches, she never said a word about it, not to my mom or me. I think she knew how embarrassed I'd be, and she had the heart not to crush me with humiliation. Hey, do you still have a wooden mantle over the fireplace?"

"It's still there."

"I bet you can still see the dent, then."

"You dented it?"

"Not with my head." He frowned. "When she startled us, I was holding the paperweight that she'd put on her notes. It went flying through the air and dented the mantle just about the same moment I cut my head."

"Well, come on. You can go take a look while I gather my things, relive some childhood humiliation."

"Sounds like a dream come true." He put the truck in park.

Once inside, Ava nodded toward the kitchen. "If you need a bottle of water for the road, you're welcome to get one from the fridge."

"No thanks. I'm good." He watched as she disappeared to the back of the house.

Standing in the living room, he took note of the sparse furnishings. She obviously wasn't one to horde things. A comfortable-looking chair, an overstuffed couch, and a coffee table were about all that spoke to her taste in furniture. The mantle that had been a part of his coming-of-age story stood as firmly as it had years ago. As he ran a hand across the wood edge, his fingers sank under the small tell-tale divot, not conspicuous in the rough wood but still visible. He called over his shoulder, "Hey, it's still here."

Three photo frames lined the mantle, the only small and movable objects in the room. One was a picture of a beaming, younger Ava standing against a brick building in a graduation gown with mortarboard and tassel, an older man and woman at her side. She looked like the perfect blend of them both.

In the next photo, she and another woman sat on a beach towel, feet buried in sand, wearing some heart-stopping swimsuits. His eyes lingered on Ava, her aqua-colored one-piece modest but evocative enough to magnify some pretty tempting features. Despite taking a few hard seconds to peel his eyes from the beach photo, the last one rapt him.

The frame, made from popsicle sticks and embellished with buttons, held a photo of Ava sitting on the side of a hospital bed with a young girl who looked almost Toby's age, the little girl's arms wrapped around a pink teddy bear. A balloon, floating above her hairless head, revealed the occasion: it was her birthday. Logan's mouth felt dry, then too parched to swallow.

Ava returned to the living room with a medical bag. "So, you found it?"

"Huh?"

"The dent? Did you find it?"

"Um, yeah." He reached back and tapped the mantle. "Right there."

"Funny that you have connections to this place. I guess it happens in a small town, though. I think I have everything I need." Ava nodded toward the door. "You ready?"

He reached for her bag. "Here, let me take that for you." When his hand inadvertently touched hers, the sensation lingered as he stepped outside, and he wondered—just for a second—what it would feel like to hold a woman's hand again.

Well, maybe not just any woman.

Chapter Seventeen

Ava

When they arrived at Logan's parents' home, the sky had put on a multicolored gown of purples and blues as the lightning bugs came out of their hiding places in the grass, and the crickets and owls began their slipshod melodies.

The gravel crunched under the weight of the tires as Logan pulled into a spot next to a house with a small, detached garage. With the truck in park, he grabbed Ava's medical bag.

Back at the restaurant, Ava first felt awkward at the notion of Logan opening doors for her and carrying her dinner tray. Then at the house, when he'd offered to take her bag, something about his old-fashioned chivalry, left her a little less guarded.

As they reached the porch, a woman who looked to be in her early 70s opened the door. When Ava appeared from behind Logan, her expression turned to surprise.

"Mom, this is Dr. Fenn. She's the one who's opening the new office in town."

Ava noted his sheepish expression but turned and held out her hand. "It's nice to meet you, Mrs. Carter."

"And you, too, Dr. Fenn. Please, call me Margaret." She waved the two inside. "He's back in the bedroom." She led the way down the hall, calling over her shoulder. "How on earth did you find a doctor so fast?"

"We ran into each other tonight." Logan side-glanced at Ava. "I'm doing work on her office. When she heard me talking to you on the phone, she offered to come check on Toby."

"You don't see doctors make house calls anymore. I'm hoping I'm worried over nothing, but you can't be too careful with children." She eased the bedroom door open.

Inside, the little boy lay propped in the middle of a queen-size bed with pillows all around. A wet washcloth covering his eyes obscured most of his face. A trash can, set close to the bed, had, no doubt, been placed there just in case.

As Margaret neared the bed, she spoke softly, "Toby, sweetheart, your daddy's here, and he brought someone to see how you're feeling."

The boy rolled over, and the cloth slipped from his face. "Dad, I threw up."

Logan sat down beside Toby and leaned to hug him. "Hey, Peanut Butter, I'm sorry you're feeling bad. This is Dr. Fenn. She came to see if she could help you feel better."

The bedroom door opened again, and an older man with a glass of orange liquid came in.

Logan turned around. "Hey, Dad."

Ava stepped forward to shake the man's hand. "Mr. Carter, I'm Dr. Fenn. I heard you had a sick little guy here."

"Name's Gus. And we do have one who's a tad under the weather. I was just bringing him a little something to drink." He handed the glass to Margaret. "I didn't know doctors did house calls anymore. That's a treat."

Ava nodded toward Toby. "When I found out your grandson was feeling sick, I thought a handsome six-year-old would be a great first patient."

"Dad, Dr. Fenn is opening the new practice in town."

"Oh, she is? You'll be a big hit if you do house calls for everybody."

"Only the special ones." She smiled.

Margaret set the drink on the nightstand. "Maybe we should let the doctor take a look at Toby before we give him anything to drink. We don't want it coming right back up."

Ava stepped to the other side of the bed and sat down. "Toby, I'm sorry your tummy hurts." She crossed her hands. "Do you still feel like you're going to vomit?"

"Not right now."

In her pediatrics rotation, she'd learned a long time ago not to come at her patients with instruments first thing. "You know, I have this tool and I thought we could let your dad listen to your tummy with it."

The boy sat up a little taller in the bed.

"Wanna hear, Dad?" Ava pulled the stethoscope out of her bag and handed it to Logan. Once he'd put the earpieces in, she took Logan's hand and guided the drum to Toby's stomach. "Right there." She pushed from her mind the little surge of energy that inched up her arm, then cleared her throat and let go. "Do you hear anything?"

"Um-hm. Could be a bear. I think he's in hibernation, and that's snoring I hear." Logan winked at Toby.

His tired eyes rolled. "No. That's *your* tummy when I hug *you*, Dad?"

Ava smiled. "Those are the kinds of sounds we want to hear. Is it okay if I listen too, just to see if I hear all the right noises?"

The little boy lay back onto the pillow. "Okay."

Ava moved the stethoscope to different areas of his stomach and chest. To put her patient at ease as she listened, Ava asked, "Do you have any pets, Toby?"

"No, ma'am. My dad says we don't have time for pets."

Logan's head dropped a little. "Taking care of one takes a lot of time and energy."

"So, I still can't have a dog?"

Ava applied pressure to Toby's left side. He didn't indicate pain.

"What purpose would a dog serve?" Logan asked. "Take a look at Milo." He turned to Ava. "That's my brother's dog. Lazy as can be."

No discomfort on the right side either.

"Milo's purpose is to be a good dog, and he's doing that like a boss." Toby grunted as Ava pushed his stomach one last time.

"Any pain now?" Ava cocked her head.

"No, ma'am. I just feel yucky."

"Let's take a look at your throat." She pulled a tongue depressor from her bag and peeled off the paper.

As Ava shined a pocket light into his throat, she asked Margaret, "Nothing unusual to eat today?"

"No. Nothing out of the ordinary."

After Ava finished looking into his ears, she turned to Margaret. "He may have a little stomach bug. Logan mentioned that you were concerned it was the appendix, but if it were, he likely would've been much more uncomfortable when I pressed on his side. If you keep the fluids going, he should be feeling better in the next day or so." Ava turned to the boy. "Toby," she whispered, "you keep working on your dad. Maybe he'll give in and get you that dog."

"Yes, ma'am." Toby smiled for the first time, the space where his two front teeth should have been showing a wide gap.

"Gee, thanks for the backup there, Doc." Logan smirked.

"That's what house calls are for, support where it's needed most." She patted Toby's hand. "I'll see you around."

As Ava packed her stethoscope back into her bag, Logan tucked Toby in tighter and kissed his forehead.

"I should probably be getting back home." She turned to Logan.

"Yeah." He stood. "Mom, instead of moving Toby, I think I'll come back and stay here with him tonight."

"Of course," she said. "And you come back anytime, Dr. Fenn."

Ava nodded her thanks. These were good people. The kind she hoped to treat all the time in Camden Grove.

As she and Logan left the room, she heard Toby ask his grandmother, "Is that Dad's girlfriend?"

Logan closed the storm door behind him as they stepped outside. "Sorry. He's not used to seeing me with anybody."

"You have an adorable little boy."

"He's a good kid. Carry that for you?"

She hesitated and handed over her bag. "Sure."

The sound of the frogs croaking from some distant pond bank left Ava filled with a sense of momentary contentment, like their summer song somehow put things in proper order. It felt good to help someone again.

On their way back into town, they chatted about mostly inconsequential things. By the time they reached her car and Logan thanked her again, she realized that the ride back had seemed a little too short.

Chapter Eighteen

Logan

The following morning, Logan woke early. The sky had just begun to lighten in shades of pink along the horizon. Toby lay by his side, breathing softly. The night before, he'd asked that Logan sleep beside him in case he got sick again.

As he rose from the bed, Logan felt the warm spot on the side of his shorts. Toby had wet the bed again. Even as a potty-training toddler, he had never had accidents as frequently as he was lately. Logan hoped it would be a short-lived phase.

He pulled a quilt from the closet and ruffled through Toby's backpack for dry clothes. When he found a clean pair of shorts and t-shirt, he raised the groggy boy from his sleep and changed him. On the dry side of the bed, Toby burrowed up in the covers and drifted back to sleep. A bath and the laundering of the linens would have to wait until he was awake.

The sun shone through the lace curtains a half hour later casting a pattern across the floor reminiscent of the doilies Logan had watched his grandmother crochet when he was a child. The woman had died fifteen years ago, but he could still imagine her knobby hands rolling and pulling and stringing thread or yarn for a new project, ever careful with her stitching.

His mother had always said he'd gotten his work habits honestly. Something about doing a job systematically and finishing it to perfection gave him great satisfaction. But lately, he'd been out of sync. Nothing had gone as planned.

Subcontractors he'd always relied on were occupied with higher-paying jobs. To keep his track record clean and money coming in, he'd have to double up on work in the coming weeks. The doctor's office and the Brashear contract would demand it.

Maybe, if Toby felt better, they would go over to the doctor's office later and see if he could knock out a small job or two. His mother wouldn't much like him working on a Sunday, but he didn't have the luxury of a lot of time.

After lacing up his shoes, Logan checked Toby's head for fever and grabbed the truck keys and his wallet from the side table. Milo would be waiting for food.

The ride to Wyatt and Lydia's left his mind wandering through the events of the previous day. A strange twenty-four hours. Meeting Ava Fenn had certainly been a twist in an otherwise ordinary weekend.

When he thought of the photoshoot, his chest tightened a little. The outfit she wore had been simple enough. Nothing like what Eliza would have sported, but he couldn't deny being drawn to look her way when he thought she wouldn't notice. Jeans, snug against her hips and her loose shirt, dripping with creek water, etched a memory in his head he didn't mind lingering on for a while.

Then, they'd had dinner together, he'd been to her house, and she met Toby and his parents. She even carried on a conversation with Toby. How many doctors took time to talk with a kid?

When she touched him last night, though, held his hand with the stethoscope, something shifted. Maybe even before then. Maybe it started at the Old Mill. But he hadn't expected whatever that was. He'd almost forgotten how a woman's touch could tilt things, how warmth could trail up his arm and settle in his chest.

He took a deep breath and slowly exhaled when the phone perched in the dashboard cradle rang and pulled him from his thoughts. A picture of Wyatt with his cheesy grin lit up the screen, and he tapped the speaker. "Hey, man. What's up?"

"What's this I hear about a doctor, and how much are you gonna hold out on me?"

"Which one already called you, Mom or Dad?"

"What do you mean Mom or Dad? Lydia was chatting with her sis this morning, and Jessie was telling her that your date yesterday was the new doc coming to town. I didn't realize we had a full-scale professional on our hands. So, what do Mom and Dad know about it?"

Logan rolled his eyes. He'd opened a door. "Nothing, she stopped by the house with me last night."

"What? To meet the parents already?"

"No, you bonehead. Crazy thing happened. I'm the contractor she hired to do the remodel on her office, and neither of us knew it until we met at her office last night." Logan decided again to leave out the details about the meal at Wigg's Place. "She heard me talking on the phone to Mom about Toby feeling sick and offered to come check on him. I was worried, so I took her up on it."

"Hm, sounds a little like destiny to me."

Logan could hear Lydia in the background.

"Lydia says, if the doc's making house calls, the doc's interested."

"She was very professional, and we both made it clear at the photoshoot that we're not open to a relationship. So, let's just drop it."

"Why not be open to a relationship?"

"Because I have a son to think about," Logan sighed. He had explained it all to his parents and Wyatt before, and now here he went again. "Look, Toby doesn't remember a lot about Eliza leaving, and that's good in my book. I can't take a chance on something like that happening again because next time, he'll remember."

The phone went silent for a moment. "But—"

"Drop it."

"Okay. Okay." Wyatt paused. "You said Toby's sick. What's wrong?"

Logan turned into the long driveway. "Dr. Fenn thought he had a stomach bug. I stayed at Mom and Dad's with him last night. He was sleeping when I left, so hopefully, he'll be better this morning. I'm pulling into your place now to feed Milo and give him some attention."

"Tell Toby we love him and that I'll be sure to get his opinion of the good doctor when I get back."

"Do me a favor and don't. Knowing you it won't stop there."

After the call ended, Logan wondered what Toby *did* think of the doctor.

Chapter Nineteen

Ava

Ava rolled over to look at the clock. The phone rang for the third, fourth, maybe fifth time from the dock on her nightstand.

Carly.

Ava pulled herself from the pillow, blew the hair out of her eyes, and fumbled toward the noise. "Don't you sleep?"

"Weren't you wondering how long it would take me to call? If it hadn't been so late when I started home from the Roxbury wedding Atlanta last night, I would've buzzed you then, but I know how you doctors like to get up with the sun. So, tell me everything."

Ava fell back on the pillow as she cleared her head. "What's there to tell? We took a few pictures, and then we left."

"That's not all. That can't be it. The few digitals Jessie sent me tells a whole different story. Good grief Ava, I could see the chemistry sizzling through the screen. Don't tell me that you didn't at least get his number."

Ava debated exactly what she should share if Carly was likely to hear about it anyway. Camden Grove didn't strike her as having the same anonymity quotient as a big city. She sat up, peeled the covers back, and spilled the news. "Turns out I already had his number."

"Wait. What?"

"Yeah, he's the guy who's working on the remodel of the office."

"You're joking. That's crazy, Ava. Maybe your best friend is a genius, and this was meant to be."

"Back up, Miss Einstein. He and I already agreed that neither of us is looking for a relationship."

"Why, in the name of all that is perfect, not?"

Ava sighed, "You know I moved here to be solo."

"Professionally, yes. But are you planning to let Corbin Simmons ruin your private life too?"

"Are you forgetting that if I hadn't stumbled on those files and started asking questions, he could eventually have cost me my license? Carly, it's professional suicide to be in an office with another doctor who's not reporting honestly. And I don't even know to what extent he was doing it. I'm still just hoping I pulled out early enough that my name won't be wrapped up in his shady practices from here on out." She tried to push the thought aside. "Look, bottom line? My trust in humanity got a good shake with Corbin, not to mention my heart. That suffered a pretty big blow too."

"I totally get the professional divorce. The burn was real. But you've got to get back on the dating horse at some point."

"I'm not looking for it anytime soon."

"That's perfect. Don't look for it. Let it hit you broadside. It'll be awesome!"

"This guy and his family are nice, but—"

"You've met his family?"

Ava combed a hand through the tangled waves of her hair. "It's not what it sounds like. I mean, I've met his parents and his little boy, but—"

"He has a little boy?"

"Yes, he does."

"How did you meet them?"

Ava tried to ignore the hint of self-satisfaction in Carly's voice. "I stopped by the office yesterday after the shoot, and he was there. We talked, and since you'll probably find out by day's end anyway, we ate dinner together." She hesitated to divulge that little nugget, but maybe Carly would ease up if she thought they'd actually gone on a pseudo-date.

"You went out?" Carly nearly squealed.

"We talked business. Briefly. And maybe a few other things. Then, his mom called about his little boy being sick. I offered to check on him, and that's how and why I met his family. On a professional level only."

"Oh, Ava, you're gonna suffocate on your own stale air. Let your guard down and have some dang fun."

"I did that once before and look what it got me. No, thanks. That road's closed."

"That road is up for repair, and it sounds like you know somebody who's a good handyman."

"He's got only four weeks to prove he's any kind of handyman. My office is nowhere near being done. And if he stiffs me, I'll be ready to—"

"What? Take him to small claims? I thought you'd had enough talk of court already."

Ava palmed her forehead. "Can we chat about something else?"

"One last comment, and I'll quit. The photos that came from that shoot yesterday were seriously usable. I need them to secure a vendor's spot for the Hartley Bridal Fair I was telling you about. You're going to let me do that, right?"

Ava drew in a deep breath. "This is just to get that spot, right? And just in Hartley?"

"That's it."

"I want to see them first."

"Good. I'll bring the proofs by today after I pick them up from Jessie's."

"I'm dropping off some boxes at the office, but if you want to come by later this evening, that'll work."

"Sure. I hope you run into your new boyfriend again while you're there." Carly snickered.

"Not my boyfriend, and that's exactly why I'm going over on a Sunday, so I don't run into him."

Ava dropped her phone into the dock and slid out of bed. "Logan, a boyfriend. Pshh." Carly was still romantically delusional from meeting her new man from Chicago. She'd have to find a way to divert conversation to that when Carly came by.

As she made her bed, a much less threatening thought came to mind. Maybe she'd call Logan later and check on Toby.

Ava passed over the Sunday dresses in her closet, scanning each item with her wet hair bound in a towel. Maybe when things settled, she'd find a nice little Southern church to attend, where after-service potlucks and summer sing-alongs edged out the angst of weekday worries. She reached for a light, printed summer skirt and a baby blue scoop-neck blouse that made her happy when she wore them together. She needed happy today.

After the previous evening with Logan, she had come home and tried to clear her mind by staying up into the early hours, continuing to purge from her belongings the useless things she'd collected over the years.

Simplify and reduce. She played the mantra over and over in her head.

Throwing out old reminders helped more than she'd have thought. With every bag she tied for the garbage truck, her emotional load seemed a little lighter. That was until she sat on her bedroom floor, surrounded by old photos, and ran across something that stopped her cold.

The gala photo of her with Corbin Simmons.

They'd been to the fundraiser that night for the Children's Hospital. At the event, several people had commented on how perfect they looked together—he, the dashing and successful doctor, dressed to the nines in black coat and tie, and she, the former resident turned co-worker, his companion in a black silk dress. It was their first public foray. She'd wanted to keep their relationship low-key, but he was ready to wear her on his arm for anyone to see.

After residency, the position in his satellite clinic came almost magically, made even more enticing by a generous business proposal. If she'd not been completely sold by his charm alone, the perks he'd offered for coming on board were enough. Even so, she still had concerns about appearing professional. With his share of coaxing, Corbin had finally convinced her to relax. At the gala that night, as he introduced her, she finally loosened up, began to bask in her success, and could hardly stop smiling. Then, the bottom fell out only two months later when she ran across the files with information that didn't add up. From there, she worried, then dug around only enough to realize that if she didn't get out, sooner or later, there would be a witch hunt, and she'd be left holding the broom.

She'd trusted Corbin blindly, given him open reign on her reputation, her confidence, her life. What a fool she had been!

She sat looking at the gala photo for a long time. Debated on whether to set fire to it. Then, she finally tossed it in an office box, determined she'd keep it. Not because she didn't hate what it represented. On the contrary, it symbolized what she'd never let herself succumb to again. Yes, she'd keep that memento. Sometimes reminders didn't need purging so fast.

Chapter Twenty

Logan

Mid-morning, after returning to his parents' house with Milo in tow, Logan found Toby at the table with his dad, eating scrambled eggs and sausage. He looked a little more chipper than last night, with his hair still damp from a bath. The washing machine spinning in the background left Logan certain that his mother already had the load of wet bed linens in the wash.

"Hey Peanut Butter, how're you feeling this morning?"

"Okay."

Margaret rounded the table with a loaded bowl of hash browns as Logan sat down. "He's hungry this morning. That's a good sign. But we decided to stay home from church in case his stomach was still uneasy." His mom and dad were regular attendees at a little country church a mile and a half closer to town. Logan and Toby went with them, too, more than not. Most Camden Grove residents found a church pew to warm on Sunday mornings.

His dad, seated on the other side of the table, leafed through the Sunday paper. "Yeah, I've been telling him if he keeps at this rate, we'll have to raise another hen or two to supply his demand on eggs."

"I'm glad you're feeling better." Logan winked at the boy. "Milo's outside. I thought we'd bring him with us today."

Toby's eyes widened. "You brought Milo to Nana and Pop's?"

"Yeah. Don't look at me like that." Logan forked some hash browns onto his plate. "I'm not caving. I'm just giving him a break from being in the house. Besides, I thought if you were feeling better, you could spend some time with me today. I've got a couple of things to take care of in town. You could keep me company and watch after Milo."

"This boy needs a dog." His dad flipped to a new section.

"We don't *need* a dog. We're away from the house too much," Logan argued.

"He could come with us, Dad, wherever we go."

Logan talked at the newspaper between him and his dad. "You started something. I've got enough work to do without keeping up with a dog." He turned to Toby. "I've never seen one that would stay right with you anyway—always gotta go off chasing after 'em. I don't have time for that."

"We could get a trained dog. Blaze from the playground says his dog is trained to do tricks and stay and sit, and he doesn't even have to say it twice." Toby took a big bite of eggs.

"I bet Blaze from the playground wasn't the one chasing his dog in circles while he was learning how to do tricks and stay and sit."

Toby shrugged his shoulders and took another bite.

"Where're you headed today? You're not going to work on Sunday, are you?" His dad closed the newspaper and set it on the table beside his plate. Expectations for quiet Sundays still took a lead seat at the table in the Carter family.

"I'm running behind, and this new account'll be taking up even more time starting tomorrow." He forked the last bite of sausage. "I need to make sure some things are in place before the week gets started."

"Why don't you leave Toby with us since he's not well." Margaret refilled her grandson's glass of water.

"Seems he's feeling better. He's eating like a starved horse." Logan smiled.

"Nana, I wanna stay with Dad today. And take Milo too."

Logan finished his plate and scooted his chair back. "That settles it, then."

"You be sure to tell your daddy if you get the least bit queasy." She turned to Logan. "And you keep him hydrated."

"I will, Mom. Stop worrying."

She propped her hands on her hips. "We don't have that nice doctor in arm's reach at the moment, so you'll have to keep a close eye on him. If he gets pale or—"

"Mom, I'll watch after him."

"Say, about that doctor." His dad raised an eyebrow. "I didn't notice her having a ring on."

Logan gave him a hooded look. "That's enough, Dad."

"Just an observation."

Logan ignored the comment. "Come on, Mom. I'll help with the dishes while Toby gets his things together."

After cleaning up, Logan and Toby stopped by the house to pack a few lunch items in a basket, then set out for work. Toby sat in the passenger seat with Milo's head in his lap, talking to the dog as they headed for the office. His one-sided chatter faded into the background as Logan thought about his dad's comment about Ava. Then, moments from the day before floated in and out of his mind, teasing him with images of her face.

Less than twenty-four hours ago, he'd effectively held hands with this woman. Though it was only on pretense, he'd laced his fingers with hers at the water's edge like they'd been together forever. And then, when she'd gotten feisty and pushed him into the water, he had pulled her in after him without even a second thought, his judgment completely abandoned in a single moment. He'd almost kissed her, for Pete's sake. What was he thinking? Getting that close should not have been in the cards at all. Touching her, seeing her smile . . .. He pushed the thoughts out of his head and exhaled a breath he didn't realize he was holding. Ava Fenn and all the work he had to do definitely could not occupy the same headspace.

Or could it?

By early afternoon, they'd spent a couple of hours at the construction office with Logan pouring over the last details for the Brashear project. When the particulars were buttoned down to his satisfaction, they loaded Milo in the cab of the truck and headed toward the doctor's office. At least, they'd be less likely to run into Ava there on a Sunday.

As they traveled down the highway, Milo sat perched in the seat between Logan and Toby, tongue hanging out and panting. Toby kept his hand buried in the fur around his neck, Milo appearing as if he expected as much.

Then, out of nowhere, Logan let a question slip from his thoughts to his lips. "Toby, what did you think of the doctor last night?"

"She was nice."

"Yeah. She was nice," Logan repeated. He curved his wrist overtop of the steering wheel. "So, I heard you ask Nana if she was my girlfriend."

"Yeah, you don't ever hang out with girls, so I thought she must be your girlfriend."

Milo moved to the floorboard beneath Toby's feet to lie down. Then Toby asked, "Dad, will I ever have a mom?"

Like enduring a punch to the gut, Logan took a moment to recover. "What makes you ask that, buddy?"

"All the kids at school have moms. They're at the parties and field trips and come to have lunch on Fridays." Toby looked out the window away from Logan. "I know Eliza doesn't want me, so I don't expect her to come back and be my mom."

Logan's heart sank. Toby had called his mother Eliza ever since he was old enough to know his family didn't look like others. Since before he was old enough to ask gut-punch questions.

"Some of the other kids at school have stepmoms. Will I ever have a stepmom? Cause if you want to have a girlfriend and she became my stepmom, I'd be okay with that."

Logan reached over and put his hand on the boy's arm. "Well, we don't have to worry about that today. Sound good?"

Toby nodded as they reached the south end of Main Street, headed toward the doctor's office.

Chapter Twenty-One

Ava

When she saw Logan's truck parked in front of her office, Ava started to turn around and go back home, but her curiosity got the better of her. Maybe he'd begun to see that the office needed more of his attention after all. But on Sunday?

A few seconds of deliberation left her reasoning that if she dropped off the boxes, she could save herself any awkwardness later of calling to ask how Toby was doing.

After parking beside Logan, she carried a tightly packed box from her car, weighing enough for her to wish she'd loaded it a little lighter. Leaning the box against the door, she stretched to turn the knob, and, as the door burst open, the box and its contents scattered on the waiting room floor.

She knelt to gather sticky note pads, file folders, and ink pens as Logan came through the hall door. "What in the—? I thought the roof had caved in."

Ava looked up, embarrassed. "No, just me."

"Are you alright?" He bent to the floor and began picking up stray note cards.

"I'm fine. Just clumsy. What're you doing here?" She brushed a strand of hair from her face.

"I came to see what needed to be in place for this coming week. Just trying to get a few things ready." He handed her the note cards. "You're not planning to do any work here today, are you?"

"Oh, no. I just wanted to get these boxes out of the house."

"Dad?" Toby came through the door with a rather hefty-looking golden retriever padding along by his side.

Ava dropped the cards into the box and stood. "Hey, Toby. How's my first patient feeling today? Any better?"

"Hey, Dr. Fenn." The little boy's eyes lit up. "Yeah, I'm okay."

The dog barked a greeting.

"I hope you don't mind us bringing Milo inside. He's my brother's pet."

"Yeah, I remember, 'lazy as can be,' right?" She cut a glance toward Logan.

His dimples deepened in his cheeks. "We're dog-sitting while Wyatt and his wife are on vacation for a few days."

She walked over and knelt beside Milo to rub his head. "What a sweetie." She smiled at Toby. "I can see why you're hoping to get one of these. Looks like Milo's a big buddy of yours."

"Yeah, he's awesome." Toby rubbed the dog's coat.

"I used to have a neighbor who had a retriever just like Milo. Got him after he came home from Afghanistan." She looked up at Logan. "PTSD. So, his was a service dog." To Toby, she tilted her head. "Which is a complicated way of saying he had an animal friend who helped him feel better." She scratched Milo behind the ears as he leaned into her hand.

"Milo always makes me feel better too." Toby leaned over on the panting dog. "Have you ever had a pet, Dr. Fenn?"

"I did once. His name was Coco. He was a chocolate lab. But a few years back, he died."

"Don't you want another dog?"

"Maybe someday, when I've settled down and have a little guy like you who can be his best buddy."

Toby smiled.

"So—" Logan picked up the box "—where do you want this?"

"In the office area would be great." She opened the hall door and followed him past the receptionist's counter. "There," she said, pointing. "You can set it on the file cabinet. Thanks."

"Do you have more?"

"One more out in my car."

"I'll grab it for you, then. Toby, I'll be right back."

"Thanks." Ava stepped over to Toby as Logan disappeared through the door. "So, you're feeling better?"

"Yeah, I'm just thirsty. My throat got sore when I threw up yesterday."

"Was your tummy hurting when you got up this morning?"

"No, it didn't have time to. Nana put me in the tub first thing, cause I . . . um . . ." He turned to Milo and started to shake the dog's paw. "Did you know Milo can shake hands?"

"'Cause why, Toby?"

The little boy sighed. He hesitated. "I don't want to tell you. You might think I'm a baby."

Ava cocked her head to the side. "I would never think you're a baby, Toby. Did you happen to wake up wet?"

He hung his head. "Yeah. That's embarrassing."

"Oh, Toby, sometimes our bodies just decide to work on their own without getting our permission first. Everybody has accidents, and you know what? Everybody gets embarrassed sometimes too. Did you know I was embarrassed that your dad saw where I'd spilled everything out of that box a minute ago?"

"Really?"

"Tell you what, don't you worry about your accident, and I'll not worry about mine, either. Deal?" She held out her hand.

"Deal."

Logan came through the door with the other box. "What're you two making pacts about?" He crossed to the file cabinet and set the second box with the first one.

Ava looked at Toby, and he looked back at her. Then he burst out, "Dr. Fenn's gonna have peanut butter sandwiches with us, Dad."

"Oh, yeah?" Logan's brow furrowed. "Um, okay."

Ava shook her head. "I didn't—"

"You like peanut butter sandwiches, don't you? Everybody likes peanut butter sandwiches." Toby stretched his arms wide.

"Let me guess . . ." Ava squinted ". . . that's why I heard your dad call you Peanut Butter yesterday? Because you're a fan?"

Toby nodded.

"I caught him buried up to the elbow in the peanut butter jar when he was little. The name kind of stuck." Logan grinned.

"So, ya want one? The basket's in the back room. I'll go get it." Toby took off out the door before waiting for her reply.

Logan lowered his gaze. "You don't have to feel obligated, you know."

"I don't. In fact, I'd love a peanut butter sandwich. I haven't had one of those in a long time."

"Okay, then. Guess we'll have a real picnic this time, instead of a staged one."

Toby burst back into the room with a basket. They first pulled out a small blanket that Logan threw onto the dusty sub-floor. Then they each took a corner with Milo at the fourth and cleaned their hands with wipes from the basket.

"Hey, you've even got the good peanut butter. This is real gourmet." Ava unfolded a napkin on her lap as Logan smeared the spread on a slice of bread, then handed her a sandwich.

"Nothing but the best." Logan shrugged. He thought about how Eliza had always hated peanut butter sandwiches, how he had to be the one to buy a jar if they ever had it in the house.

Toby opened a water bottle and chugged half of it before he stopped.

"Thirsty, buddy?" Logan opened the bag of chips.

Toby capped the bottle and set it on the blanket. "Dad, can Dr. Fenn come to my birthday party?"

"Um, yeah." Logan set the chips in the center of the blanket. "She may be busy, though."

"You're not busy on Saturday, are you? It's my seventh birthday at Nana and Pop's house. You already know where that is, and it's at five o'clock. We're gonna roast hot dogs and hamburgers and have cake and ice cream. You'll come, right? Milo'll be there too. Cause Uncle Wyatt and Aunt Lydia's coming."

Ava hesitated as she looked to Logan for a reaction.

He rubbed the back of his neck. "Like I said, Tobe, the doctor may have some other plans."

"Yeah, I don't want to impose. I probably need to work here at the office that night."

"Please. You gotta come." The little boy's pleading eyes melted her resolve. Ava stole another glance at Logan.

He shrugged. "Yeah. You . . . should come, unless you can't get away, that is."

She somehow coaxed words from her mouth. "Okay. I'll be there."

"Yes." The little boy pumped his fist.

"Ever get the feeling you've been played by a first grader?"

Better than being played by an adult, she thought.

The rest of their impromptu picnic passed with easy conversation and some laughs over Milo's antics. Then, Ava looked at her watch. "I should probably get back home. My friend Carly's coming to see me in a little while. I shouldn't keep her waiting."

Logan rose as she stood and brushed off her hands.

"Here." She pointed to the blanket. "I can at least help you clean up since you shared your peanut butter with me." When she bent down, Logan leaned over for the same corner of the blanket, and her shoulder rubbed against his. She didn't dare look at him.

"Oh, sorry."

"No, it's my fault." He took the blanket from her and changed the subject. "So, enjoy your visit with your friend."

"Yeah, I will." She decided against telling Logan that Carly was bringing the photos from their shoot by her place. For him to think she had any interest in them . . . in him . . . would be sending the wrong signal.

"So, I guess we'll see you Saturday, if not here at the office this week." He tossed the folded blanket in the basket.

"I'll probably just stay out of the way and let you get your job done." She turned to Toby and handed him the jar of peanut butter. "I'm glad you're feeling better."

"Thanks, Dr. Fenn." He grinned. "See you Saturday."

"You bet." With a half-wave, Ava stepped out of the room and, by the time she got to her car, wondered why she'd let someone—this time a child—lead her right into another occasion involving Logan Carter.

She started her car and pulled out of the clinic parking lot, smiling. Something about that little boy made her heart a little warmer every time she thought of him.

Chapter Twenty-Two

Logan

Logan had plans for a chat with his son on the way back to Wyatt and Lydia's about not putting adults on the spot, but his phone rang just as they were locking up Ava's office.

Dakota Renshaw's name flashed on the screen.

"Hey, man." Logan opened the truck door to let Toby and Milo in. "I was hoping to hear from you soon."

"Yeah, I wanted to check on you after our run-in with the doctor. She didn't seem so happy with us. You smooth things over?"

Logan looked over at Toby as he slid into the driver's seat. "I guess you could call it that. We've still got the job."

"That's good."

"Maybe, but since I picked up the Brashear contract, time's gonna be tight.

"I haven't seen you leave a contract undone yet. You're in luck, though. The installation job I had lined up got pushed back.

Owner's waiting on special-order supplies, so I should be able to help at the end of next week."

"Don't guess you could bump me any sooner, could you?"

"We'll get it by your deadline. You worry too much."

"Next week, then. I'll be on site."

When Logan ended the call, his thoughts revolved around Ava, then how to meet deadlines. Then Ava some more. She really was good with Toby. Something genuine in her voice, in her actions, softened his hard-earned aversions to the whole idea of a woman being in his thoughts in the first place. And man, did she know how to wear baby blue.

He shook the vision from his mind, and mid-way through the trip back to Hartley, when Logan again considered the would-be conversation with Toby, he glanced to his right. A tired little boy lay atop Milo in the seat, sound asleep. Their man-to-man would have to come later.

Chapter Twenty-Three

Ava

On Sunday evening, a short-lived thunderstorm dropped enough rain to rinse the pollen off the porch rails. Ava sat out in the swing taking in the musky scent of the wet trees, heavy with water. An occasional car passed or turned around at the keyhole, but the neighborhood remained quiet.

As she waited for Carly to show, her thoughts meandered between Logan and Toby and their afternoon at the office. If she were being honest, the spur-of-the-moment picnic had been a highlight of her first weeks in Camden Grove. The little boy being there had been fun, his personality a mix between impish and lovable, wickedly smart and unusually intuitive for someone his age. She wondered what events in his life had molded him into such a child. Maybe he was a weekend warrior, seeing his dad only during summers, holidays, and every other weekend. Or what if his mother had passed away? Or something worse.

The SUV, crackling against the wet drive, drew Ava from her thoughts as Carly pulled in from the street. She got out and rounded the vehicle, calling across the lawn on the way to the porch, "Look at you! Do you own a rocking chair too? Sitting out here like an old maid watching the grass grow. What's up with that?"

"You don't have to watch me in my pathetic state." Ava's voice dripped with sarcasm.

"Yes, I do. I have to find a way to make something of this sad existence you call a life." Carly stepped up on the porch, sauntered over to her friend, and kissed her on the top of the head.

"So glad you care."

Carly set a large, leather-bound photo album in Ava's lap.

"Should I be scared?" Ava cocked an eye toward the book.

"You should be petrified because they are *that* good." She pointed a thumb over her shoulder. "While you peruse those magical pages, I'm gonna use your little girls' room and grab a bottle of water."

"Help yourself."

Carly disappeared into the house as Ava anxiously flipped to the first page.

The scenery almost took her breath, and it wasn't the trees and water. It was him, so close to her, looking into her eyes. Page after page, she soaked in every picture.

When they'd taken off the blindfolds.

After they sat on the blanket.

When they'd skipped across the steppingstones.

Then she came to the one in the creek after they'd emerged from the water soaked and laughing . . . and she was in his arms.

Logan Carter. She touched the photo. She could almost feel the water dripping from his hair. The physical distance between them in the photo was negligible, but Jessie had captured something else, something besides two people standing close together.

She stole a quick glance at the door, hoping Carly would be a minute longer.

Then, she let her eyes linger, traced the outline of his face.

The story told itself, with each page she'd turned, in a progressive wordless narrative.

Seconds later, Carly cleared her throat, standing in front of Ava with a Cheshire grin.

Ava closed the album with a thud and looked up. "Wow." Her voice came out abrupt, firm. She tried not to sound overly impressed. "Jessie did a good job."

"Oh, don't sit there and try to minimize and analyze and do whatever else it is that you doctors do. Just look at it for what it is. You two are a steamy mess." Carly plopped into the swing beside her and turned again to the first page of the album. "See how he's looking at you? Can you even stand it?"

"I promise you, Jessie just caught a millisecond glance here, and she—or you—did a good job of doctoring it up with those soft, romantic filters of yours. He wasn't giving me any scorching looks if that's what you're thinking."

"Ava, you may be trying to kid yourself, but you're not pulling one over on me. I know because I happen to have experience with this. Remember?"

"Your experience with Jex and that Chicago trip this spring has nothing to do with Logan and me, though."

"I'm telling you, it has everything to do with it. When I went to Chicago to meet Jex, he was a total stranger, and he taught me about the magic of strangers in these kinds of settings. Remember, he even demonstrated. Carly raised her eyebrows."

"You should focus on the two of you, then, because you've got your hopes up for nothing with Logan and me."

"I plan on spending some serious time focusing on Jex, but neither you nor I can deny that you two have some serious chemistry going on."

Ava turned more pages, acting as if to satisfy Carly. Honestly, Logan was just plain hot. By the time she got back to the photos where they were in the creek, her heart hammered in her chest. Then, she shut the album again—another thud. "Okay, he's a good-looking guy. I'll give you that much."

"Are you out of your mind? He's sizzling. And you're not half bad yourself with those dripping locks and sultry eyes."

Ava laughed. "So, because we both look like river rats who happen to be exchanging a glance, that means we're into each other?"

Snatching the album from Ava's lap and opening it a third time, Carly sighed. "Let me show you *my* favorite. This one." She pointed. "The water around you two, how it's dripping from your clothes and his hair. There's so much movement in these photos. They're too good for you not to be into each other." She closed the album and fanned her face. "Whew, it's hot as blazes out here. I can't wait to show these at the bridal fair."

"I thought you were just using them for getting a vendor's spot."

"Exactly. That's what you do at a bridal fair. Vend. With potential brides with potential weddings for potential bookings. And this, my dear" –she tapped her finger on the album— "is exactly what's going to vend our business out of the shadows. The novelty of it being a blind date shoot? Trust me, people are going to go wild over the romance factor here."

"But how many people are going to see this?"

"I don't know." Carly waved a dismissive hand. "You've got to stop worrying. It'll be fine."

Ava pushed herself from the swing. "That's easy for you to say." She turned, leaning on the banister. "You haven't had to worry about your professional life being flipped upside down in the last year, nor have you been concerned that you'd eventually have to answer for every professional act you've performed over the course of your employment." She threw her hands up in the air. "While I was in Nashville, I feel like I should've documented every move I made down to the band-aid, just in case. So wouldn't you be a little protective of your reputation too?"

Carly sighed. "Ava, look, I know it's not been easy for you, but no one's going to think you're unprofessional here. No one even knows the circumstances of your coming to Camden Grove."

"And that's exactly the way I intend to keep it. And as far as having a relationship, you've got to trust me on this. I'm not desperate. I'm not even interested. I just want to get started with my practice and move forward."

Carly rose from the swing and took Ava's hand. "I want that for you, too, Ava. I just don't want to see you live in the past like I did before I met Jex. I'm telling you this friend-to-friend because I love you. Corbin Simmons is the past." She gave Ava's hand a squeeze. "Don't let him rob your future."

Ava sighed. "Do you really think the photos'll help you?"

"That spread will make a *huge* buzz if you let me use it."

Ava kneaded the tightness in her neck. "Okay. I get that they look like we were having a good time."

"They look like you were meant to be."

Ava cut her eyes.

"In the shoot together." Carly raised her hands in defense. "Meant to be in the shoot. But just in case you eventually decide you'd like to explore the possibilities, you know, way in the future, when you're old and gray, wouldn't you like to know what I've found out about him?"

Ava folded her arms.

"No pressure. Just asking. Thought you might be a smidge curious." Carly pulled Ava back to the swing. "Oh good, I knew you'd want to know." She rubbed her hands together and continued. "Jessie was telling me that her sister Lydia—the one that's married to Logan's equally hot twin brother—said Logan's been single for three or four years now . . . and the ex is in California . . . and he's not dated since then either, according to Lydia."

So, that's where Toby's mom was. "Yeah, he told me he had a twin brother."

"What else did you two talk about?"

Ava smirked and shrugged her shoulders.

"C'mon. You can't leave me hanging like this. You said you went to his house?"

"His parents' house. To check on his little boy, Toby." She pushed the swing with her feet. "He's an adorable kid."

"Yeah. And?"

"And there's not much more to tell. I'm sure I'll get to know more about him since he's working on the office. And, despite it being Sunday, I did bump into him and Toby there again today when I dropped those boxes off."

"So, you've seen him now on two different occasions besides the shoot?"

"Should that be a big deal?"

"No." Carly plastered a frown on her face as if it were the least substantial nugget of information she'd heard all day. "Of course, it's not a big deal. Just two people who happen to bump into each other twice in two days. Who in their right mind would call that destiny?"

Ava elbowed Carly from the side and nodded at the closed album. "Those are some pretty good photos, aren't they?"

Logan

Logan carried a sleeping Toby into Wyatt and Lydia's house and tucked him in for a nap as Milo found his own bed and nuzzled into a comfortable position. For a long while, Logan sat on the back porch overlooking the meadow and thought about his son, about how he'd cornered the doctor into coming to his party, and about how he'd asked if he'd ever have a mom. Toby didn't really know his own mother, but Logan could tell that her absence had taken a toll. It showed in the little things, like his attentiveness to what his Nana and his aunt Lydia wanted or needed.

Last year, Lydia had been hospitalized overnight at the beginning of their first pregnancy. The miscarriage had left her depressed, and no one seemed to be able to pull her out of it. One especially hard evening when she'd pushed even Wyatt away, Logan went to spend the afternoon with his brother. While they were talking, Toby played with Milo in the field adjacent to the house, hiding and skipping among tufts of Johnson grass and wildflowers.

When Logan called him back to the house, his little fist bore a handful of daisies and Queen Anne's lace for his aunt Lydia because she was sad. Knowing the lace would likely be laden with chiggers, Logan told him that Lydia would probably want to keep his bouquet outside. He didn't realize she'd been watching from the screen door. Lydia put them in a vase and kept it in the front window until the daisies and lace wilted and the threat of chiggers had died in the sunlight of the window.

She later told Logan that Toby gave her hope that her own children would someday pick wildflowers to put in her window. It was the day she began to heal. All from the hands of a little boy.

But now, what else was in the hands of this little boy? Logan's reservations last night about Ava stopping by to check on Toby had multiplied with her coming for something as personal as a birthday party. Should he put a stop to it? Maybe it was innocent enough. She'd come to the party. They'd have cake. Toby would open a few presents, and then she'd go home.

Maybe he was making more out of it than he should. But what if he wasn't? Saturday was just a few days away, and something told him that a visit to a kid's party wouldn't be the end of the story. Something told him maybe he didn't want it to be.

Chapter Twenty-Five

Ava

When Saturday rolled around, Ava spent entirely too much time looking for an outfit to wear—a good reason, she thought, to purge her closet next. Simplifying and reducing hadn't made its way to her ample wardrobe yet.

After flinging hanger after hanger of summer combinations on the bed, she asked herself why she was agonizing over something as silly as clothing. It was just a kid's birthday party. But then, Logan would most definitely be at his own son's party, and she wanted at least to be presentable. Who was she kidding? She wanted to wow him. But why? It was all so ridiculous. Her thoughts had run the gamut since seeing those photos. One minute her stomach would flutter with anticipation, and the next, she'd push away thoughts of being with another man.

Pulling another couple of outfits from the closet, she settled on a summer dress she'd bought back in Nashville but had never worn. The light and flowy fabric had no memories weaved into it, and if she were lucky, after today, it still wouldn't. Before leaving, she loaded a gift bag containing a set of movie-themed Legos she'd bought earlier in the week into the car and headed for the party.

Balloons decorated the mailbox at the Carter house, and hand-sharpied signs pointed the way toward the back yard. She smoothed her dress as she stepped from her car and took a deep breath, conscious that her heartbeat had kicked up a notch.

As soon as she rounded the corner of the house, Toby came running to her, his little legs moving in a blur. "Hi, Dr. Fenn. I knew you'd come. Dad said he didn't think you'd be here, but you told me you would."

Logan jogged up behind Toby and ruffled the boy's hair. "I said I thought she might be busy."

Ava shrugged her shoulders. "How could I not come? When somebody serves me a peanut butter sandwich like you did last weekend, I can't pass up the chance for more."

"No peanut butter today, but we've got other stuff." Toby took her hand, tugging her toward the party. Balloons and streamers, a birthday banner, and gifts covered a table to the side while small clusters of adults sat around the yard. Weaving between chairs, a handful of kids played a game of tag.

A man who looked nearly identical to Logan except for his clean-shaven face walked toward them. "Logan, you didn't tell me the doctor was such a knockout." An attractive, woman sidled up beside him.

Ava smiled and held out her hand. "I'm almost certain you must be Wyatt."

A broad grin lit up his face, and he shook her hand. "Either my reputation or my good looks precede me."

"Or the doctor is smarter than your average bear and can see the resemblance between you and your brother." The woman held out her hand. "Hi, Dr. Fenn. I'm Lydia. Pay no attention to my husband. He's a charmer." Then she whispered, "It's how he wrangled me into marriage, but he's harmless."

"It's nice to meet you, and please, call me Ava." She looked down at Toby. "This is for you. Will you put it over on the table for me?"

"I knew you'd bring me something." Toby took the bag and skipped away.

Logan called after him. "Toby. Manners."

"Thank you," the boy yelled back.

"Sorry. We're still working on politeness."

Lydia piped in. "His Uncle Wyatt is still trying to figure that out too."

Wyatt wrapped his wife in his arms and nuzzled her ear. "You know you like me rough around the edges," he said. Then to Ava, "Come sit with us before Mom or Dad steals you away."

Ava followed Wyatt, Lydia, and Logan to a round table decorated with the latest action figures. Gus, Margaret, and a handful of other adults, whose names she'd never remember, came over to welcome Ava. They asked all the proper questions—whether she'd gotten settled and found all the best stores and restaurants. Questions that she might have heard on occasion in Nashville but that seemed much more commonplace in little Camden Grove.

In the next two hours, Gus grilled hot dogs and hamburgers, Margaret fussed over the breeze-blown decorations, and a troop of children played games with clothespins and blindfolds. Before the cake cutting, Margaret called to Logan and Wyatt, "Boys, come over and set up my circle."

Wyatt wagged his eyebrows. "Here goes Carter family tradition at its best." He leaned over and pecked Lydia on the lips, then said to Ava, "Bet you thought you were coming to a kids' party."

Logan rose from the table along with his brother. "Just so you're prepared, Mom believes in everybody being involved in the games."

As Margaret's two grown *boys* weaved around the tables toward their mother, Ava stole a glance at Logan's broad shoulders. Lydia scooted into the seat beside her. "They're an eyeful, aren't they?"

Ava dropped her gaze, embarrassed that she'd been caught.

"Don't be shy. I'd worry about you if you didn't soak up some of that scenery. Logan's a real head-turner. And of course, my Wyatt too."

Something about Lydia breaking the ice with the hard stuff made Ava relax a little. "They're both very handsome." She conceded.

"Are you feeling claustrophobic coming from a big city and landing here in the metropolis of Camden Grove? Or is that another phobia?" She fanned herself with a napkin.

"That obvious?"

"I can usually tell a transplant when I see one." Lydia angled her seat and crossed her long, slender legs. "I heard you were from Nashville. I'm an Atlanta move-in myself, so I get it. Not a lot going on here, but it sure is a great place to slow down and unwind." She admired her husband from across the lawn and waved his way. "Wyatt says Logan's converting the old newspaper office in town into a clinic for you."

Ava wondered how much Logan had talked about her to his family. "Yes. I'm hoping it'll be finished in time for my opening."

"If Logan Carter's doing the work, he'll finish it in time or die trying. Not many in the world like that set of men, right there." She nodded toward the brothers. "Wyatt's a little more . . . um . . . unreserved than his brother, but both of them are as good-hearted as they come. And hardworking."

"So how did you and Wyatt meet?"

"Have you seen the bookshop in town?"

"The one on the square beside the boutique? Whirlwind?"

"Yes, Whirlwind Books. Logan and I met in a bookstore a few years back—a long story for another day—but he decided pretty quickly he couldn't live without me. He found out that I always wanted to own a bookstore, so he bought that real estate to lure me to Camden Grove."

"It must've worked."

"Easily." Lydia grinned. "And his brother's made from the same cloth." She twisted a lock of her hair and nodded toward Logan. "So, how much has he told you about himself?"

Ava shook her head. "Oh, we haven't talked much at all. Mostly just business."

"Well, from one woman to another, he and that little boy have had their share of hard knocks. He's had to work his way out from under a load of debt his ex-wife left. And he takes care of Toby like he's a prince."

At first, Ava hesitated, but then she decided that Lydia was consciously inviting conversation about Logan. "What happened with the ex?"

"Eliza?" She huffed. "Her mind always changed with the wind. She got married, didn't want to be married, wanted a baby, didn't want a baby, had a baby, then left them both. Nobody's figured that girl out. Least of all Logan. He's still trying to understand what happened."

"Does he have Toby full-time?"

"Um-hm. She left for California and never looked back. He's got full custody."

Wyatt called from across the yard, "Lydia, you exquisite woman, come sit by me."

"See what I mean? Unreserved." She rose from the chair but turned back to Ava. "This game's always a hit," Lydia said. "For better or worse, it's become a tradition at Carter birthdays. Hope you enjoy getting to know people on a whole different level." She motioned for Ava to join her.

"Should I be afraid to ask what that means?"

"C'mon. It's a riot with this crew."

Margaret waved all the guests to a circle of chairs the two brothers had set up. "Everybody take a seat. Toby, bring your friends over."

The nervousness Ava curbed when she first arrived, came back. Exactly sixteen people, both kids and adults, scrambled to grab a seat. Before she could ask Lydia where to land, she was swept up in a group of kids vying for empty chairs.

Toby pulled at her hand. "Come over here, Dr. Fenn. Sit by Dad and me."

Ava shuffled behind the boy and sat to his left. Logan had already claimed the seat to his right. Directly across the circle sat Lydia and Wyatt, and a smattering of adults and kids of all ages occupied the other chairs.

"Okay, everybody," Margaret called out over the noise of the crowd. "I'll ask a question, and if you can answer yes, you'll move one seat to your right. If you answer no, you stay put until the next question. Oh, and the last rule: if you're ten or younger, you get to sit on rather than be sat on. We don't want to give Dr. Fenn any reason to have to work today." She winked. Everyone else chuckled. "Whoever gets back to their original seat first wins."

Ava remembered playing this game once at a bridal shower for one of her college friends. The questions got rowdy enough that she eventually bowed out. Though the mixed company wouldn't allow those kinds of questions here, she still knew they could get embarrassing, and she started thinking of reasons to excuse herself.

From her seat, she knew staying ahead of the old man they called Uncle Bart was a priority. She would not be sitting in his lap nor he in hers, even if she had to lie with every question. She also knew that she'd have to stay far enough back from Gus's mother, Helen. Her walker was parked at her side, and she looked as if she'd break if anyone sat in her lap. At least Wyatt was on the other side of the circle. That could be awkward. But what if she had to sit in Logan's lap? The knot in her stomach tightened a little as Margaret got everyone's attention.

"Alright, first question. Have you ever laughed so hard that milk shot out of your nose?"

Ava spontaneously giggled as almost the whole circle of people rose to move. She and Lydia stayed in their seats.

Wyatt pointed to his wife. "Lydia's lying." He teased.

With a smirk, Lydia rolled her eyes as the crowd laughed and settled into their new seats.

Margaret's voice carried over the ruckus. "Next question. Have you ever cried at a movie?"

Ava glanced at the old man to her left. He moved. She got up, too, but it wasn't a lie. Logan and Toby rose and shifted to the right.

"It was the movie about the whale, wasn't it, Logan?" Wyatt taunted his brother across the circle.

"My secret." When Logan stretched his arm over Toby's chair, his fingertips brushed against Ava's shoulder. She turned to see his forearm, corded with muscles, resting against the back of the chair, and, for a split second, wondered what it would feel like to be wrapped up in those arms. She pulled her gaze back to the crowd and noticed Lydia, who'd obviously caught her noticing Logan. Lydia simply smiled and winked.

A few questions later and Uncle Bart was two chairs away, catching up fast while she, Toby, and Logan were back in their original sequence side by side.

"Next question. Do you wear earrings?"

"Rigged! This game is rigged," Wyatt shouted. Lydia slid from her chair as Margaret shushed him.

The silver hoops that Ava wore kept her honest on that round. The crowd shuffled and chuckled as they moved positions. She slid into Toby's seat next to Logan, and because of rule number three, Toby hopped into her lap as if he'd sat there plenty of times before. Uncle Bart snapped his fingers in disappointment three chairs away, and Lydia took a spot on her husband's lap. Wyatt wrapped his arms around her waist and perched his chin on her shoulder. "Grandma Helen, you'd better put that walker in high gear. I see those long danglies on your ears."

The old woman laughed and waved off his comment as she scooted her walker to the next empty seat.

Ava tried not to let the butterfly swarm inside her stomach distract her from how much fun she was beginning to have watching all the banter among the Carter family.

The next few questions roused a lot of hoopla: "Have you ever stayed in your pj's all day? . . . Have you ever had your tongue stuck to an icy lamp post?"

From his spot overseeing the grill, Gus reminded the crowd of the Carter twins reenacting the scene from *The Christmas Story* and him having to pour warm water on the lamp post outside the kitchen door. "That was the movie you *both* cried over." Gus snickered.

"It's a rite of passage," Wyatt called out. "What kid hasn't done that?"

"Um . . ." Lydia pointed to herself and Ava. "Take note, babe."

"Well, we can't all be perfect, my little Georgia peach." Wyatt rose from beneath her and shifted to the next seat.

With everybody still laughing and chattering, Margaret read through the next few questions. Then came the one that changed the game: "Do you want or have a pet?"

At this point, Toby was back in Ava's lap, and they sat next to Logan with Uncle Bart still two chairs away.

Logan poked Toby in the ribs. "Did you tell your Nana to ask that question?" The boy giggled and shrugged his shoulders.

As mostly kids and a few adults shifted, Toby jumped off Ava's lap and turned to her with a big smile. "We both want a dog. Remember, Dr. Fenn? You told me someday when you have a little boy, you'd want a dog?" He turned to Logan. "Guess you'll have to sit still for this one, Dad."

A grin spread across Logan's face as he raised his eyebrows at his son. Ava smiled, too, at the little boy's craftiness.

Toby took Ava by the hand and tugged. She stood and nervously shifted toward Logan.

Wyatt called from across the circle. "Go ahead, Doc. Serves him right for calling my dog lazy for so many years."

Logan opened his arms in submission as Ava took her spot in his lap. Toby climbed on top of them both, and Ava wrapped her arms around the little boy's waist to hold him in place.

Giggling even more, Toby turned to look at his dad. As Ava sat in Logan's lap, she tried not to think too much. Her cheeks turning warm made her glad to have Toby in front of her to conceal the blushing.

Once the noise died down enough for Margaret to be heard, she called out the next question. "Have you colored a coloring page in the last month?"

Grandma Helen moved to take her place on Lydia's lap, who sat on Wyatt. "Rigged! I'm telling you," Wyatt called. "Grandma, you just see if I get you another one of those adult coloring books for Christmas this year." The laughter roared as the woman parked her walker and settled in comfortably with beaming smugness written across her face.

Uncle Bart still sat two chairs away, with empty places between them, while Toby hopped with gusto from Ava's lap and moved on to the next seat.

As Wyatt beefed up the theatrics beneath his loaded lap of women, Ava turned to Logan. "Are your legs squished yet?" His face eased into a satisfied grin as he leaned back contentedly with arms draped across the chair backs.

"Not at all. You're light as a feather."

"What are you smiling about?"

Logan nodded toward his brother. "From his caterwauling, it sounds like I'm in much better shape than my brother. That's always cause to smile."

Something about how comfortable this family was around each other, how much fun they had together, settled her nerves. But more than that, Logan's genuine disposition led her to enjoy the feel of once again being close to a man. This man. And for just a moment, like someone thirsty in search of a cool glass of water, she enjoyed his smile. She allowed herself to drink him up.

"Hurry, Mom. Ask the next question before my legs give way." Wyatt's pretentious moaning pulled Ava's attention back to the game.

Adding to the fun of the moment, Margaret stalled.

"Dad," Toby tugged at Logan's arm, pushing it around Ava's waist. "You're supposed to hold onto the person sitting in your lap, like Uncle Wyatt's doing, so they don't fall off."

Before Logan could say anything, Margaret moved on to the next question. Ava felt his hands slide tentatively but without argument into place along her waist.

"Okay, here's the next one." Margaret held up a hand to gain attention. "How many of you have done something you regret in the last week?"

Wyatt continued his exaggerated teasing. "This game, that's what I regret. And that's in the last fifteen minutes."

A few people shifted. The kids lamented about not eating more candy or playing more video games, and the adults remarked about getting out of bed or eating that spicy food on Tuesday.

Ava honestly tried to think of a reason to move. Then, she felt Logan move beneath her.

He leaned closer to her ear. "I regret what I said that upset you at your office last weekend."

Ava didn't get up but instead turned to him. "I wish I hadn't been so irritable with you."

"Are you sorry we met at the Old Mill?"

"No." She looked directly into his eyes.

"Neither am I." He wrapped his arms around her waist and lifted her as he stood. Startled, she let out a little squeal of laughter. Then, he sat down in the next chair over, with her in his lap again.

As the adults continued to banter around the circle and the children giggled at each other, Ava realized something. Maybe she didn't really want her answers to be different from Logan's, at least for the remainder of the game. She was having fun sitting right where she was.

Chapter Twenty-Six

Logan

After the game, Logan's mother directed the kids to the decorated table for Toby to open his gifts while the others visited and enjoyed hot dogs and hamburgers. Wyatt circulated to the table where Grandma Helen sat with her walker to the side, while Lydia snapped pictures with her phone and chatted with Ava. Uncle Bart moved to the grill to commiserate with Gus over the best way to cook a burger as chatter continued among different pockets of people in the yard.

The circle game had left Logan clenching his fists again. But not out of frustration. Not even out of nervousness. It was more from a sensation he couldn't pinpoint—or maybe chose not to. Though, regardless of how hard he tightened down on his own fingers, they still easily retained the feeling of having touched Ava again.

As she'd eased into his lap earlier and Toby climbed in hers, he realized he liked where she was, as if she could be his if he let it be so. The same feeling had come over him at the Old Mill, but he'd shut it down then before it gained momentum. Then, when Ava and Toby sat together in his lap, the world tilted on a different axis. She held Toby with her chin perched on the top of his head, like he mattered . . . like he wasn't some throw-away kid.

After a moment, he loosened his clamped fists, letting the blood flow back into his fingers as he watched Ava from across the yard laughing and talking with Lydia. With every second that passed, more feelings surfaced—strong feelings he didn't know he'd ever allow himself to have again. And they scared him.

His relationship with Eliza had been one-sided. He knew it was a train wreck after a few months and endured it long after that. Coming home nightly to a filthy house, Toby crying in his crib, and her piled up on the couch scanning through online forums for casting calls left a still-sour taste in his mouth.

His clenched fist again involuntarily pumped with the same rhythm as his heart. He kept it under the table, out of sight as Ava approached and sat next to him, leaning forward, her fingers laced together on the table. At first, she didn't speak but smiled as she watched Toby and the other kids playing. Logan didn't talk either but sat without filling the space between them with idle talk.

Eventually, he leaned forward too, his arm almost touching hers. "What do you think?"

Ava's brow wrinkled. "About what?"

"I don't know. Anything, really. I'm almost afraid to ask what you think about this crazy family of mine." He rubbed the stubble on his chin. The eye contact between them was fleeting but long enough to stir again his attraction to her.

They both turned to watch Toby's face light up as he opened Ava's gift.

"Thanks, Dr. Fenn," Toby held the Lego set in the air and shouted from across the lawn. Ava waved at him.

"I think you've got a special little boy." She shifted to face him. "He makes people feel good . . . needed."

"I'm sure you know the feeling of being needed with the profession you're in."

"I think it's different with a family."

"What about your family? Those photos I saw on your mantle the other day. Tell me about them."

She tilted her head as if considering. "Not all of them are my blood relatives. Just the graduation picture. Those were my parents."

"You mentioned before that they'd passed away?"

"In a car accident a few years back, not long after that photo was taken."

"I'm sorry."

"That's why I ended up so close to Carly. You may have recognized her in the other picture."

Logan's mind wandered back to the beach photo. His pulse surged a little at the thought of Ava in that swimsuit. "Yeah, I remember seeing her around town a few times."

"We went to college together. After my parents died, she kept me going to classes, on a good path, in her own crazy way."

"What about the other picture? The one of the little girl?"

"Ariel? She's not family, but we met each other during my residency at Vanderbilt. I got to know her on my oncology rotation." Ava looked at the kids playing across the yard. "I always thought doctors were supposed to heal patients, but with Ariel, it was the other way around."

"How's that?"

Ava's expression changed to wistful. "After I got over the initial shock of being an adult orphan, I kind of took Carly's advice to the extreme and jumped into school like the deep end of a pool. Only I didn't come up to take a breath for a long time. Not until I met Ariel."

She continued. "I used to go in after hours and take her for wheelchair rides around the Children's Hospital, to give her parents a break. We'd sneak into the lounges on each wing and raid the ice cream freezers for her favorite flavor." Ava shook her head. "She thought that was so mischievous, but the truth was I just needed her to eat something. I never told her that they stocked the freezers on every wing just so all the kids would have their favorite flavors."

"Ice Cream Espionage. That's what we called it, and every day we'd wheel down all those halls, I grew a day closer to realizing that Ariel wasn't getting any better." Ava turned and looked at him. "I didn't see my parents die, but Ariel? I watched her fade away a visit at a time. Before she left, though, she helped me remember to enjoy my ice cream. That's when I started going to midnight movies and Titan's games and the Grand Ole Opry." She smiled.

Logan wondered why she'd walked away from it all and—even more—why she'd come to such a small town.

"So, there were no other pictures on the mantel. No significant other in your life?" Logan forced his eyes toward Toby, opening another gift.

"No, I haven't found the right man, I guess."

His fingernails dug into the flesh of his palm.

From across the yard, Logan's mother called, "Come light the candles, Logan, so we can sing Happy Birthday to this boy."

He rose from the table almost instantly. "C'mon, my mother makes a mean double chocolate cake." Relieved for a moment, he stood aside and waited for her to lead the way.

Chapter Twenty-Seven

Ava

After the party, the kids played in the yard with Milo and a frisbee that Toby had gotten as a gift. The adults began to say their goodbyes and leave as Ava helped fold chairs and clear off tables.

"You don't have to do that. We can get this cleaned up." Logan threw a paper plate in the trash can close by.

"I don't have anything pressing to get back to. Thought I'd help."

He paused, then drew closer. "Do you like fishing?"

"Fishing?" Ava squinted. She'd had men ask her to go to some unusual places before, but never fishing.

"Yeah. Mom and Dad have a pond just over the hillside. Every so often, when I have a few minutes, I take Toby at about this time of the evening when things are cooling off. Fish tend to bite a little better then."

"Um." She glanced at her clothes. "I'm not exactly dressed for it."

"It's a clear path to the pond, and Mom has some rain boots she keeps around here somewhere. I bet they'd fit."

Ava cocked her head. "If I say no, does that mean I'm an automatic wimp?"

"Pretty much, but that's easy enough to remedy." The spark in his eyes was a challenge, the same kind she'd seen when they'd been at the Old Mill. The kind that made the butterflies in her stomach take flight again when his dimples deepened with his smile.

"Then, by all means, let's go fishing."

Chapter Twenty-Eight

Logan

Logan first checked on Toby, who sat on the steps resting as the other kids' parents began to arrive to take them home. Then, he went to pull gear from the small garage to the side of the house while Ava slipped on his mother's boots.

He hadn't planned to invite her fishing, hadn't even planned to visit much with her at the party other than to say hello. It was a risk he didn't need. Neither did Toby. But when she got out of her car in that dress, the June breeze blew against her and hit all the right curves. Then, during the game? Well, there wasn't much else to say after that.

He needed to take this girl fishing. Maybe she'd show her true colors when she got behind a rod and reel. Maybe that would be the turn of events he needed to cool off the burners. If she acted even remotely like Eliza had when he'd taken her out on the lake, squealing at the sight of a worm and nearly gagging at the smell of a fish, that would be all the reinforcement he needed to remind him of why he was happily single.

As he checked the tackle box and pulled a container of nightcrawlers from a small bait cooler, Wyatt stepped in the door, arms loaded with the last of the lawn chairs.

Logan could see it coming before his brother even opened his mouth. "Don't start." He pointed a finger, cutting him off the minute he began wagging his eyebrows.

"Aw, c'mon, man. Lighten up. She's a babe, and you know it."

Logan couldn't deny it. His heart seized up every time he let his mind wander to that silly lap game. Any straight, red-blooded man with a set of eyes would've reacted the same way. "She's a friend. Of Toby's more than mine. The only reason she's here is that he invited her."

"Good for Toby. At least somebody's got some sense about him."

"Not in the market, man." Logan picked up the tackle box.

"Why not?" Wyatt put his hands on his hips. "You've been solo for a long time. Don't you think it's good for Toby to have a female figure in his life?"

"He's got his aunt Lydia and his Nana."

"That's not what I mean."

"Wyatt, I don't plan on bringing somebody new into the picture and risk turning things upside down for Toby when she doesn't stay."

"You don't know that she won't stay if you don't give it a try."

"She's not planning for the long-term in Camden Grove. I already know that. She told me that her goal is to eventually go back to big-city living."

Wyatt folded his arms across his chest. "If you're not interested, then why are you taking her fishing? I saw you bring Mom's boots out, and here you are pulling out gear. What's up with that?"

Logan shrugged. "Maybe taking her fishing will prove to you and everybody else that she's not our kind. Run her off, even. You know how squeamish women are about stuff like smelly fish and worms."

"It's a good thing Mom or Lydia isn't around to hear you say that, or I'd be mailing your next birthday gift to you. And, hello, I don't think doctors are allowed to be squeamish." He pointed a thumb toward the yard. "Logan, this one's not Eliza. She doesn't strike me as even being on the same playing field as your ex. You'd better perk up and take notice. Mark my words, the ravishing Dr. Fenn is somebody to be reckoned with." He grinned. "Or at least someone to be caught in a cold thunderstorm by a warm fireplace with."

"Will you stop trying to play cupid?"

"Will you stop looking for reasons not to like her and loosen up?" Wyatt squeezed his brother's shoulder. "Now, speaking of naked cherubs. I think I'll go get that way with my wife. She's supposed to ovulate anytime." Wyatt thrust his chin out.

"Too much information, man."

"Wish me luck."

Logan waved his brother out the garage door.

As he made a last check of the tackle box, he wondered if he *was* looking too hard for reasons Ava was all wrong for him.

Then, he snapped the box closed and grabbed his gear. He'd settle this right now.

Chapter Twenty-Nine

Ava

While Wyatt loaded Milo in the car, Lydia sidled up to Ava. "Looks like you're getting ready for some fun."

"So I gather."

"Just keep him honest. I've heard more fish tales out of this set of Carter men than I can count. Better yet, take the big one out of that pond yourself, and humble them all."

"The big one?"

"Yeah, a few years back, Gus had the pond stocked, and they put in a four-pound bass. Even named him Walter." She smirked. "Anyway, you two have fun." Lydia patted Ava's arm, then waved over her shoulder as she trekked across the yard. "It was nice to meet you."

Wyatt opened her car door, kissed her on the cheek, and turned to Ava, cupping his hand to his mouth. "Hey Doc, I've got a bet against Logan says you catch the first fish. Don't disappoint me."

"Oh yeah, what's it worth?" Ava grinned.

"A steak dinner. We'll buy yours, too, if I win." He slid in the driver's side with a wave.

Tires crackled against gravel as Wyatt and Lydia pulled onto the road and sped away from the house. Milo's nose jutted out the back window, his tongue catching the wind.

With arms folded, Ava waited as Logan emerged from the garage with a tackle box and rods in hand.

"You ready?" He tilted his head.

The roped muscles of his forearms drew her eye yet again. She cleared her throat. "Yeah, I hear Walter's waiting."

"So, you've heard of the legend of Carter Pond."

"Um-hm." She nodded. "I'm planning on catching him."

Logan's raised an eyebrow. "We'll see about that. Always good to have a little friendly competition."

"Lead the way." She tucked her hair behind her ears and fell in behind him, another view she didn't regret.

The path to the pond was as clean as Logan had promised. A small dock about fifteen feet square came into sight as they crested the hill. The pontoons bobbed, rippling the water, as Logan boarded it. He held out a hand for Ava.

When she accepted it, he tightened his grip until she steadied herself, then set the tackle box down and handed her a rod. "This one's Toby's. It's a little easier to cast. Don't want you to be at a disadvantage right off the bat."

"Thanks for thinking of me." She looked toward the house. "Did Toby not want to come too?"

"No, I think he's tired from all the running and playing. And he's not at a hundred percent after being sick last weekend, either."

"Hm." She examined the rod. "You sure you're not hindering yourself by giving me the easier caster?"

He huffed out a laugh and touched his brawny chest with a wide-spread hand. "You're talking to the teen champion of the Camden Grove Bass Fisherman's League."

"But that's been a few ago. You think you still have a leg up?"

"A Carter man doesn't lose fishing talent. It just ages like a fine wine."

"Or smelly cheese?" Ava giggled but didn't give him time to respond. She stepped to the middle of the dock where the tackle box sat. "Can I see what kind of artificial bait you have?"

"Don't you want to fish with some big, juicy nightcrawlers?" He held up a Styrofoam container.

He was testing her. "I've fished with nightcrawlers before." Then, in an exaggerated girly tone, "I've even baited my own hook." She drew her shoulders in a shrug and bent down to open the tackle box. "I just plan on showing you up, eating a paid-for steak dinner, and meeting Walter tonight. So"—she pulled a small white lure from the box, examining it at eye level— "I think I'll take my chances with this rooster tail."

She could see from her peripheral, Logan's mouth opened slightly as he watched her attach the lure to the line with a perfect clinch knot.

Ignoring his ogling, she tilted her head. "I bet right now you're trying to convince yourself that I only know how to tie a good knot because I've stitched up a few cuts at the office. You may be wondering if I even know how to cast a rod."

At that, Ava drew the rod to her side and, with the flick of her wrist, whizzed the lure across the pond. It landed in prime shallow water close to the bank's edge to her left. When she looked back over her shoulder, she offered him a self-assured grin. "Let's just put your curiosity to rest right now."

Logan reared back in laughter. "I not only have a kid who knows how to play me; I've got a doctor too."

"You need me to bait that hook for you? Might not want to give me too big a head start. Walter's eying my lure as we speak."

After that, Logan wasted no time getting his own line in the water. Ava steadily drew the wiggling lure across the pond and recast as he lobbed his bait to the right of the dock and waited for a nibble. A few minutes passed of her casting and reeling and Logan waiting patiently.

"So that's the second time you've surprised me. What else are you hiding, Dr. Fenn?"

She pulled the lure from the water, drew the rod to her side again, and purposely sent the line to the far corner of the pond, into a small row of cattails lining the bank. It snagged on a reed, leaving her with the excuse she needed to evade his question. "Must've cast it a little too hard. I'll go over and get it out."

"Don't bother. It's just a cheap lure. Give it a yank. It'll come loose."

"It won't take a minute."

Walking to the other side of the pond, Ava hoped her tactic hadn't been too obvious. She pulled the hem of her dress higher above her knees as she waded into the edge of the water to unhook the lure. When she looked up, Logan was eyeing her.

She gave the line a gentle tug, and it released from the cattail reed that had been holding it fast. As she trudged to the bank and returned with the lure in hand, he shook his head. "I don't think I've ever seen a girl go in after a snagged lure before, especially in a dress. You're a mystery in the making."

You have no idea, she thought. His comment dredged up thoughts of Corbin and the mess she left in Nashville, the fiasco she hoped wouldn't follow her to Camden Grove. She wondered if she'd ever be rid of worry over that part of her life.

As she continued to cast and reel and he waited for a tug on his static line, they quietly soaked in the remnants of the late afternoon sunshine. The clouds on the horizon spread in layers of orange and pink. But instead enjoying the surroundings, she reminded herself that this was just a party for Toby, that once this day was over, she'd go back to being an acquaintance with a working relationship with her contractor. After all, she didn't even know if he'd get the remodeling job done as promised. And, despite what Lydia had said about his work ethic, she still hadn't seen any proof other than him showing up at her office a couple of times.

She slowly reeled in the lure. "So, how's the work coming along?"

"At your office? Why? Are you still worried?"   "Should I be?"
He grinned. "No."

"People have told me before not to worry." Corbin always had a dismissive attitude toward her concerns.

Logan turned, looked her directly in the eye, and said, "I'm not a con artist. I'll treat you right."

Ava almost dropped her rod. In the lingering heat of a warm, June afternoon, a cool shiver trailed up her spine.

Chapter Thirty

Logan

Twenty minutes later, Logan stood beside Ava on the dock, her casting like she'd been born for it and looking like a little piece of heaven while he struggled to keep his mind focused on his line. When he'd reassured her she could trust him, the look on her face was strange, like what he said had somehow hit home.

Finally, his distraction got the better of him, and he bent down to close the tackle box. While straightening the compartmentalized lures, he stole a glance at her slender frame. The summer dress she had on showed off her legs even though most of them were concealed in borrowed rubber boots. Most women would have looked a little ridiculous in boots and a dress, but she was nothing short of beautiful.

Before his mind could roam further, Ava's pole bobbed in a quick, unsteady tug. She jerked the rod to snag her catch and then began the fight to bring it to the dock. "I got him!" she squealed.

Logan slammed shut the tackle box and crossed the dock. "Give it some slack. Don't let him break the line."

Ava laughed uncontrollably and tugged at the rod, arching it above her head.

"Give it some slack, now." Logan jumped behind her, guiding the pole to its snapping point, then giving in.

Ava leaned into him, pulling at the rod again, then straightening it and winding the reel in a quick motion to gain ground. "He's huge!"

Logan laughed over her shoulder, her hair brushing against his whiskers. "This is a minnow."

Ava screamed again as they fought to bring her catch to shore. Then, a trophy-sized bass flopped above the surface of the water, the silver blade of the lure flashing in the waning light. Mid-air, the fish turned at just the right angle and unhooked itself from the lure. The line went slack, then the rod. With his arms still wrapped around Ava, he stepped back, tripping over the tackle box and taking Ava with him to the ground.

Both Logan and Ava were a little shocked at first. Then, with her lying in his arms, laughter began to bubble up between them. Logan rested his head on the plank beneath him while Ava dropped her face against his chest. A few seconds later, their laughter stopped.

Ava slid to his side and started to get up.

"Wait," he whispered.

He leaned over her as she lay back on the dock, his eyes following the line of her jaw, searching the crease of her lips. His fists didn't clinch this time. Instead, he reached out and slowly laced his fingers into her hair. Tracing the hollow of her throat with his thumb, he drew closer. Neither of them spoke. His breath caught, then quickened. His heart rammed against the wall of his chest. Ava's eyes locked onto his. He felt the warmth of her breath.

Then, a voice, a woman's voice—no, it was a scream—echoed beyond the hillside. It was his mother shouting his name.

Something was wrong.

Chapter Thirty-One

Ava

They left the rods and tackle box where they lay and ran up the path toward Margaret's voice. Logan, a few feet ahead, rounded the corner of the house to find Toby on the ground, heaving and vomiting, and Gus and Margaret holding his head.

The concern on Gus's face mirrored that of his wife's. She looked up. "Logan, something's wrong. He started looking a little more peaked during the party. While the other kids were playing, he sat on the steps and watched. Dr. Fenn, do you think this is more than a stomach bug."

Toby wretched to the side as Ava moved closer. "Mr. Carter, can you go get a wet washcloth for him?"

"Of course." The man hurried away.

Ava looked at Logan. "Can we get him inside in front of some cool air?"

Logan waited until Toby could handle the move, lifted him from the ground, and took him into the bedroom. "Do you know what could be going on?" He eased Toby onto the bed while Margaret got a trash can.

Ava sat on the bed beside him. "We'll try to find out." Gus returned with a washcloth, and she placed it on Toby's forehead. "Hey, sweetheart." She took the boy's wrist in her hand to feel for a pulse. "Do you think you ate too much cake a while ago?"

Toby barely shook his head.

"He had only one small piece and a bite or two of ice cream," Margaret reported.

"Toby, do you remember what I did the other day when I pressed on your tummy. I'm going to do that again, and I need you to tell me if it hurts at all."

Toby endured the pressing without the kind of pain that would alert Ava to appendicitis.

"Has he had any other episodes of being sick this week?" She turned to Logan. "Or have you seen any other symptoms? Fever? Mood changes? Confusion?"

"He's been tired. He slept a lot on Sunday when we got back from your office, and he's been going to bed a little earlier than usual."

She turned back to Toby and washed his face with the cool cloth. "What about anything else? Trouble concentrating? Diarrhea? Headaches? Trouble breathing?"

"He complained of a headache a couple of times."

Ava looked at the little boy's eyes. Darkening circles deepened the hollows above his cheeks. She saw them earlier in the day but thought it might have been the lingering effects of the weekend before. "Toby, is anything hurting you right now?"

"Just thirsty." The little boy whispered.

Margaret started for the kitchen. "I'll get you a drink. What about a ginger ale to settle your stomach?"

Ava asked, "Could we change that to a little water for now?"

"Of course." Margaret disappeared into the kitchen as Ava's suspicions gained ground.

When she returned, Logan took the glass and held it for Toby. He took a large drink.

"Whoa, pal. Slow down."

"Has he been drinking a lot lately?" Ava felt Toby's head for fever.

"He stays thirsty, but when he runs and plays out in the heat, we keep him hydrated." Margaret handed Ava a fresh, cool cloth.

"Okay, Toby." Ava smiled at the boy and patted his hand. "I'm going to let you rest for a little bit, and I'll check on you again in a few minutes to see if you feel any better." Ava stood from the couch and squeezed Logan's arm. "Could I see you for a minute?"

Gus and Margaret took her place on the bed as she and Logan stepped into the next room.

Concern clouded Logan's eyes. "You have some idea what's going on with him, don't you?"

Ava shifted into physician mode. "I think it would be best to have him checked out further." She spoke casually, unwilling to worry Logan more than necessary before she had any definitive answers. "I would do it myself, but I don't have the means to do anything here or even in the office."

"Should we give it some time or go now?"

"Since he's still sick and has been for a few days now, I think it's worth checking out sooner than later."

"Okay. I'll take him to Hartley tonight." Logan ran a hand through his hair.

Ava saw the worry in his eyes. "Would you like me to go with you?"

"I don't want to ask you to do that."

She placed her hand softly on his arm. "You're not."

Chapter Thirty-Two

Logan

Logan had driven to Hartley a thousand times, but the ride never seemed as long as it did the two nights he traveled to the hospital for Toby's sake.

The first night, fear gripped him in the chest like a giant vice. He'd come home from work that evening and found Eliza standing at the bathroom counter, a puddle of water at her feet, spitting curse words at him with every pained breath. She'd been having contractions off and on for weeks, nothing that the doctors were alarmed about.

Then, at four weeks before the due date, neither of them expected Toby's early entry into the world. The road between Camden Grove and Hartley grew by miles that night, and now, it was doing him the disservice again.

Having Ava along did give him comfort. Relieved she'd offered to come, he'd loaded Toby into the truck and told his parents he'd call when they had news.

As they sped down the parkway toward the hospital, he glanced over at Ava in the passenger's seat. Toby, buckled between them, lay his head in her lap. Her gentle stroking of his hair pulled at Logan's heart more than he would have admitted just hours earlier. Toby had taken to her quickly, inviting her into their lives without reservation. And tonight, he had welcomed her company too.

As they neared Hartley's city limits, Logan drove in silence, his mind battling against the questions in his head. The uncertainty about why Toby was sick caused the biggest of his concerns. Then, as he pulled into the emergency room parking lot and watched Ava rouse Toby with the gentleness of . . . a mother, thoughts tore through his head with the force of a tidal wave. What if letting Ava into their lives was a mistake?

Chapter Thirty-Three

Ava

By the time they arrived, Toby was more than tired. Lethargy had set in, and he didn't have the energy to walk. Logan carried him inside, and Ava followed.

At the check-in desk, Ava promptly took over. "Hi, my name is Dr. Ava Fenn. We have a little boy here, possibly in DKA. He needs to be seen immediately."

The receptionist, a pleasant-looking woman in her 40s, immediately picked up the phone and dialed. Cradling the phone against her shoulder, she began punching on her keyboard at the same time. "What's his name, Dr. Fenn?"

"Toby Carter."

The receptionist's fingers flew as she keyed in his name. Then she spoke to someone on the other end of the line. "I have a male. Toby Carter. Possible DKA. Age . . ." She looked at Ava and Logan.

"Seven." Logan held Toby against his chest. "Seven today."

"Seven," the receptionist repeated into the phone.

With another few clicks on her keyboard, she dropped the phone to its cradle and stepped from behind the desk. "Come with me. The nurse can key in the other information after he's in a room."

They followed the woman to an entry door. She swiped an authorized card, a buzzer sounded, and the electronic door eased open. On the other side, a petite woman dressed in pink scrubs met them with a sympathetic smile. "Hey there, little man. I hear you're not feeling so well." She patted Toby on the back. "Let's get you into a room and see if we can make you all better." She turned down a long hall and spoke as she walked ahead of them. "My name is Marissa, and I'll be watching after Toby tonight."

"Thank you, Marissa." Logan glanced down at his son, who'd been completely quiet the whole trip there.

As they passed the nurse's desk, Marissa called to another woman at a computer, "Hey, I'll need a workup in Room 4. Can you call the lab?

"We'll put you right in here." Marissa opened the door to a small room with two chairs, an exam table, and a mural on the wall of an ocean scene. "I'll be right back with a warm blanket and a special pair of pajamas for you, little man."

Logan gently lowered Toby to the exam table while Ava circled to the other side and tucked a small pillow under his head. A TV mounted high on the wall, played a classic cartoon and momentarily took Toby's attention. Logan turned up the volume a notch and stepped over to Ava, putting his back to Toby. "What is DKA?"

Ava knew this question was coming. On the way to the hospital, she'd weighed heavily whether she should mention it at check-in at all, at least within hearing distance of Logan, but she was afraid if she hadn't, Toby wouldn't be triaged as quickly, and they'd be waiting longer. If she was right, Toby didn't need to wait.

She took Logan by the hand and pulled him away from the bed. "I'm still not sure what's going on, but they'll do a blood test to get a better idea."

"That's not an answer." He was determined. "If you know what's wrong with Toby, I need you to tell me now."

"DKA is an imbalance in the body that causes the buildup of ketones. High ketone levels are toxic and could cause a person to feel stomach sick, cause them to be thirsty, to urinate frequently, even to the point of bedwetting. Several other symptoms could show, but those are the big ones."

Logan ran his hands through his hair. "But what causes DKA?"

Ava lowered her gaze. "Diabetic ketoacidosis happens when your blood sugar is high, and your insulin levels are low."

"Wait a minute. Are you telling me you think Toby is diabetic?"

"I just think it's important to check for diabetes when a child is experiencing the symptoms Toby is. It's a simple blood test."

"But he doesn't even eat a lot of sugar." Logan turned his back to her and paced to the door. "Maybe a piece of cake or a cookie occasionally, but we don't keep candy in the house. And he's not overweight."

"Type 1 diabetics are not necessarily overweight, and it has nothing to do with how many cookies they eat." Ava stepped closer and touched his arm. "Logan, we don't even need to speculate at this point. He was getting lethargic, and I wanted to get him in without a wait. I just wanted them to rule this out before moving forward." She continued. "Toby's been sick for a week now. Once the bloodwork comes back, you may be able to take him home and let him rest, knowing that it's probably just a persistent stomach bug. If not, he's in a good place."

The exam room door opened, and Marissa came back in with a warmed blanket, a child's hospital gown, and a rolling-cart computer. After taking Toby's vitals and draping the additional blanket over his legs, she asked Logan a few questions and gave him paperwork to sign.

The door opened a second time, and another woman came in with a small monitor, a bottle of glucose strips, and some alcohol swabs. She left the items on the rolling cart and stepped back out. As Marissa pulled a set of gloves from a box mounted to the wall, she generated small talk. "I'm so glad I get to be the one to take care of you tonight, Toby. Are you comfortable?"

Toby barely nodded once. Logan stepped closer to the little boy and took his hand. "You okay, buddy?"

Toby turned his head toward Logan, and a tear rolled down his cheek.

"Hey, now. It's okay." Logan wiped the tear away.

"Aw, it's alright, sweetheart." Marissa loaded the monitor with the test strip. "Toby, did you know your body has secrets?"

As she spoke, Toby lay on the table with little response.

"Now, I'm going to clean your finger and get all the germs off, and then we're going to get one little drop of blood from your finger to see what secrets your body can tell us."

As she tore open the alcohol swab, Toby buried his head in his daddy's arm. Logan dropped his head to Toby's while Marissa discharged the lancet and pricked the little boy's finger. Logan flinched at the noise, but Toby barely moved.

Ava watched as the nurse collected the drop of blood into the strip. As the monitor beeped, she placed it to the side and wiped Toby's finger clean. "Okay, all done. And you were a champ." Marissa collected the supplies, then opened the door, "Mom, Dad, I'll let the ER doctor look at this, and we'll be back in shortly." The door closed behind her before either of them could correct her.

"Did you see what the monitor said?" Logan either didn't hear or ignored the nurse's mistake.

"No, it takes a few seconds to register. I'm sure they won't be long, though."

The nurse's assumption had taken Ava by surprise. *Mom?* Though the comment didn't seem to affect Logan, she let it simmer for a moment, tried on the name in her thoughts. Had it not been like a handmaiden donning a queen's robe, she might have let it stay a while. Instead, she shook her head. As they waited another few minutes, Logan sat, then stood, then paced the floor.

Ava never expected what happened next. As she sat bedside, Toby slipped his hand over into hers, his fingers small inside her palm. "Thanks." It was the first words he'd spoken since they'd left Camden Grove. His eyes were sickly, and his skin pale beneath the stark lights.

Logan turned to face them when he heard Toby speak.

"What?" Ava leaned closer.

"Thanks for being here."

"You bet, sweetheart," she said. "I wouldn't want to be anywhere else." Strangely, despite all the objections she'd voiced to Carly about getting involved with a new relationship, at that moment, she couldn't have spoken a more truthful statement.

Chapter Thirty-Four

Logan

The doctor who walked through the door stepped in with his hand extended to greet first Ava, then Logan. He patted Toby on the shoulder and introduced himself.

"Hello there, Toby. Mr. and Mrs. Carter, I'm Dr. Jameson, the ER physician on call tonight."

Logan ignored the second mistake in Ava's identity and went straight to business. "Do you know what's wrong with Toby?"

The doctor looked in Toby's eyes, scanned his overall appearance, and began a typical examination as he talked. "The strip test the nurse took a few minutes ago told us the story." The doctor's expression changed, like he had something to say that required sympathy. "Toby's blood glucose is currently 682."

Logan stepped closer. "What does that mean?"

"The normal range for someone his age is typically anywhere from 80 to 180." He paused. "Mr. Carter, Toby has type 1 diabetes."

For a moment, Logan couldn't breathe. The air stopped at his throat, and his lungs refused to work. Then, the exam room door opened, and a woman in red scrubs entered the room with a tray of needles and vials. The ringing in his ears became violently loud, and he suddenly felt hands on his arms, shoving him into the hall. Then nothing.

Chapter Thirty-Five

Ava

Logan began to falter seconds after the doctor broke the news. When he held his breath and locked his knees, Ava knew what would come next. As the lab technician opened the door, she shoved Logan into the hall and onto a nearby gurney. He slumped onto the stretcher as he succumbed to the rush of blood from his head.

A nurse in the hallway and the ER doctor converged as Ava rolled Logan to his back and propped a pillow under his feet.

"Mrs. Carter, I'm so sorry." The doctor turned to Marissa. "Can we get a wet cloth over here, please?"

The nurse returned quickly with a cloth, and Ava began to wash Logan's face. "I'm not Mr. Carter's wife. My name's Dr. Fenn. I'm a friend."

Dr. Jameson raised the rail on the gurney. "I'm sorry about Toby. You did catch it early, and I'm sure you know, that's the best news."

Logan started to come to.

"Marissa, if you can see to Mr. Carter, I'd like to have someone with Toby now as we get blood drawn." He turned to Ava. "Dr. Fenn, I think the sooner we get a bead on this little guy's situation, the better."

Ava looked at Logan, his bleary eyes taking her in. "I'm going to Toby, now. You stay here. He'll be fine, I promise." She squeezed Logan's hand and stepped into the exam room.

Chapter Thirty-Six

Logan

By 11 p.m., when all the preliminary tests were completed, they'd put Toby in a room and given him his first shot of insulin. Logan had regained his composure after the initial shock of hearing the diagnosis and had begun the long road of processing his son's illness and what lay ahead.

As Toby finally lay asleep, Logan sat in a window seat, gazing over the darkened parking lot below. A couple of employees in scrubs, leaving after shift change, weaved through the cars until they found their own and pulled out of the lot. *Their* world kept moving in routine circles—get up, send the kids to school, go to work, go home, go to bed, and do it all again. *His* world had come to a screeching halt.

All the *what-ifs* plagued him as he watched taillights disappear around the bend of the building. What if he'd brushed Toby's illness off as a stomach bug and kept waiting for him to get better at home? What if he'd allowed his reservations about Ava coming to the party to take root? What if he'd diverted Toby's invitation, or she hadn't even wanted to come? She wouldn't have been there to recommend taking him to the hospital.

He finally shook off all the thoughts tormenting him in search of something more consoling. When he turned from the window, he saw Ava curled up in the sleeper chair close to Toby's bed. She had closed her eyes too, though she couldn't have been sleeping—not well, anyway.

He sat in silence and watched her, the rise and fall of her breathing, the way she was turned toward Toby, within reach of him. He thought about his and Ava's moments at the pond, how playful she'd been, telling him she was going to show him up and catch Walter, how confident she'd been casting her rod. Then came images of her wading in the water, smiling at him over her shoulder, her brown hair glowing against the fading sunlight.

His eyes closed as he thought of her. These were the first seconds since earlier that afternoon that he'd felt the turmoil inside him diminish.

What he wouldn't give to go back to that moment before everything in his and Toby's lives changed. To freeze it in time so things wouldn't be as they were now. So that his boy would still be just a boy instead of one with a diagnosis.

Back to the moment when he almost kissed Ava.

After a few seconds, he opened his eyes again and refocused on Toby. He had to stop thinking about Ava. His reality had just changed. He had no reason to wish and dream. Now, more than ever, he had to concentrate on his son and their new reality. And thoughts of Ava would just muddy the waters.

When he rose from the window seat, Ava inhaled deeply from the chair, opening her eyes and looking at Toby. When she turned toward Logan, he pushed his hands into his pockets.

"I'm sorry I've kept you here. You should go home. I can give you the keys to my truck or have Wyatt and Lydia come pick you up."

"That's not necessary. Carly's usually up late. I'll give her a call . . . unless you want me to stay."

"No, you've already done more than enough, helping with Toby and keeping me from cracking my head on a hospital floor." He didn't want to think about how much he wanted her to stay. Instead, he returned to the view of the parking lot. "I'm sorry you had to deal with all that. Still not sure what came over me earlier. I've never passed out, not even when I saw Toby born."

Ava stepped closer and put a hand on his shoulder. "You got some hard news tonight. It's not uncommon for somebody to get a little weak in the knees when it's their baby, but Toby's going to be fine. You know that, right?"

He didn't respond. His shoulders rose with the deep breath he took. "He's got to be."

Chapter Thirty-Seven

Ava

Carly stepped into the third-floor hospital room at a quarter past midnight, Ava waiting in the sleeper chair while Logan snuggled against Toby in the undersized hospital bed.

"Hey," Carly whispered.

Ava rose from the chair and hugged her. "Thanks for coming."

"Of course, I came." She crossed to Logan and held out her hand as he stood to stretch his back. "Hi, I'm Carly. It's nice to meet you, though I'm sorry it's under these circumstances."

He gave a weary smile. "Likewise. Name's Logan."

"Yes, Jessie told me about you. Thanks so much for helping us with the photoshoot."

He nodded.

"How is he?" Carly glanced toward the bed.

"Finally resting." Ava crossed her arms. "They'll be trying to regulate his blood sugar throughout the night."

"I was so sorry to hear the news, but maybe having a good doctor close by will help ease your worries." Carly gave a sympathetic smile and a quick nod toward Ava.

The IV drip beeped, and Toby stirred in his bed.

"I should probably get back to him." The concern in Logan's eyes never wavered. "He's been restless. All this has been pretty overwhelming for him."

"I'm sure it has. Yes, by all means. It was nice to meet you."

Ava walked with Carly toward the door. "I'll be ready in just a minute. I want to tell Logan something."

After Carly slipped into the hall, Ava turned from the door to face Logan, the tired expression on his face deepened in the shadows of the room. Ava stepped to the bed and placed a hand on Logan's arm. "If you need anything, you have my number. Please, call me."

He nodded. "Thanks for everything. If you hadn't been with us . . . well. I guess what I'm saying is you were there when Toby needed somebody. That mattered to him . . . and me."

On the ride home, Ava answered questions. About Toby's condition. About how Logan was *really* doing. About the whole day. Had she not been exhausted, she probably would have been more engaging, but the events over the last few hours had drained her too.

"At least you caught it early enough that he'll be okay, right?" Carly sped down the parkway toward Camden Grove.

"It definitely could have been much worse." Ava rubbed at the stiffness in her neck.

After a few moments passed, Carly began to fidget, and Ava took notice. "What's wrong? Why are you so jittery?"

Carly shrugged her shoulders.

"You know you can't keep anything from me. I can peg you across a dark room with my back to you. What's up?"

Carly tapped the steering wheel nervously and blew a curl from her eyes. "Now may not be the best time to tell you this, but I got a call from Nashville this afternoon. I was planning to wait until tomorrow when I saw you, but it might be best if you have time to prepare."

"Prepare for what?" Ava's tone of voice hardened.

"Corbin called me asking for you. Said he'd tried your old number, but there was no answer."

"Yeah, my phone died earlier. That's why I called you from Logan's phone."

Carly turned off the parkway.

"So, how did Corbin get your number?"

"I asked him the same question. He's so arrogant. He never did say. Maybe he dug up your emergency contacts from personnel or something." Carly glanced at Ava. "Anyway, he wanted to talk to you."

"He can keep on dreaming."

"Yeah, that's what I thought, too, but just so you know, he was pretty insistent. I don't think you've heard the last of him."

"Is that all he said?"

"That's it."

As they drove to pick up Ava's car, she and Carly speculated over Corbin's motives. Whatever they were, it wouldn't be good.

Just past 1 a.m., Ava arrived home. She showered, dressed in a cotton t-shirt and pajama shorts, and sank into the comfort of her cool sheets, hoping to find sleep. But thoughts of Toby and Logan, of Corbin's call, of having the office ready in time for opening—all of it swirled in her head like whirlwind.

Tossing and turning, she finally found a comfortable position clutching an extra pillow. After that, sleep began to close in fast. Just before she drifted away, the image of Logan lying on the dock at the pond slipped into the edge of her awareness. She tried to push the thought away. Tried to argue with that dream-laden part of her brain that insisted she think of him. She could be a friend . . . but that was all . . . a relationship now . . . too much . . . Then . . . he pulled her to him . . . kissed her . . . so softly.

The next morning, a knock on the door reverberated through the living room and down the hall. Ava rose from the bed dazed, her extra pillow still in her hands. She looked at the phone docked on her nightstand: 9:02 a.m. She didn't remember ever having fallen asleep but did recall the last image of Logan that lingered from her dream.

Brushing hair from her face, she rose and started for the door, silently condemning herself for not waking up earlier to quell the dreams before they ever started.

With a peek through the viewer, Ava saw the fishbowl image of a man with a suit and tie. She hesitated, then opened the door.

"Dr. Fenn?"

A quick assessment told her he was likely in his 50s. His salt-and-pepper, clean cut gave that away. A wedding ring said he was married and, based on his dress, probably pretty conservative.

"Yes. I'm Dr. Fenn."

"My name's Dennis Ranier." He handed her a business card. "I'm with the Department of Commerce and Insurance. Would you have a minute to speak with me?"

"A Sunday's an odd time to make a business visit, isn't it?"

"I apologize. I won't keep you long."

"I just got up, but okay." She opened the door wider. "Come in."

The man stepped inside with a black binder under his arm.

Ava twisted the blinds open and offered him a seat. "Would you like something to drink?"

"No, thank you, ma'am. I have just a few questions."

"I'm sorry." Ava shook her head and glanced at the business card. "Did you say Department of Insurance?" She sat in the chair opposite the couch where Ranier settled.

"Yes, Commerce and Insurance." He scooted to the edge and laced his fingers together. "I'm here to ask about your work at Dr. Corbin Simmons's practice in Nashville."

Ava's stomach sank as she heard him speak Corbin's name. She tried not to appear affected. "Is there something wrong, Mr. Ranier?"

The man opened the binder and set it on the table. He slid it toward her. "I have here a list of some of Dr. Simmons's patients. Do you recognize any of the names?"

Ava pulled the binder closer and scanned the list. "No, I don't."

"Recently, we contacted the caregiver of one of those patients. The insurance company had been billed for services the patient had never received. Mrs. Leta Nylander. Her name's at the top of the list there. But you don't recognize it?"

"No." Ava's stomach began to churn. "What's this about?"

"The attending physician who signed off on that paperwork, Dr. Fenn, is you."

The sinking feeling became a weight pressing into her core. It was the same sensation she had the day she discovered one of her patient files in Corbin's office, and questions started to surface. She looked up from the list. "Mrs. Nylander is not one of my patients. Are you suggesting that I falsified information?"

"I'm asking what your role was at Dr. Simmons's office?"

Ava sat, her lips parted, staring at the list. "Mr. Ranier, I can assure you I've never fraudulently billed an insurance company if that's what you mean. I'd like to keep my license."

"Did you ever review and sign forms based on treatment Dr. Simmons may have claimed to provide?"

"Why would I do that? He's authorized to do that himself. He's a physician."

Ranier shifted on the couch. "Honestly, I'm not sure why you'd take such a risk unless you were covering for him."

"Are you serious? I have no reason to cover for anybody. I am an honest doctor trying to run a reputable practice. If my name's on something I didn't personally sign, that's because someone besides me put it there. Forgery, Mr. Ranier, not aiding and abetting."

The man never flinched at her defensiveness. "Dr. Simmons's receptionist, Paige Westerfield, seems to think you're on the up and up. So that's why I'm here."

His candidness was both upsetting and appreciated. Upsetting because she'd never done anything to cause anyone to feel she wasn't on the up and up, and appreciated because someone had vouched for her honesty, and he was at least telling her about it.

"You've talked to Paige?"

"She's the one who first made us aware that something was wrong and supplied the list." He nodded at the paper in front of Ava. "And she pointed me in your direction because of those suspicions, thinking you might be able to offer some insight. Ms. Westerfield no longer works at Dr. Simmons's practice. Since you also left, I have reason to believe that either she's right and you've never knowingly fraudulently billed an insurance company . . . or things were getting too risky, and you decided to bail . . . or your conscience bothered you enough to quit and establish a new practice a state away."

Ava cradled her head in her hands. "I can't believe this. I'm not a criminal, Mr. Ranier."

"Quite frankly, Dr. Fenn, the more I researched this case, the less convinced I became that you were. You're too new to the scene. Magna Cum Laude at Vanderbilt. Star resident. Bet I couldn't even find a traffic ticket if I looked. Most people in the business of fraud have a little less of a squeaky-clean profile and work ethic than you. Truth is, we've suspected Dr. Simmons for a while." He nodded toward the binder. "Before we got the communication from Mrs. Nylander's caregiver, we had reason to believe that Dr. Simmons was a part of an insurance scam of larger proportions than just a couple of misrepresented files. But we haven't been able to prove it."

"That's it." She shook her head. "That's why he didn't want me digging into the files."

"What do you mean?"

She shook her head. "We had a falling out." Hesitant at first, Ava didn't see a reason to elaborate on the personal details of that disagreement, but the business end of it could keep her head off a chopping block. "It's partly why I left Nashville. I was worried he was doing something he shouldn't be." She leaned back in the chair. "That's what this is all about."

Sitting upright again, she stabbed at the binder. "Back a couple of months ago, I went into his office to get his opinion on a case. He was with a patient, so I set the file on his desk for review. That's when I spotted another file—one of my patients—in a stack waiting by his computer. It had documents, reports of treatment I hadn't rendered. When Corbin came into his office and saw that I had the file, he took it from me and said he visited with the patient on a day I was booked—a telehealth visit. Except the billing code wasn't for telehealth."

"How do you know that? Doctors aren't always up on the codes."

"Yeah, but I had just been over that with Paige the day before when I was reviewing paperwork for another patient. Corbin had signed off on the wrong code. When I tried to point it out to him, he became fidgety, defensive even, and ushered me to my side of the clinic. From that point on, he tightened security on the files, and I didn't ask any more questions. I dug just enough that day to realize I was very uncomfortable not knowing everything that went on with my patients' paperwork."

"Dr. Fenn, were you in a personal relationship with Simmons?"

The question cut Ava to the quick. "Why is that important?"

"It could be very important to this investigation. It could tip the scales and even mean your license if your name is tied up with his."

"Mr. Ranier, I've always tried to be honest and professional. When I began to suspect Corbin of practices that weren't above-board, I decided to leave professional and personal interests behind and start over. I didn't give him much notice because I didn't want to deal with the repercussions. I left knowing I had done nothing wrong. I'm opening an office here in Camden Grove, knowing I'm starting with a clear conscience."

"That's not a direct answer. Look, Dr. Fenn, if fraud charges are brought against him, he'll likely pull you into the mix to share the conviction. The more personal the connection, the worse it looks for you unless we drum up evidence to the contrary."

Ava took another tack. "So why haven't you called all the patients on the list to check their bills?"

"We've tried, but Dr. Simmons didn't get where he is by being stupid. From this list, the three people we've been able to find are all Alzheimer's patients in a local facility with no memory of what treatments they've received from Dr. Simmons's office. And it's not all just billing of services not rendered. Those are just the skim on top. We suspect kickbacks and bribery, and false issuance of prescription drugs that may end up on the street. We've got the whole menu."

Ava felt sick. "But why would he have needed my signature?"

"Doctors involved in criminal practices have to be savvy. They prescribe medications under co-worker's names, so they won't get flagged for overprescribing. Their kickbacks come from multiple referrals to specialists, all too often for unnecessary procedures. Too many of those referrals under one name, and they draw unwanted attention from people like me. You get the picture. He needed your license and name." Ranier pointed to the list. "He's got a system—"

"And I was the trusting fool." Ava dropped her head into her hands. "I thought a big-city doctor wanted to hire me because of my ability." She stood and paced the room, the sick feeling in her stomach growing into a knot. "What do I do? How do I get cleared of all this?"

"We need evidence and your testimony."

"I'll testify, of course. But evidence?"

"We need the paper trail. Do you have access to your old files?"

"No. Like I told you, Corbin tightened down on access. I left that all behind when I broke ties." She shook her head. "Mr. Ranier, it's like I told you. I'm starting over here. I'm waiting now for the licensing board to approve my application to practice in Alabama. That should be in place any day. My office is supposed to open here in just a few weeks. You said yourself you don't think I'm involved. Can't I just go on with my life?" Ava already knew his answer.

"Unfortunately, what I think doesn't make your case. I need proof, and if all this comes before the licensing board, it'll be just cause for them to dismiss your application, maybe even rescind your license to practice altogether. Dr. Fenn, this has to be resolved and soon." Ranier stood. "I'll continue to dig for more evidence.

In the meantime, if you have any revelations about how to obtain the documentation we need, you have my card."

Ava followed the man to the door. "Mr. Ranier, am I going to lose my license or . . . go to jail?"

"You seem like a good person who got caught up in the wrong situation, Dr. Fenn. For your sake, I hope not." He opened the door. "I should tell you that news of this investigation broke over the weekend. Dr. Simmons will be aware, which is why I wanted to visit you as soon as possible." He shrugged his shoulders. "On a Sunday, even. Because this investigation is pending, doctor, I'd counsel you not to discuss our visit with anyone. It could land you in even more trouble."

Ava nodded.

The knot in her stomach grew as she watched the man get into his car and pull away.

Before she stepped from the door, she heard the phone ringing in the bedroom. As she rounded the corner from the hall, Corbin's name flashed on the screen from the dock on her nightstand. It stopped her dead in her tracks. She stared at the phone, her stomach knotting more with each passing second until the ringing stopped.

Chapter Thirty-Eight

Logan

The two days Toby spent in the hospital were a fire storm of learning. The doctors handed Logan pamphlets and books of information to digest about carb counting, insulin dosages, measuring ketones, and calculating ratios. He learned how to give a shot by practicing on a piece of fruit and then giving one to his son, something he had to demonstrate proficiently before leaving the hospital with Toby. It was mentally exhausting.

Wyatt, Lydia, his mom, and dad had all come to visit on Sunday with balloons and a change of clothes for Logan. Their moral support cheered both him and Toby by the time they left that evening. Ava had also called the hospital that night to see how they were faring and encourage Logan in his efforts to learn all the new medical protocols. He'd already put the hospital and Toby's new endocrinologist on his phone's contact list. After thinking long and hard, he ended up editing Ava's place in his contacts to a more prominent spot too. Just in case of an emergency.

On Monday afternoon, one of the nurses handed Logan a new backpack with materials from the Juvenile Diabetic Research Foundation and presented Toby with Rufus, the diabetic teddy bear. According to the nurse, they were his graduation gifts for passing the crash course in diabetic care with flying colors. The nurse then wheeled Toby to the front door of the hospital in his complementary wheelchair ride, where Logan loaded him up, and they started home.

Ten minutes into the drive, Toby asked Logan, "Dad, do you think we could stop by Nana and Pop's house and ask if she could fix me some of her chicken and dumplings? I didn't tell anybody, but I didn't really like that hospital food."

Logan squeezed the boy's shoulder, a lump forming in his throat. "You bet, Peanut Butter."

Toby's eyes widened. "Do you think I'll be able to have peanut butter sandwiches anymore?"

"I checked to make sure. And you can have other things you like too."

"But no more cake or cookies?" Toby's head dropped.

"You can even have cake or cookies. We just have to be a little more careful when it comes to those things. That's all."

A smile worked its way across the boy's lips.

"You know, I'm really proud of you, taking those shots and finger sticks. You're more of a man than a lot of grownups I know."

"I don't like it." He looked out the window at the trees passing along the roadside. "How long do I have to do this?"

Logan's chest swelled with the pressure of heartache. He never considered that Toby might not realize there wasn't an end in sight. He took a deep breath. "Let's just worry about today, first." One day at a time. Those had been the words Logan recited over and over in his head in the days, weeks, and months after Eliza left. If he could get past today, tomorrow might come easier.

Logan looked over at the fragile little boy beside him—so small, but he had such a big spirit. "I wish I could take those shots for you." Logan cleared the lump in his throat. "I'd do it in a minute."

Toby glanced up at him. "I know you would, Dad, but I wouldn't want you to."

Logan turned away toward the window to wipe away the anguish trailing down his cheek. *One day at a time.*

At his parents' house, Logan parked the truck, and his mom and dad opened the door before he and Toby even reached the porch.

"My heavens, look at you," his mother said, giving her grandson a soft hug. "I bet you feel so much better. I can tell the difference now from when we visited you at the hospital yesterday. Your color is better."

Logan held the screen door for Toby to step inside.

"Look, Nana, they gave me a Rufus bear. He's got places where you practice giving him his shots, and he's got a bracelet just like I do. It tells he's got diabetes."

Margaret's eyes misted over, and she hugged Toby again. "I think that's just amazing, dear."

"Come on inside, and let's take a look." Gus took Toby's backpack as he closed the screen door.

Logan followed Toby and his parents into the living room, where they sat down to talk. He watched as his parents examined all their grandson's new medical gear and teddy bear as if they were the most awe-inspiring things they'd ever seen. Toby showed them his glucose meter for the second time and told them how he had to get lots of finger sticks and shots every day. They bragged about his bravery and told him how impressed they were that he knew all these new things.

As they talked, Logan stepped into the kitchen. He ran water from the sink to splash on his face and filled a glass.

"You okay?" His mother came into the room and placed her hand on his shoulder.

After taking a long drink, he set the glass on the counter. "He's always been so healthy. How am I going to do this?"

"Just like you've faced every other challenge that's been thrown at you." She wrapped her arms around him. "Logan, when you were little, I was always amazed at the differences between you and your brother. Twins, and yet so different. Wyatt would plunge right in and fight his battles like a dragon, not giving a second thought to how it could turn out. He was like a wildfire spreading across a dry field, and I could always tell if he was trying to hide something. Sure as the world, I had trouble on my hands if he was pulling on his ear."

Logan smiled. She was right. He remembered catching Wyatt tug at his ear just days ago, when he came to the office. He always had something up his sleeve when he started for the ear.

She rubbed his arms as if she were trying to warm him. "But you? Oh, you were so different. You were always the analyst. You studied every angle of every situation and then studied it again. And you were so independent. Never wanted any help. You resolved every problem before it ever showed its ugly face and took pride in doing it on your own."

"There's no resolving diabetes, Mom."

"No. But you've got family to help you. This isn't something you have to do alone. Remember that." She nudged him to face her. "You look tired. Go lie down and rest awhile. We'll visit with Toby."

"I couldn't sleep if I tried. I do need to take care of something, though, just a quick trip to the office. Toby asked earlier if we could stop by for your chicken and dumplings. Do you mind making him dinner? I think he'd like that. And, if I can step out for a bit, I'll be back in time to help with his insulin."

"Of course, sweetheart." She cupped his face in her hands. "Go get a breath of fresh air. I'm sure you could use it."

Logan spent the next few minutes with Toby, checking his blood sugar to make sure it was in a safe range and talking over the measures with his parents in case Toby dropped low. "He has juice boxes in his backpack and glucose tabs. If you suspect anything, I'm only a few minutes away, and I'll have my phone. Call me for any reason."

"It'll be okay, Dad." Toby smiled.

"We'll watch after him." Gus nodded as he patted Logan on the back. "Go on, and don't worry."

When he reached his truck, he started it and rested his head on the steering wheel, wondering if he should go back inside. Would it always be like this now—him worrying about leaving Toby? Or feeling guilty? He suffered enough with that before the diagnosis.

He drew his hand to the keys, ready to turn off the ignition and go back inside, but then he glanced toward the pathway to the pond and thought again of Ava. Since being with her at the dock, he'd fought to keep her out of his mind, battled against remembering the moment she landed in his arms, and how simply touching her had somehow begun to repair something in him that had been broken for years.

After a few more seconds, he put the truck in reverse and backed out of the drive. He had to breathe, had to sort out the hundred thousand thoughts running through his head.

When he parked the truck again, he hadn't arrived at the office where he'd first planned to go. Instead, he was sitting in front of Ava's house.

Chapter Thirty-Nine

Ava

Ava had already spent hours agonizing over what to do. Her thoughts had volleyed between Corbin and Mr. Ranier, then Toby and Logan. She finally resolved that, at least, Toby had the medical care he needed, and Logan, by now, had been trained with the basics in how to watch after him.

Since talking with Ranier, though, she couldn't sit still knowing that Corbin and his greed could pull her into some big, black pit with him. So, she spent the better part of the worrisome hours following Ranier's visit on her couch, in front of her laptop, researching insurance fraud.

The thought of getting an attorney had crossed her mind the minute Ranier started questioning her, but she didn't even know if Camden Grove had an attorney, much less one versed in something like this. In Nashville, the flip of a digital Rolodex would have produced twenty, but here? Not likely.

Then came the thought of finances. If she got to the point of needing legal counsel, the fees would bury her financially, even if it did keep her out of jail. The more she thought about it, the more worried she became.

Minutes turned into hours as she poured over case reports and news articles, looking for examples of documents submitted as evidence. She'd read legal journal articles and made tons of notes. If she was going to clear her name, she had to understand how to do it.

By the time she took a break from researching, her head ached with disgust for the methods and practices some people used to generate illegal cash flow. Finally, she set her notes and laptop on the coffee table and trudged to the shower for relief.

As the water trickled and fell in ribbons on her skin, she tried to imagine all the worry that had knotted up in her shoulders going down the drain with it. Though she liked cooler showers in the summertime, she turned the heat up and deep-breathed the steam to take the edge off. The truth was nothing about the last months had alleviated her stress. Not one thing.

Then she thought of Logan.

Not one thing, except for being with Logan.

No matter how much she wanted to, she couldn't deny that the hour they'd spent alone at the pond over the weekend had built up tension, but it was a force of a different kind—one that caused her to forget about Corbin and the trouble she'd left behind in Nashville. One that compelled her to relive that moment with Logan on the dock, even while she slept.

She inhaled another deep breath and allowed herself the indulgence of wondering what it would *really* feel like to kiss him.

Finally, she shut off the water in a quick jerk. She had to clear her head of Logan Carter. In fact, he was the last thing she needed to think about right now.

A half-hour later, when the doorbell rang, Ava turned off the hairdryer with hair still damp and stepped barefoot from her bedroom in a summer button-up and a pair of shorts.

As she opened the door, Logan raised his eyes to meet hers. "Sorry, I should have called." A sadness emanated from his expression.

"No, it's fine. Come in." When she stepped back to allow him entry, her heart fluttered a little as he brushed past her. The scent of musk and wood lingered behind him, and she thought of her dream.

For a moment, Logan stood with his back to her.

"Where's Toby?"

"At my parents' place. He was just released from the hospital this afternoon. Mom's fixing one of his favorite meals." He lowered his head.

"How's he doing?"

"Toby's doing okay. Incredible, considering."

"And you?"

He didn't answer, but instead stepped to the mantel and picked up the photo of Ariel. "This little girl. The other day, when you talked about her, you said you watched her fade away. How do you handle watching a kid be sick every day for the rest of their lives?" When he turned to face her, the anguish in his expression had deepened. "You're a doctor. You've probably seen this kind of thing a million times." He swallowed hard. "But . . . I don't know how to do this."

"Of course, you do." She spoke softly. "And Toby's condition is completely different from Ariel's. Toby can live a happy, healthy, long life, the same as you or I can."

"What if his blood sugar goes low, and I don't know it? What if it's at night and I'm asleep, or he goes high, and I can't bring him down? What do I do then?" Logan's breathing quickened. He turned away from her again. Ava watched him touch the dent he'd created on the mantel so long ago.

"You know, there was a time when I didn't even want to be a dad. I was selfish, wanted to spend time doing other things, not tied down being a parent. But then I married Eliza, and somewhere along the line, she decided she wanted a baby. Our marriage was already a catastrophe. I thought maybe that could salvage it. I didn't know I'd fall in love with this little baby, that he'd become the center of my universe. I just want to take care of him."

She hesitated. Then, Ava tugged at his sleeve, turned him toward her, and wrapped her arms around his broad shoulders. At first, he stiffened. Then, a yielding, pulling her to him, burying his face in her hair.

Despite the history with relationships that, at first, had left her reluctant, she now simply wanted to comfort him, felt motivated to forget for a moment all the barriers she'd put up. Her memory, shortened by a touch she didn't realize she wanted, now recorded all the sensations he created. She abandoned every doubt just to be the solution he needed in that second.

As he lifted his face from her shoulder, the stubble of his beard brushed her cheek, his lips, in search of hers, giving tender hints against her skin. In seconds, the soft touch of his mouth pressed against hers. Not urgent. Not demanding. A butterfly on a petal. An aching need for connection, for reassurance. In that moment, time floated like the seed of a dandelion.

Then, came the wind.

The sound of the doorbell faded into existence, and Logan began to back away. He whispered, "I shouldn't be here. I shouldn't have—"

She touched his lips, cut off his words. "Don't." Her fingertips slid to the cleft of his chin.

"I didn't come here to . . . I just wanted to talk. I—"

The doorbell rang again. Ava's eyes followed his. "Wait. We'll talk more." She bowed her head and slipped away toward the door.

Without looking through the peephole, Ava turned the knob and came face-to-face.

With Corbin Simmons.

The self-righteous smirk, the memories of all he'd done, should have given Ava warning and reason enough to slam the door shut, but she couldn't gather her thoughts fast enough to register any response beyond shock.

"Ava, wow, you look beautiful as usual." He stepped inside, kissing her on the same cheek Logan's beard had just brushed.

Energy drained from her body as she stared at him, dumbfounded.

He stepped further into the room but turned back toward her. His eyes remained fixed on Logan. "I'm so sorry. I should've gotten here earlier, sweetheart. It's been a busy month." He paused. "Now, who might this be?"

Ava tried to regain her voice, but thoughts of Ranier's warnings began coursing through her head. "Wh—what are you doing here?"

He crossed the room and held out his hand to Logan. "I'm Dr. Simmons, and my sweet Ava's so surprised I don't think she's going to introduce us."

Logan returned the doctor's handshake, though he looked guarded.

Ava stepped between the men. "This is Logan Carter. He's a contractor, doing some work for me." She hugged her own arms.

"Ah, the new office." He looked over to Logan, eyebrows raised. "Got it all ready?"

"No . . . I've, uh . . . been delayed." His brow furrowed, eyes refocused on Ava.

"Well now, that's fortunate for me"—he grinned— "since I'm planning to bring this lovely woman back with me to the city. A lot of people are missing her there. Not the least of which is me, of course. And I've got an offer I don't think she'll be able to refuse." He glanced back at Ava.

She tried to cover the anxiety welling up inside her chest. She had to get him away from Logan. Surely, he wouldn't mention anything about the insurance investigation. Ranier had said Corbin knew. If anything came out about that and put doubt in

Logan's mind about her professional life, everything she'd started in Camden Grove would disintegrate.

"Really?" Logan eyed the man and nodded. "Well, sounds like you two have plenty to talk about, so I'll get out of your way." He spoke in a cool, business-like tone to Ava. "I'll get an inventory of what's left to be done on our contract. You can let me know if there are changes to your plans for the office."

As he passed Ava, moving to the door, she followed. "But you and I—we still have some things to discuss. I, uh, understand you've had a big hit over the weekend. I know you'll need time to figure things out." She stumbled over her thoughts. "Maybe we can talk again soon?"

Logan opened the door and looked back inside. "Dr. Simmons," he tipped his head in a nod goodbye, glanced once more at Ava, then left.

Before she could follow him further, he was off the porch and headed to his truck parked in the driveway beside a convertible Porche, no doubt Corbin's newest, guiltless pleasure.

She closed the door after a moment and faced the man who'd caused her flesh to crawl. He glowered at her. "A new boyfriend already? I'm hurt."

"He's my contractor." Ava's voice hardened.

"And I suppose his 'big hit over the weekend' had nothing to do with your being a cold fish, leaving him without so much as a warning?" Corbin's expression condescended. "Looking at him, I didn't think I had much in common with your poor chump handyman, but maybe we do, after all."

All the sour memories began to bombard Ava as she stood across the room from this man who'd changed her. Back in Nashville, despite ignoring her instincts about dating a co-worker, Ava had stayed firm, refusing Corbin's sexual advances. Now he wanted to make sure she didn't forget it. His sharp words felt like a slice to her flesh, one of many he'd inflicted since she'd started to pull away, but more because it was a cut to Logan than to her.

Bitterness, like molten lava, began to bubble up beneath the surface. She wanted to erupt with details about a little boy who'd just been diagnosed with a life-threatening disease, about Logan's struggle to absorb the blow, and how that should matter in the eyes of a compassionate human, certainly a doctor. Corbin couldn't have cared less about anyone else's struggles, though. The longer she knew him, the more surprised she was that he'd even become a physician.

Instead of exploding in anger, Ava pulled back and began to rummage her thoughts for ways to get Corbin out of her house. The threat from him she'd come to recognize in Nashville had now slithered into her home. If she'd only listened to her instincts a long time ago.

Ava glared at him. "Why are you here?" She folded her arms, trying to brush off the threat she felt.

"Like I told your boyfriend, I came to make you an offer."

"You've got some nerve showing up here. I know about the fraud allegations."

He sauntered away from her, away from the door. "Oh, Ava, I was hoping you'd overlook my minor infractions and help me out of this silly fix."

"Look, whatever proposition you have, I'm not interested." There wasn't an offer this side of the moon with enough sway for her to do anything for him.

Corbin shrugged his shoulders. "Okay, call it a bribe, call it blackmail, call it whatever lights your fire. I need something from you, and I plan to get it because you'll be unable to resist." He smirked and splayed out on the couch, propping his feet on the coffee table, inches away from her open laptop screen.

She walked to the table and closed the laptop, hoping he hadn't seen her search results. Every nerve that had been tantalized only moments ago in Logan's arms now stood on end in the same room with Corbin.

"I left Nashville to get a new start. Why do you think you can show up and just lay claim to me? And how did you find me?"

Corbin picked at the underside of his fingernail. "My former secretary sang like a bird just before I fired her for misrepresenting all that information on our insurance claims."

After visiting with Ranier, Ava knew that Paige had nothing to do with Corbin's claims. "What? Did you need a scapegoat?"

"Unfortunate, losing a good secretary, but I had to make everything look compelling for my case, which is where you come in."

Ava's voice lost force. "Leave me out of this, Corbin. I just want a simple life where I can build a business on my own."

"So you and your country bumpkin can settle down and have a yard full of hayseeds while I decompose in a prison cell? Pshh, Ava. You're better than that. Did you not learn anything from serving in a well-respected office?"

"I think it's time for you to go." Ava turned the doorknob.

Corbin ignored her. "This is how it'll go." His voice hardened. "You'll testify on my behalf in this misrepresentation rap they're trying to hang on me."

"They're coming after you because you're guilty."

Corbin ignored her. "Because of my good nature, in exchange—if you don't want to come back to your old office, that is—I'll set up a new one, in Nashville, another satellite clinic, if you will, all-expenses-paid, with your name on the shingle. I'll even staff it for you. All you have to do is walk in and start work. We'll call it even at that point."

"You're out of your mind. Why would I do that? I would testify for the other side before I would do business with you again."

"I thought you might say that." He pulled his phone from the pocket of his sharply pressed slacks, swiped the screen a couple of times, and threw it on the table in front of her. "Take a look." He smirked. "Start there, and scan to your heart's content."

Ava picked up the phone. She began to swipe from picture to picture—all of them photos of records with her signature, for services she'd never rendered.

"If you want to testify against me, rest assured right now that I have enough documentation to incriminate you for long enough that you'll probably need hair dye when you get out. And look at the dates on those files, sweetheart. You've been complicit for a long while. Feds will take a peek at that and see your testimony as a vain attempt at wiggling out of a long-term scam of epic proportions. Oh, and I've got a few witnesses that'll say we were pretty cozy the night of the gala too. I think that'll cement your feet in a nice, long partnership with me, don't you?" He scraped his shoes across the coffee table and slammed them to the floor.

Ava flinched.

"My clientele wants me where I am, Ava, and having you as an asset to keep me there is well worth their money. Fact is, if I go down, you go down with me."

Ava had heard a handful of entertainer's names spoken in Corbin's office before, though they had never darkened the door. She now wondered how many favors he'd slid under the table to them. Or what streets on Music Row he had supplied with drugs to support his lifestyle.

Regardless, reality set in, and Ava clearly understood why Corbin had tried to seduce her in the first place. He'd already been using her. He needed someone to take on some of the patient load on paper so he wouldn't raise suspicion. Tossing her a few cases of her own was just a nice cover. But, when she refused his advances and then left him altogether, he had to resort to more extreme measures. "You want me in Nashville so you can keep your thumb on me. You need insurance for your insurance scam and a doormat in case this all goes south."

"I knew they gave you a degree for some reason, smart girl. And, yes,"—he nodded— "I'd say that's a fair assessment."

"I told you, I'm not interested, Corbin." She opened the door.

"I wasn't asking if you were." He stood and sauntered toward the door. "You have forty-eight hours to mull over my offer. If you decide not to accept, I'll slide those documents to the authorities. And it won't be just you behind bars. I've made accommodations for Paige as well. You decide to cross me, and both of you will float right down the river beside me. So, don't keep me waiting, sweetheart." He crossed in front of her, leaned over, and in a quick, repulsive yank, pulled her face to his, kissing her on the mouth. Then, he walked out the door.

Ava couldn't lock the deadbolt fast enough. She wiped her lips with the back of her hand. Corbin Simmons had effectively turned her evening into a living nightmare.

Chapter Forty

Logan

After Logan spun out of Ava's drive, he forced himself not to look back at her standing in the door. The image of the overconfident doctor, who strutted into her living room like he owned the place, was enough to make a believer out of Logan. Just what the man laid claim to, he had no intention of caring enough to find out. And Ava obviously saw Logan as only the contractor. Nothing more, nothing less. He shook his head. That was best anyway. Why did he ever let himself kiss her?

The further he drove into town, the more he tried to block out the thought of holding Ava just moments earlier, the image of kissing her. He fought to push away the comfort he found with her in his arms, kept reminding himself that she was an emotional liability neither he nor Toby needed right now. They had bigger mountains to climb. Getting his head straight, getting back to work, figuring out what his and Toby's lives looked like now were his priorities—not thinking about her.

He picked up his phone and called Dakota as he turned toward Ava's office. When his friend answered, he asked if they could meet at the job site, pronto. He probably sounded shaken. Dakota agreed without question. As he drove toward the other side of town, he rolled the window down for some fresh air, but it didn't help.

Inside the office, he went from room to room, looking at all the work left to be done. With his fist clenching like a pumping machine, he wondered what Simmons meant when he said he was taking Ava back to the city. He mulled over whether he should dive into work in the morning or wait to hear if she was leaving Camden Grove behind just as she was getting here.

A few minutes later, Dakota came in with a couple of tall Styrofoam fountain cups in his hand. "Hey, man, thought you might need a drink."

"What is it?"

"You know me. Dr Pepper's my poison." He offered a consoling smile. "Gus and Margaret told me about Toby. Man, that's tough. How's he doing?"

Logan nodded. "A lot better than I would be if I had to take a shot every time I ate" –Logan lifted his drink— "or had a Dr Pepper."

"You want to talk?"

Logan sat down in an office chair, exhausted from the drain of worry. "Dakota, I'm a self-insured contractor, and I've got a boy with type 1 diabetes. I'm scrambling for jobs and trying to cover the few I've got. I don't know how to take care of Toby now physically, much less financially. How am I going to do this?"

Dakota shrugged. "The same way you always have, Logan. You're a man of sheer grit. You've raised that boy on your own from the time he was tiny and look at what a great kid he is. You've got people around to help you. Don't be too proud to ask for it."

Dakota walked to his side and put a hand on his shoulder. "Listen, there was a time in my life when I didn't know if I'd get through, and you helped me. So, I've called in a few favors from some sub-contractors I know. You've got the Brashear building to finish, and I'm pulling the grunt work off your plate on that job. Give me a list of deadlines, and we'll make sure to catch 'em."

"Man, I can't ask you to do that."

"You're not. I'm telling you it's already done."

"I already owe you, remember?"

"Yeah, well, buy me a Dr Pepper some time."

Logan looked up at his friend. Dakota was a quiet man with wounds, just like everybody else. His were deeper than most. But here he stood, ready to take on what another man couldn't see clear to handle.

"Thanks, Dakota." Logan wiped his glassy eyes and cleared his throat. "I'll put the time in with you when I get this place caught up." He looked around the room.

"Come on. I'll help you inventory what's left here so you can get your supplies in hand and know where to put your focus next."

"I don't even know if the doc's gonna stay here to use the place."

"What're you talking about?" Dakota squinted his eyes, confused.

"She may be going back where she came from."

"She tell you that?"

"Not exactly." Logan started to tell Dakota about Ava and her visitor but decided better of it.

"Well, until you do know, a little work my be good, you know, to get your mind off your troubles."

Logan nodded and took a deep breath. "I'll need to take some measurements. Surely she's got pen and paper here somewhere."

Turning to the desk, he opened the drawer, and in the bottom lay a photo. The rock that had been sinking in the pit of his stomach for days, finally hit bottom. Staring up at him from a glossy image stood Ava in a sleek black dress. She looked beautiful . . . happy . . . wrapped in the arms of Dr. Corbin Simmons.

Dakota stepped up beside him. "Wow, pretty lady." He drew closer. "Hey, where have I seen that guy?" He tapped his chin with the straw of the fountain cup. "I know. That's the doctor up in Nashville. Been on TV."

"What're you talking about?"

"That guy." Dakota pointed. "I saw him on the news when I was at a mall job site up in Franklin, Tennessee this weekend. He's a doctor for some of the big names in country music. If I remember right, he's being investigated for insurance fraud." Dakota took a sip from his drink.

"Are you sure that's him?"

"Yeah, he was trying to get past reporters. Slipped into a nice-looking Beamer. Nearly ran over a cameraman when they tried to interview him." He plucked the photo from Logan's hand. "Yeah, that's him alright." Dakota's expression went dark. "You don't think this lady doctor's mixed up in all that, do you?"

Logan's mind started reeling. The image of the man in the photo waltzing in the door at Ava's house and kissing her. Of her total shift in demeanor toward him when the guy showed up.

"I don't know, but something's not right."

"What do you mean?"

Logan crossed the room and stood at the window, slowly putting pieces of the puzzle together in his head. "She showed up here in Camden Grove less than a month ago. I met her just before the two of us saw her here at the office, remember?"

Dakota nodded.

"Funny, she didn't even want to say she was a doctor at first. Nor did she want to give me any details when I asked questions." The feeling in his stomach expanded to an ache.

"May bear checking out before you spend any more time or money on this office. If the feds are coming after her, you don't want to be mixed up in that business. You won't get a cent out of it if I'm guessing."

Logan threw the photo on the desk. "You may be right." He paused. "I think I'll hold off on those measurements and see what I can find out in the next few days." He turned to Dakota. "Sorry to bring you over here for nothing."

Dakota shook his head. "Not nothing. Far as I know, we've still got each other's backs, right?"

Logan bowed his head and nodded.

"I'll check in tomorrow and get your plans on the Brashear building lined out." He turned to leave.

"Dakota?"

When his friend looked back, Logan raised the Dr Pepper in the air. "Thanks, man."

"Yep." And with that, the door closed, and Logan was alone.

He picked up the picture again. *Well, Dr. Ava Fenn, you tried, didn't you? Tried to get under my skin.* He shook his head. *I should've known better.* His eyes lingered on Ava's smile, the dark brown waves of her hair, her curves accentuated in that black dress.

Then, he opened the desk drawer and threw the photo inside, scanned the office one last time, and locked the door on his way out.

He had a son to take care of.

Chapter Forty-One

Ava

The look on Logan's face when she'd introduced him to Corbin as her contractor burned through Ava's thoughts like a steamroller. Confusion. Betrayal. She didn't know what exactly he'd felt, but the sting of his cool response left her keenly aware that she'd left a bruise.

She crossed to the window. Corbin's car was gone. A minute later, she changed into a pair of jeans and slipped on some shoes. Grabbing her purse and keys, she locked the door. Leaving things as they'd been dropped wasn't an option. She had to find Logan. He'd said Toby was at his parents' house, so she'd start there.

When she came in sight of the Carters' drive, Logan's truck was nowhere to be seen. She almost turned around and headed back into town, but the thought of Toby nudged her to pull into their drive.

Gus answered the door. His face lit up when he saw Ava. "Dr. Fenn, what a pleasant surprise. Please, come in."

"Thank you. Please, call me Ava." She stepped in the door. "I'm sorry I'm coming unannounced. How's Toby doing?"

"Come see for yourself. He's right in the kitchen with Margaret. Logan needed to take care of a few things, so he stayed here with us. He'll be thrilled to see you."

She decided not to mention being with Logan earlier. Gus led her to the kitchen, where Toby sat at the table with a steaming bowl in front of him.

"Dr. Fenn!" Toby jumped up from the table and ran to her, wrapping his arms around her waist in a hug.

She squeezed him back and knelt to eye level. "Hey, there, sport. You must be feeling a lot better."

He nodded, his eyes wide. "A lot better. I never got the chance to say goodbye to you at the hospital. Or to show you Rufus." He held up a bear dressed in a white and blue t-shirt. "The nurses gave him to me. He has places where he gets shots too."

Ava took the bear and stroked the designated blue "injection sites" in his fur. "Oh, wow, how's that going?"

"I don't like shots."

She smiled and took his hands in hers. "That's not fun, is it?"

The little boy shook his head.

"Do you know, I think you're one of the bravest patients I've ever met. And, I'll bet Rufus, here, would agree."

Margaret wiped her hands on a dishcloth. "Would you like to stay for dinner? We have plenty."

"Yeah," Toby jumped in. "You can sit by me."

"Oh, no, I wouldn't dream of it. I'm sorry I interrupted."

"Perfect timing. We were just letting our food cool. We'd love to have you stay. Logan should be coming back any minute now. He's supposed to give Toby his insulin."

"I could help with that." She looked at the little boy. "That is if you want me to, Toby."

At first, he bowed his head and didn't respond. Ava looked up at Margaret. "Or we can wait for your dad."

Toby stayed quiet.

"Tell you what." Ava gave his arm a gentle squeeze. "What if you tested my blood sugar and showed me how you do it? It's been a while since I've had mine tested. Then we could check yours and see how much insulin you need."

Toby raised his face to hers. "You mean we stick your finger?"

"You have a new meter, right?"

Toby ran to the table, where a small backpack hung across the chair. When he returned to her, he pulled out a small glucometer. "The finger poker is in here."

"Ew, the dreaded finger poker." Ava grinned. "Can you show me how it works?"

"Sure." Toby took her hand and led her to a chair. "First, you put one of these blue things in this hole." The little boy loaded a new lancet into the pen device and slid a test strip into the slot on the meter. "Then you pull back the trigger on this thing, and it's ready." He got an alcohol swab from his backpack and tore the flat packet open. "I'll have to clean your finger first. That's what they told me to do at the hospital."

Gus walked over to Margaret and put his arm around her shoulder. They watched the little boy take charge.

When he finished wiping her finger clean, he asked, "Ready?"

"Okay, poke away." Ava held out her finger, took an exaggerated breath, and blew it out.

Toby held the lancet pen on her finger and pushed the trigger. With a click, a drop of blood rose on the pad of her index finger. The little boy then let the test strip soak up the droplet of blood. In a few seconds, the meter beeped with a number.

"Wow, you're pretty good at that. Ever thought about becoming a doctor?" Ava cleaned the remainder of the blood droplet from her finger with the alcohol swab.

"Not really."

"So, how do we get the meter ready for you to check your blood sugar?"

"We have to put in a new poker and strip." Toby began to pull the necessary items from his backpack.

"That's right. You've learned so much, Toby. I'm so proud of you," Ava bragged.

"I don't think I'm hungry anymore." His brow furrowed.

Ava glanced at Gus and Margaret, their faces troubled. Then, she lifted Toby's chin. "Are you worried about the finger stick and shot hurting?"

He nodded.

"Tell you what, your bowl of chicken and dumplings smells really good, and I think I heard your tummy growling a second ago. What if we get everything ready for you to eat, and I teach you a little trick to help you with your shots and finger pokes?"

Toby hesitated, then nodded again.

The expression in his eyes warmed her heart. He trusted her. "Why don't you go into the bathroom and wash your hands extra clean, and I'll be ready when you get back." When he left, she turned to Gus and Margaret. "I hope that's alright. You don't think Logan will mind, do you?"

"Of course not." Margaret's brow furrowed. "He'd appreciate anything you can do to help Toby."

Ava looked to Gus. "If you'll go delay him for a couple of minutes, I'll calculate his insulin and draw it up so that doesn't cause him any more anxiety than it already does."

Gus nodded and stepped into the other room.

"May I wash up at this sink?"

"Paper towels are on the counter, there." Margaret pointed.

Ava turned on the water. "Do you have his medical log?"

"Should be in here." Margaret pulled his backpack from a kitchen chair. "Logan said he had everything in his bag."

Ava took a quick look at the calculation for insulin recorded in his log, did a carb count of what he would be eating from the nutrition book the hospital supplied, and unpackaged one of his syringes. She finished drawing up a tiny dose just as he and Gus returned from the bathroom.

Ava set the syringe aside. "Toby, I've been thinking. You like dogs, right?"

"I love dogs." He sat down in front of her in a chair she'd pulled from the table.

"Okay. We're going to make up a little rhyme. I'll start each line of our rhyme, and you get to finish the last word. But the trick is to see how fast we can go. Okay?"

Toby smiled. "Okay."

Ava slipped a new test strip into the meter and began her line of the rhyme. "There once was a dog who could . . ." She waited for Toby's response.

"Talk," Toby answered.

She wiped his finger with an alcohol swab.

"Okay." She thought. "There once was a dog who could talk. He decided to go for a . . ." She placed the lancet on his clean finger.

"Walk." She pulled the trigger. Toby winced only slightly.

"Oh, good one." The meter beeped, and she glanced at the number. He was in an acceptable range, so the insulin she'd drawn up would be sufficient. "Okay, so there once was a dog who could talk. He decided to go for a walk. The neighbors were . . ."

Toby looked at the syringe. "Scared."

She turned him slightly sideways. "The neighbors were scared, 'cause he talked as they . . ."

"Stared?"

"Stared." Margaret and Gus laughed, and Toby did too. Ava plunged the tiny needle into the fleshy part of his arm. "But still, he enjoyed his walk."

Margaret and Gus applauded as Ava removed the needle and rubbed his arm.

"Is it done?" Toby's eyes were wide with wonder.

"It's all done. And you are an amazing poet." Ava capped the syringe and set it to the side. "I'm so proud of you."

Toby's eyes glistened as he turned and wrapped his arms around her neck. "Thank you for making it not hurt."

"You're so brave, sweetheart. You just say our new rhyme every time you take a shot or poke your finger and think about our talking dog. Deal?"

"Deal." He tightened his hug. "Dr. Fenn, I'm naming our talking dog Coco."

Ava's throat tightened a little. She sat there, wrapped in the arms of a seven-year-old boy, trying to help him be brave during one of the most tremendous challenges of his life; yet, in her own, she had been a coward and tried to run away, leaving her fate to the odds.

At that moment, with Toby's arms wrapped so tightly around her, she knew she had to find her own courage.

Then, she knew exactly what she had to do.

Chapter Forty-Two

Logan

As Logan pulled into his parents' drive, he saw Ava walking across the yard toward her car. He parked beside the Prius and stepped out. "What're you doing here?"

"I, uh, wanted to check on Toby, and I was hoping to talk to you about what happened this afternoon."

"What's to talk about? Nothing really happened." He started to walk toward the house.

"Logan."

He stopped and turned. "Look, I let all the chaos from the last couple of days get to me, and you happened to be there in a shaky moment. It was a mistake."

Ava's expression changed. "I see."

He nodded toward the house. "I really need to get to Toby. He's probably ready to eat, and he'll need his insulin."

"I just gave him his meal dose."

"You did?" His eyes narrowed.

"Yeah, I hope you don't mind. His dinner was ready, and he did great."

"Actually, I should've been the one to do that. I need to get comfortable with the whole process, and the more I do it, the better." He knew it was a lame excuse, but she needed to get the picture that she couldn't walk in and take over.

She paused, a flicker of surprise stealing across her face. "I'm sorry, I didn't mean to . . . Well, I guess I should go then."

Logan continued, "And just so you know, I decided to shift my focus to another big contract tomorrow. It's been waiting on me, and I can't let it set any longer."

"Okay. What about the office?"

"Sounds like you still have some things to iron out. I can't tie up my resources when there's uncertainty. Let me know when you've got it figured out, and we'll go from there." He could feel the sharpness in his voice cutting into his conversation with Ava.

"Yeah. Okay."

He crossed the yard without so much as a wave goodbye. When he got inside, he pushed the door closed and leaned against it, torn between his anger that Ava had misled him and some small measure of gratitude that she'd helped Toby. Whatever she was, Ava Fenn was a complexity he didn't want to unravel.

"Logan, is that you?"

"Yeah, Mom." He stepped from the entry into the kitchen where Toby and his parents sat at the table eating.

"Dad, you won't believe it. Dr. Fenn poked my finger and gave my shot to me, and it didn't even hurt."

His mother dabbed her mouth with a napkin. "Yes, she stopped by to see how Toby was doing. Wasn't that nice of her? And while she was here, she worked magic. We were going to wait for you to give Toby his insulin, but she settled his fears and had his dose given before he even knew it was happening."

"Was that all she wanted? To check on Toby?"

"Yeah." His dad shook his head. "She's a fine doctor. Never seen one able to make a kid get along with a shot, but she did it."

Logan kept quiet.

"Get a bowl, and sit down with us." His mother prompted.

Logan pulled a dish from the cabinet and managed to serve up his meal while preoccupied with thoughts of Ava. He continued to question why he'd gotten close enough to kiss her, why he'd even stopped by her house in the first place.

He could justify it if he tried. All the stress—one thing snowballing into the next—caught up with him, left him in a moment of weakness where her touch had been a temptation he wasn't ready to push away. He knew where that could land him, though. It had already spelled trouble. The second he'd begun to let her in, Dr. Simmons's put him back in his place, where he should have stayed to begin with. Yeah, after seeing the picture of Ava and Dr. Simmons all cozied up, it was a good thing he *had* stopped by and more so that her doorbell *did* ring that afternoon. Now at least, he had a much clearer understanding of Ava Fenn.

Toby finished his meal and slipped into Logan's lap. "Dad, I really like Dr. Fenn. We've got a dog now."

"A dog?" Logan looked at his mother. She grinned.

"Dr. Fenn taught me a rhyme about a dog. She told me to say it when I'm taking my shots and finger pokes to help me not be scared."

"I see." He pulled the boy close. "You're really brave, Toby."

"That's what she said too."

"Well, she's right about that." He squeezed a little tighter. "Why don't you go get your backpack together and give Pops and Nana hugs. We should get back to the house and call it a day."

Toby slid out of Logan's lap and pulled his backpack from the chair. When he left the room to tell his pops goodbye, Logan turned to his mother. "Thanks for watching after Toby."

"Of course, I'm gonna watch after him. I'm still watching after you, too, you know." She patted his arm. "Logan, Ava didn't come here just to see Toby. Now, don't get me wrong. She had him in mind too. It's in her blood to care about her patients—that much is obvious—but that wasn't the sole reason she showed up at our door tonight."

"Mom, don't let your imagination get started."

She poked a finger at Logan's chest. "And don't you go telling me what to do with my imagination. I know what a girl's eyes look like when she's starting to think sweet thoughts toward a man, and that's what's happening with Ava Fenn."

"Well, she has some other interests, and I'm not stepping out on a limb for anybody else in this lifetime. There's room for only one important person in my world right now, and that's Toby."

"I'm not trying to tell you what to do. I'm telling you she's a good woman with a good heart. I saw it not half an hour ago in how she treated that most important person in your life. You always were the one to think too much. Maybe it's time to stop thinking with your head and start feeling with your heart."

"I love you, Mom." He kissed her on the forehead. "I should get Toby home."

"Stop thinking. Start feeling," she called as he waved goodbye over his shoulder.

Chapter Forty-Three

Ava

When Ava called Carly the next morning, she breathed a sigh of relief that her friend didn't answer. She didn't want to go into the long explanation she knew Carly would demand. Too many things fought for attention in her brain, and she couldn't handle one more added to the mix.

The night before, when she'd returned from the Carters', she'd spent the first hours trying to push away the memory of her conversation with Logan and how cold he was toward her. The silver lining of stopping by had been helping Toby with his fear.

Then, after wrestling with her thoughts about Logan, she'd gone back through her research, making the plan to face her own fears. That was the reason for her morning call to Carly.

When the perky voice recording prompted, she left a message as innocuous as possible. "Hey, Carly. I just wanted to let you know I'm going out of town for a few days. I'll call you when I get back. No worries. I'm just taking care of some business." Maybe her voice message would put a conversation with Carly on hold until she could get a plan lined out.

Ava finished packing her bag and loaded it in the car. From the coffee table, she picked up the letter she'd written to Logan the night before and stuffed it in her purse. She decided that leaving it at her office, where he'd hopefully find it at some point, would be best. From the conversation they'd had last night, the less she talked to him now, the better. His words and tone had stung only slightly less than the sensation of Corbin's repulsive kiss at her door.

When she pulled in at her office, the empty lot left her relieved. She placed the letter on a makeshift workbench Logan had fashioned from two sawhorses and a piece of plywood. He would find it if he came into her office at all. After one last look around, she began to think of the possibilities for her little Camden Grove practice and how they'd now have to be put on hold. With not much more than a ray of hope, she stepped out the door. The road back to Nashville would be long and worrisome.

Chapter Forty-Four

Logan

Toby's first night home from the hospital lasted what seemed like a month. Logan made a bed for him on the living room couch while he slept in the recliner, mostly afraid his son's blood sugar would go low and he wouldn't catch it.

By 6 a.m. Tuesday morning, he'd checked Toby's blood three times, and his breathing thirty-two. It reminded him of the days when they'd first brought him home from the hospital as a baby, and Logan sat up at night to make sure he was still breathing while Eliza slept in the other room.

The endocrinologist at the hospital had encouraged Logan to try not to lose sleep, but that suggestion didn't even register as logical. How was he supposed to sleep soundly when Toby was at risk?

By 8:00 a.m., his mom had already called to check on the two of them and asked Logan to bring Toby to their house if he had work to do. She assured him several times that she would call if there were any problems. With a little persuasion, Logan finally agreed to go long enough to do some morning business.

His first stop was Ava's office to get some of the tools he'd need for the Brashear project. When he arrived, he'd already begun to load tools when he found her letter. Sitting on the edge of a sawhorse, he peeled the envelope open.

Logan,

When I left you last night, I knew I'd somehow managed to lose your trust before I ever fully had it. That moment you shared with me—the one you said was a mistake—got lost in the confusion Corbin created the moment he walked into my home.

I know I should be honest with you, with everyone, even with myself—something I've avoided since coming to Camden Grove. So here it is. My move to this little town wasn't a choice I leaned into. Sometimes, circumstances we don't create force us into change we don't expect. And, though I didn't welcome Camden Grove, the Grove truly welcomed me.

Meeting your family, taking a small part in your lives, has left me with an understanding of what I have to do. I learned it best from Toby—life sometimes requires courage.

Even though I can't explain right now why I'm going back to Nashville, I want you to know that I'll honor our contract, regardless of what happens, and maybe you can finish the office as you have time. I know your attention has to be with Toby right now, so if that's too much to ask, I understand. You know how to reach me.

I hold Toby and you in my thoughts,

Ava

Logan wadded the letter up and threw it across the room, a storm rolling up in his chest. Ava had stepped into their lives just long enough to open old wounds and remind him of what being left felt like. Why had he let her in?

He sat for another few minutes stewing again on the last days and weeks, on the first time they met at the Old Mill, on when she sat in his lap, and their evening at the pond. On her kiss.

That kiss.

When his phone rang, he shook his head. Wyatt always did have intuitive timing.

"Yeah, what do you want?" His voice was sharp.

"Whoa, man. What's got you all torn up?"

"I'm waiting for some good news for a change. You got anything?"

Wyatt sighed. "I could make something up."

"I'd almost welcome it, but life's never been a fairy tale around here. Don't suppose I should start asking for it now."

"How's Tobe?"

"He had a decent sleep, despite me poking his finger all night long."

"Poor little guy. What do you say you two come over for dinner tonight? Maybe he'll feel up to playing with Milo, and you and I can talk."

"Between you, Lydia, Mom and Dad, Toby and I don't spend much time at our place."

"Too lonesome there anyway."

Logan stayed quiet.

Wyatt waited. "Look, if I know you, you've probably thought through every scenario that could possibly happen with Toby, to the point that you've worried yourself nearly sick. And if we're being honest, you can't sustain that kind of load on your own.

You've gotta open up sometime." He paused. "Tell you what. You two come over tonight. We'll pull the old ping pong table from the garage and see if you've got any ping left to my pong."

Wyatt and Logan had spent many nights after Eliza left playing round after round of ping pong. Logan held no false notion that Wyatt just wanted to play a game. He knew one of the ways his brother helped him worked out the hardest of problems was when a couple of paddles were swinging.

He finally let out the breath he'd been holding. "What time?"

"Six-thirty?"

"Toby doesn't need to eat anything with a lot of carbs right now."

"It's okay. You know Lydia. We'll have something ridiculously healthy. Even her junk food has only two-item ingredients you can pronounce."

Logan finally agreed. "See you tonight." He pushed the button ending the call and brushed a hand over his stubbly shadow of a beard.

He had to get a grip.

Chapter Forty-Five

Ava

Ava drove across the Fulton Memorial Bridge above the Cumberland River as it snaked its way toward the city two miles to the south. The iconic structure that Nashvillians had dubbed the Batman building stood in the distance with its twin steeples piercing the sky, flanked on all sides by several other steel and glass skyline contributors.

Just less than a month ago, she'd put this city in her rearview mirror, planning to forge a new future in quiet little Camden Grove. Now, she was returning to the metro to salvage her reputation with a desperate hope that there would even be a future to go back to.

Even having been weeks removed, something about the city now seemed menacing, no longer the same draw it had been only weeks earlier. At the sight of it, all she wanted was to go back to the Grove. Something about it now felt more like home.

As she exited the interstate, a dull ache settled in her stomach. Getting the advantage over Corbin wouldn't be easy, but she had no choice if she wanted her name cleared. What if, in the process, she buried them both and brought Paige Westerfield down too? Her fingernails dug into the vinyl of the steering wheel.

Paige. She had to find Paige Westerfield.

Catching the custodian at Corbin's office building as he was carrying out the trash was her first stroke of luck that afternoon. The older man was the only person Ava knew of who seemed well enough acquainted with all the office workers to help. Ava had once heard Paige tell one of the nurses that he reminded her of an uncle she had in the service. That he knew where Paige lived was the second stroke of luck.

With the address he'd given her plugged into her GPS, she crossed town in sluggish afternoon traffic and finally pulled into an oil-stained parking space in the lot of an old apartment complex. A dumpster that looked as if it hadn't been emptied in a month stood to the left of the gray brick building, and a rusted Buick with a raised hood sat four spaces down. A few other older-model cars littered the lot, along with a bike or two.

At first, she waited and watched, trying to work up the nerve to step out. An apartment door opened in the next building down, and a man with greasy, black hair and a sleeveless shirt straddled a motorcycle and started it up. The roar of the machine nearly rattled her teeth as he pulled out of the lot.

After he rounded the corner of the building out of sight, Ava took a deep breath. When she left the safety of her car, she wished out loud that Logan was there. The thought was so impulsive, it didn't even register, but when she heard herself whisper the words, they took her by surprise.

She climbed the graffitied stairs to the second floor of Building C and found a paint-chipped door marked with a rusty number twelve. Across the landing at the top of the stairs, someone's door stood open, and a bag of burnt popcorn lay on the concrete in a putrid-smelling cloud of smoke. An older, gray-whiskered man with a potbelly and veiny arms sat just inside watching a game show and fanning the smoke toward the door. Ava hoped she wouldn't draw his attention.

The knock hadn't even had time to echo across the landing before the old man's sand-papery voice called to her. "You trying to find that little lass?"

Ava turned around, and the man stood from his perch, still fanning away smoke.

"If you get her to come to the door, I'd be surprised. She don't answer to nobody around here. Hadn't much come out since she moved in a few weeks back."

Ava nodded. "Thank you for telling me." She pulled her purse close in front of her and knocked again, louder than before.

In a few seconds, she heard a scraping on the other side of the door and the bolt click. The knob turned, and a cautious gap appeared. "Dr. Fenn?" Paige's eyes widened. "What are you doing here?" She opened the door wider. "Come in, please."

From behind, the old man wheezed out a wet cough and yelled across the landing, "It's a miracle!"

Ava slid inside the darkened room as Paige bolted the door behind her.

"I never expected to see you here."

"How are you?" Ava scanned the dim apartment.

The slim woman ignored the question and pulled a ladder-back chair from beside the door, setting it close to a worn, brown couch. "Come, sit down."

Paige had a naturally welcoming smile and a pleasant face—the kind most girls would envy for her ability to go without makeup and still look fresh as a morning glory.

Ava sat in the chair and, after a moment, shook her head. "Why are you here, Paige? This isn't a very safe place to live."

Wrapping a thin robe more tightly around her, Paige dropped her gaze to the floor. "It's not much of a place, but I keep it clean." She turned on a lamp and peeked into a small bedroom door just off the living room, where Ava could hear noise from a TV. When she came back, she slid into the spot on the couch across from Ava. "Sorry, it's a little dark in here. We keep the lights off and the blinds drawn, so it stays cooler."

"We?"

"My daughter and me." Paige tucked a strand of dark-blonde hair behind her ear.

"Why didn't I know you had a daughter?"

"I guess we didn't have much chance to get to know each other back at the office."

A little girl, dressed in a blue princess gown, stole a look from the bedroom door. "Mommy?"

Paige motioned for the little girl to come to her side. Whisps of brown hair fell into her tell-tale, almond-shaped eyes as she dawdled into her mother's arms.

Ava bowed her head. Not only did she have no idea that Paige had a daughter. She wasn't aware that her little girl had

Down Syndrome. Now, with her sitting in Paige's arms and light illuminating her face, Ava could see those indicators that every doctor knew to be the signposts.

When she worked at the clinic, she'd kept a professional distance from all the employees—that is, besides Corbin—but now embarrassment at not taking more interest in her co-worker clouded her thoughts. When she looked up, the little girl's blue, judgeless eyes pierced her.

"What's your name?" Ava asked.

"Emerson." She brushed the wayward strands from her face.

"I call her Emmie." Paige tilted her head to face the little girl. "Are you hungry, sweetheart?"

Emmie nodded.

"There's a snack on the counter. Why don't you take it into the bedroom and watch cartoons for a bit while I talk to Dr. Fenn?"

The little girl shuffled to the countertop, picked up a bowl, and disappeared into the other room.

"Your daughter is adorable. I wish I'd gotten to know you both while I was here."

Paige's lips stretched into a thin, unexpressive line.

"You didn't answer my question, Paige. Why are you in this place?" Ava was more persistent.

"I can't afford anything else since Dr. Simmons fired me. And now, with all the accusations, I'm just praying to stay out of prison." Paige's eyes welled with tears. "I'm trying to find a job and save money for a decent lawyer, but I haven't had any luck yet." She paused and rubbed her arms. "Dr. Fenn, I can't lose my daughter. She's all I have, and I'm all she has too."

Ava looked away, anger simmering to a slow boil inside her. The thought of Corbin causing a mother and child to live in a dive like this while he soaked in a hot tub in a cushy skyline apartment sickened her. "Are you afraid here?"

Paige spoke as if each word required energy she didn't have. "The man on the other side of the staircase is on the state sex offender's registry. I've heard gunshots in the parking lot, and I bar the door day and night with the chair you're sitting in."

Ava's hand covered her mouth as she soaked in the details Paige shared. "Do you have family who could help you? Parents? Siblings?"

Paige rolled her eyes and let out a deep breath. "We're on our own."

"Anyone?"

"No, no one." The tension in her voice drew tighter. "Look, when I got pregnant with Emmie, my parents kicked me out, and if it matters, her father had other plans besides being a dad." She shifted on the couch, propped her elbows on her knees. "I had to waitress, clean houses, pick up whatever job I could to pay for daycare, and take a night class at a time." She wiped her eyes dry. "When I went to Metro's job fair and landed the interview at Dr. Simmons's clinic, I lied at one of those cash advance places and took out a loan just so I could buy some clothes and makeup to make a good impression. I thought I'd moved up when I got that job. I had a decent apartment, a good sitter for Emmie." She shrugged her shoulders. "I wasn't afraid. Then everything fell apart."

Outside the door, a couple, cursing as they ascended the stairs, reverted to banging against the outer wall to make even more noise, rattling the windows of Paige's apartment. Emmie opened the bedroom door and stood anxiously in sight of her mother.

"It's okay, sweetheart."

The little girl came to her mother's side again.

Ava stood, resigned with a new thought rolling in her head. "Paige, I need your help."

Another banging on the wall from the corridor outside drew their attention to the door, and Ava took the opening to make her pitch. "When Corbin Simmons fired you, he implicated me as well. I have an idea about how to get this straightened out, but I'm going to need your help. Do you have a car here?"

"No, I sold it."

Ava scanned the room. The few furnishings looked as if they'd been bought second-hand or come with the apartment. No pictures hung on the walls, and nothing of note was visible that couldn't be moved. "I want you to pack your things. Everything you can carry that means something to you. The rest we can replace later. This is no place for you or your daughter. We're leaving here."

"B-but I can't afford another place."

"You won't have to worry about that for now. If you can help me, it won't be a worry later, either. Let's just get things packed up before it gets late. We shouldn't be outside here after dark."

Paige looked at Emmie, who buried her face in her mother's shoulder. Then, she looked at Ava with hope in her eyes. "I can't pay you anything right now."

"I'm not asking for money. Just help."

Paige looked at her daughter again, then back to Ava. "That's the only thing I have to offer."

"Then, let's get going." Ava smiled. "We've got work to do."

Just before dark, the women had loaded three garbage bags of clothing in the back of Ava's car, along with two suitcases, a couple of small boxes, and a booster chair in the back seat. The pot-bellied man commented for every trip they made to the car, asking questions and fishing for information. Ava had slipped past him a few times, his game show keeping his attention, the burnt popcorn slowly becoming a roach feast. On the last trip, he asked Paige, "Are you moving, little lady?"

As Paige closed and locked the door to the apartment, Ava took Emmie by the hand and led her down the stairs. Paige followed close behind. They never answered the man, nor did they look back. The smell of burnt popcorn still lingered in the stairwell.

Chapter Forty-Six

Logan

"Trypanophobia. It's a real thing. Look it up." Wyatt sipped on a glass of lemonade, the two men taking a break from the ping pong tournament that had loosened Logan enough to talk a bit.

On the back porch, they sat with their Adirondack chairs pointing toward a clover field where Toby tossed Milo a tennis ball.

"I believe you." Logan's gaze landed on Toby hurling the ball over Milo's head. "Giving shots was never on my list of fears to overcome."

"There's a reason why you and I didn't go into the medical field, though you've got more of a stomach for it than I do." Wyatt stretched his long legs and glanced at Logan. "You look beat, man. You're not sleeping at all, are you?"

"They tell me it gets easier—not worrying about them through the night. Don't know that I believe that yet." He yawned. "I used to be so glad for nighttime to come, so he would finally sleep. Kid's always had so much energy that putting him to bed was like a welcome piece of heaven. Now, I dread to see it come."

"You do have the advantage of knowing a good doctor."

"Don't even start with Ava."

"See there?" Wyatt raised his lemonade. "You're on a first-name basis."

"Yeah, well, let me just put those thoughts to rest right now. She's involved with somebody else and made it pretty clear that I was just her contractor, not that I was looking for anything in the first place."

Toby threw the ball into the side yard and chased Milo out of sight around the house.

Wyatt shrugged. "Seems odd to me that she'd move to a small town and not bring that 'somebody else' with her if she were really serious about him. Did you give her any reason to believe you were interested?"

Logan's thoughts rolled back to the moment he kissed Ava. The smell of her skin, the dampness of her hair. Every cell in his body ignited like a match to a flame the moment he'd kissed her. Never, even when he'd been married, had he been so drawn in by a woman's touch as he had with Ava. He brushed his fingertips across the stubble on his face, the memory still lingering when Wyatt interrupted.

"Hey." Wyatt cocked his head and squinted at Logan. His eyes widened. "You kissed her, didn't you?"

"Yeah, well, like I said. She's spoken for. And . . ."

"And what?"

"I don't know. This guy she's with—I looked him up last night. He's some doctor up in Nashville, got a big, cushy practice. Ava was the only other doctor listed on his website."

"So? Maybe she wanted to put some distance between her and this guy."

"That's not all. There's something shady about him. Dakota saw him on the news recently. Something about an insurance case. It's got me wondering if she didn't come here to get away from the law."

"She's trying to open a practice, though, right?"

"Yeah."

"I'm sure all kinds of paperwork has to be submitted somewhere for her to practice in another state. If she planned on skipping town to hide, why would she do something as conspicuous as opening a new practice?" Wyatt shrugged. "I don't know, bro. All I see is a woman who's really good with Toby. I mean, she went to the hospital with you. Mom told me she worked wonders getting Toby to take his shots. And Jessie's business partner, Carly—well, I know she's on the up and up. I don't think she'd be best friends with a con artist. Those all seem like really good reasons to at least give her the benefit of the doubt."

"Dr. Fenn is a good person, Dad." Toby peeked around the corner of the house. "She had a dog named Coco, and she taught me how to not be scared."

Logan sat up on the edge of his seat. "Hey buddy, how long have you been there?"

"What's a con artist?" The boy scrunched up his nose.

"Nothing you need to worry about, Peanut Butter."

Toby trudged around from the side of the house as if his shoulders were weighed down. "That's what grown-ups say when they don't want to explain things to you."

"Smart kid." Wyatt winked at Logan.

"Why don't you go get your things and tell Aunt Lydia thank you for dinner. We need to be getting back home."

Toby sighed. "Guess I'll have to look up what a con artist is on Wikipedia."

Wyatt snickered.

"No doubt." Logan shook his head. "Go on, now."

When Toby stepped inside, Logan ran an impatient hand through his hair. "He's already gotten attached to her. I never wanted that. It just means more heartache for a kid that's got too many battles to fight right now as it is."

"Maybe neither of you needs to fight those battles alone. That's all I'm saying. Logan, I know you've been hurt, and I know you're trying to protect Toby, but in all this, have you ever wondered at the timing?"

Logan tilted his head. "What do you mean?"

Wyatt put the empty lemonade glass on the porch at his feet and scooted to the edge of his seat. "A new doctor shows up in town. You meet at a photoshoot only to discover later that you're her contractor. Then, she happens to be around when Toby's diagnosed. Probably prevents that situation from becoming more serious than it could have been. Not to mention she's able to help him with his shots—something most adults still have fears of." Wyatt shook his head. "Sounds a little more than random to me. Some would probably call it destiny, or maybe somebody on the high up has you in His sights. Either way, I don't think you should be looking a gift horse in the mouth." Wyatt pointed at him. "Instead, you should pursue this woman."

Logan shook his head. "Not much use in that. She's already gone back to Nashville."

"What do you mean 'gone back to Nashville'?"

"That doctor showed up at her place, said he planned to give her an offer she couldn't refuse."

"Well, what he plans and what she plans may be two different things."

"I don't think so. I went over to the office earlier today, and she's gone. She left me a letter telling me to finish the place as I saw fit. It doesn't sound like she's coming back anytime soon."

"Maybe she had some loose ends to tie up." Wyatt nudged Logan. "Don't you think it's worth exploring? I mean, what if she's the one? What if a relationship with her was meant to be, and you're not giving it a chance?"

Toby came out the door with Lydia and put his backpack over his shoulder. He clutched Rufus in his arms.

"You two aren't leaving now, are you? It's movie night. I can make some popcorn." Lydia dried her hands on a dishtowel.

"Thanks, Lydia." Logan stood, leaned over, and kissed her on the cheek. "Dinner was great, but we should get home."

After Toby hugged his aunt and uncle, he headed for the truck. Logan stepped off the porch, and Milo sidled up to him for a final goodbye. "See you, boy."

He scratched the old dog behind the ears and remembered the day they picnicked on Ava's office floor with Milo when Ava told Toby about a dog she once had. Seemed like most things brought up thoughts about her lately.

As they pulled out of the drive and Milo stood by watching them go, that conversation tried to surface again. Like a memory that refused to be summoned, something about that day buzzed just outside of his consciousness for the rest of the ride home.

Chapter Forty-Seven

Ava

The extended-stay hotel didn't hold ranks with a high-end Hilton, but it offered a clean, safe place for Paige and Ava to set up their plan. After booking a third-floor room, they unloaded suitcases from the back seat of the car, and Ava pulled her own luggage from the trunk. Though she hadn't foreseen the extra company in her room, Ava took comfort in knowing that Paige and Emmie would be safe and that she would have help clearing her and Paige's names and pinning Corbin with criminal acts he alone perpetrated.

Emmie climbed on the bed while Paige put the suitcase on the floor to the side. "Mommy, I'm hungry."

"I know, sweetheart."

Ava pulled her phone from her bag. "How 'bout we order some pizza? How does that sound?"

The little girl's eyes lit up as she nodded.

Paige moved closer to Ava. "Dr. Fenn, I—"

"Paige, we've got a lot to accomplish together, and I'd like it if we became friends. Why don't you call me Ava?"

The woman's face looked gaunt and tired in the yellow lamplight of the hotel room. She hesitated, "Ava, I can't pay you for any of this. I might be able to get a few groceries, but—"

She rested her hand on Paige's shoulder. "Let's call in for some pizza, and then we'll talk."

While she placed the delivery order, Paige bathed Emmie and dressed her for bed. An hour later, they all devoured a large cheese pizza, then after teeth brushing and a few extra hugs, Emmie curled up in the soft pillows of one of the two queen beds and fell asleep.

Once she tucked Emmie under the covers, Paige looked at Ava on the adjacent bed and broke a long silence. "I knew about you and Dr. Simmons, you know, dating each other."

"Yes," Ava sighed. "He took me to the hospital gala, and we had a few other dates."

"So, what happened?"

Ava leaned back on the stack of pillows against the headboard. "When I began to suspect something wrong with our patient files, Corbin downplayed everything but turned up the heat in our personal relationship, tried even harder to push past boundaries I'd set." She twirled a strand of hair around a finger and looked toward the city lights beyond the window. "For a while, I kept quiet, thinking things would get better. I had a great job. I loved working with my patients. It had to get better. But the night of the gala, he crossed the line. That's when I decided that leaving was the best option."

Paige sat on the edge of the bed, facing Ava. "Dr. Simmons was furious the day you resigned. The whole office tiptoed around, trying to stay out of his way. It was like that for the next couple of weeks. That's when he fired me." She shook her head. "He said I'd coded some files incorrectly, and he canned me for incompetence. But I checked every file two, sometimes three times, especially if I was interrupted by a phone call or a patient with a question. I'm meticulous about my work. You won't find anyone more particular. I know I coded everything properly."

"I have no doubt you did, Paige." Ava sat up. "I talked to Mr. Ranier a couple of days ago."

"Yes, I gave him your cell number."

"He paid me a visit and showed me the list of patients you gave him."

"Those were just a few of the names I could remember filing claims on. I had questions about those accounts because Dr. Simmons's reports didn't add up. When I asked him, he got frustrated, told me I wasn't paid to think, and said to file the claims as they were." She shrugged. "I did what he asked, almost certain they were wrong, but I needed that job. I didn't have time to gather proof before he fired me. Shortly after that, I got word that I was under investigation. That's when I contacted Mr. Ranier with the names and your phone number. I pointed him toward you thinking you might have information I didn't. I knew you weren't mixed up in anything dishonest."

"Why didn't you call me yourself?"

"Paranoia, I guess. I didn't want us to be connected on a personal level in case they thought we were running some kind of fraud together. I decided to give it a little while—maybe until things got desperate—before I called you."

Ava shook her head. "The truth is, things have gotten desperate, and if we sit back and don't do anything, we could both end up in big trouble."

A shadow of panic crossed Paige's face. "That's why I'm saving every penny I can for a lawyer."

"We don't have time for a lawyer. That's why I came to see you. If we can prove Corbin's involvement with the right documentation, I think we can extricate ourselves, and that's where you come in."

Paige nodded. "What do I do?"

The two women moved to the room's small dining table and, for the next hour, outlined Ava's plan. Afterward, Paige sat back in her chair, looked over at her sleeping daughter, and sighed. "Do you always come in and swoop people out of miserable places and situations?"

"As altruistic as that sounds, I didn't at first come here to take you with me, but I do owe you for believing in me. And I do think we can help each other."

Paige folded a paper napkin into a small square, then folded it again. Tears welled up in her eyes. "I just want to do right by that little girl. She's the best thing that's ever happened to me."

Ava reached across the table, above the napkin that was now in tatters, and squeezed Paige's hand. "This is going to work. We'll make sure of it."

Paige wiped her cheek. "How long do you think it'll take?"

"I have no idea. I don't see him giving me access to the files, but if we're lucky and I can convince him I'll testify on his behalf and work at the office on his terms, maybe I can find a way to get to the documents we need. If not, we could be here a while."

Paige nodded.

"We should get some rest. Tomorrow will be a big day."

***

The following morning, Ava awoke early. She showered, dressed, and brought in a tray with a continental breakfast for Paige and Emmie. When they finished eating, she did a mental recap of their plans, then left some cash for the two to get lunch at a restaurant across the street and began the dreaded trip back to her old office.

The lobby was deserted but for two patients waiting behind opened magazines, the smell of morning coffee wafting from the courtesy table in the corner. A new secretary looked up from her perch behind the partially glassed-in counter and greeted her with a plastic smile. "Hello, may I help you?"

"I'm Dr. Fenn. I'm here to see Dr. Simmons. Could you tell him, please?"

The receptionist's condescending gaze lingered as if she'd been trained to snarl should Ava show up at the office. Corbin had doubtless hired her to be his front-door watchdog as much as a receptionist. Given the recent questioning of his reputation, it was a practical move.

"Take a seat, please."

Ava took a deep breath. She would have to be convincing. "No, thank you. I'll see him now." She stormed through the door leading to the exam rooms and back offices, leaving the receptionist stammering.

When she arrived at Corbin's personal office door, he was sitting at his desk, the woman who'd chased her down the hall, now at her heels, no longer wearing a plastic smile or a condescending glare. She instead bore an expression of astonishment.

"Dr. Simmons, I asked her to—"

"It's alright, Belinda." Corbin waved the woman away. "Could you close the door behind you, please?"

Ava waited for the privacy Corbin requested. "If you want me to work here, you'll have to call her off first thing. I'm not going to have Belinda over my shoulder all the time."

"Why, Ava, it's nice to see you too. Aren't you Johnny-on-the-spot this morning? You must've been anxious to accept my offer." He leaned back in his chair, cradling the back of his head in his hands.

"Don't be under the false notion that I'm here because I want to be."

"Why *are* you here, sweetheart?"

The sickening endearment turned her stomach. "Because I need to keep my license, and I want to practice. And despite having to work alongside you, I love what I do."

"Well, well, you have come to your senses, then."

Ava remained silent, biting the inside of her lip to keep from saying anything that would tip him off. That would be the hardest part until she had his neck in the noose.

"Yes, that's right." He stood and circled from behind his desk, drawing closer to her. "You've realized that I'm the key to keeping you from wearing an orange jumpsuit." He walked behind her.

Ava felt his eyes scanning her.

"The view from this side of the bars will be much better. You'll see."

Ava spun on her heel to face him. "What do I have to do?"

"You know, Ava, you had a shot at having all you ever wanted, being with me. I could have given you a good life."

"Everything but honesty, safety, and integrity. Those are things you don't have the faintest clue about."

He returned to the other side of the desk, ignoring her remarks. "You'll first testify at the hearing on my behalf, claiming that the files you signed are legitimate."

"You mean the files you forged."

"Heavens, no." He grinned. "You should get that straight quickly." He pointed a finger. "And don't tempt me to let some compromising evidence slip into the hands of the authorities. Implication is such a nasty business."

Ava kept quiet again. "When's the hearing?"

"A week from Monday. So, you came just in time."

"Where's my office key, and when do I start back?"

"Oh, you're no longer welcome in this office. I can't have you scouring the place in search of things with which to incriminate me. That's why I offered to set up a satellite office for those times when we need to coordinate."

Ava's heart sank. "You mean those times when you want to use me?"

"That too." He smirked. "Anyway, you should go ahead and find a nice little apartment somewhere. I already took the liberty of securing a little rental space with some basic medical equipment. The rest should be set up by the end of the week. Belinda's been working on staffing for you, which means you should be up and running by the time you get unpacked. Oh, and see to it that your licensing paperwork is in order for the state of Tennessee. We don't want a snag with such insignificant things as red tape."

"What if the investigators find discrepancies because we aren't at the same physical location?"

"Don't worry about those matters. Leave the heavy lifting to me. I've been at this a little longer than you." His voice turned gruff. "In the meantime, get in the habit of answering your phone when I call." He returned to the other side of his desk and sat down. "I'll have Belinda get in touch with you when all the details are settled." He began scrolling through patient files. "Now, if you'll excuse me, I have things to do. You can go."

Ava fumed over his arrogance. She blew past Belinda without even a side glance. By the time she reached her car, panic had set in, and she began deep breathing to fend off a full-scale attack.

Chapter Forty-Eight

Logan

Logan woke up in the recliner much later than he'd planned. He fumbled toward the couch to check on Toby, his back aching from sporadic and awkward sleep in the chair. Despite the late morning hour, Toby still slept soundly and stirred only mildly as Logan checked his blood sugar. When the meter beeped with a number in a good range, he tucked the supplies back in the backpack and stroked the multiple days' growth on his cheeks to further tug him from his sluggishness.

As he pulled the makings of an early lunch out of the refrigerator, his mind wandered again to conversations with Ava. He'd taken pleasure every time he'd watched her talk to Toby. Their back-and-forth had covered all the topics Toby loved: peanut butter, Milo, dogs in general. That was his favorite subject lately. He'd watched Toby's eyes light up when Ava told him about the pet she used to have. He was equally enthralled when she talked about the neighbor with the service dog.

And then, how she handled everything at the hospital and took care of Toby when he couldn't? Those images all found a home in his thoughts. He couldn't erase from his mind how beautiful she was—the kind of beautiful that made his heart hurt, made him clench his fists with the anxiety of a kid on a first date.

He finally shook his head as if to shut off the thoughts, determined to go to work and not let her cross his mind again. Instead, he began a mental list of the afternoon's tasks, and the first thing on tap was checking in at the Brashear site. He knew if he kept Dakota's workers supplied, his friend would see to the business of finishing the job. He dreaded to think what a mess he'd have been in had Dakota not helped him out of his jam.

After lunch, he dropped Toby off at his parents' place and dived into the rest of the day's tasks. With trips to administer insulin and phone calls to check on Toby taking up a good portion of his time, his mother finally broached the topic of his needing to teach her how to give Toby's shots, too, or asking Ava to teach her.

With the mention of her name, the thin thread separating his thoughts from Ava broke, but, despite the fist-clenching anxiety and all the images flooding back, he didn't fight too hard to push them away again. In fact, he welcomed them.

Chapter Forty-Nine

Ava

Ava sat at the table in the hotel room, her hands laced together as a prop for her hanging head. "How can I get the evidence we need without working in the same office?"

Paige tapped the remote to locate a kid's show, stroked Emmie's hair, then sat down at the table across from Ava. She sighed. "We'll get it. We've just got to be smarter than he is." She paused. "Look, I've been thinking, and I may have an idea. It's risky, but—"

"It's time for risk." Ava sat upright, waiting to hear more.

Paige nodded. "Do you remember Mr. Naples?"

"The custodian at Corbin's office? Of course," Ava paused. "He's the one who helped me find your apartment." Then, she began to see where Paige was going. "You're thinking we could get him to let us in after hours."

"I know he would. I used to bring him donuts every Monday morning. He'd let me in Fort Knox if he had the key."

Ava looked out the window. "If Corbin found out, we could get in a lot of trouble."

"We're already in a lot of trouble. What's he gonna do? Threaten to incriminate us twice?" She began to shoot off thoughts in rapid-fire. "I could get things set up with Mr. Naples. I'd call him ahead of time, get him to let us in the back door."

"You have his number?"

"Yeah, he gave it to me in case I needed to work late some night. He wanted me to call him so he would know I was in the building, and we wouldn't scare each other." Paige continued, "Anyway, once we got in, all we'd have to do is copy the files we need and slip out the back. It wouldn't take more than a half-hour at most."

"But that still doesn't solve the problem of accessing his files. That *would* be like trying to get into Fort Knox. We don't know his passwords."

"You know custodians have more than the keys to the building, don't you? They're one of the most under-appreciated, under-utilized assets in a business."

"Yeah, but I don't think he has Corbin's passwords."

Paige grinned and nodded. "Back a couple of months ago, Mr. Naples was cleaning Dr. Simmons's office. He asked to show me something. When I followed him in, he dropped to his knees and pointed beneath the desk to a piece of paper that was hanging by a shred of tape from the middle of the desk."

"Corbin's list of passwords," Ava whispered.

"Mr. Naples didn't know whether to rip it off and set it on his desk or leave it. I told him to leave it. The next day, I went into Dr. Simmons's office for some signatures. He was with a patient, so I took a quick peek underneath his desk. There it was, that piece of paper neatly taped in all four corners back in its place. My guess is it's still there, with all his current passwords. He's a dinosaur when it comes to security."

"What if he's changed hiding places?"

"Do you really think he's that smart?"

Ava tilted her head. "Arrogant, yes. Smart, no. But, to get the files we need quickly, we'd have to know exactly which patient accounts to search. We're now looking at lifting information in a half-hour dump and run, not accessing files over the course of days or weeks."

Paige chewed at her lip. "If we could just narrow down our search, we could make better time."

"Mr. Ranier told me that the discrepancies he identified came from Alzheimer's patients. Is there a way to filter the patients by age or condition?

"I may be able to do that through the coding filter. Can you come up with an external hard drive? We'll need some significant storage space."

"I can get that." Ava took a deep breath. "Think we can pull this off?"

"We've got to. All we need now is one thing." Paige looked over at Emmie. "A sitter."

When Ava made the call, Carly picked up the phone in an exasperated rant. "Ava Fenn, if you ever leave town mysteriously again without giving me the full scoop, I'm going to rent a billboard and plaster your mug on it with a missing person caption."

"Hey, Carly, I'm sorry. I knew you'd be upset, but I've got a big favor to ask."

"First, tell me where you are and what you're doing."

"That's a really long story."

"I've got a really long time to listen, so start talking."

After Ava laid out the entire scenario and the plan she and Paige devised to implicate Corbin Simmons, she could almost hear Carly over the phone rubbing her hands together in anticipation.

"You've got to be the gutsiest chick I've ever met. I'm so proud to know you. So, what's the favor? How do I get to help put this Neanderthal in the slammer?"

"First, I need a babysitter." Ava paused. "Tonight."

"Wait. What? A babysitter? Tonight? I was supposed to have a Facetime date with Jex tonight."

"You two have resorted to Facetime for dating?"

"Long distance isn't exactly easy. And it works for the moment, at least until I can meet him in Atlanta next week."

Ava sighed. "Could you just do this for me, please? Paige and I think we should get the evidence we need in hand as soon as possible before he has a chance to alter anything. We're planning to pull this off tonight. She has to go with me to the office, but we need someone to watch after her little girl while we're gone."

"But it's four hours away."

"I know, and I'll owe you big." Ava paused. "Look, I'll release those photoshoot proofs for you to use wherever you see fit if you'll just do this for me."

"Wherever?"

"As far as I'm concerned, wherever." Ava nodded to Paige. "How soon can you get on the road?"

"I'll just need to grab my purse and gas up the tank."

Ava snapped her finger. "Oh, wait. I'll need you to stop by the office too. I dropped some boxes off there a few days ago. Inside one of them is a red external hard drive. Can you bring that?"

"Sure, but how do I get into your office?"

"Call the number I'm texting you now. It's Logan's number. He has a key."

Carly sighed. "Ava, what if this all goes south?"

"Then, I'll need you to babysit a little while longer. I'll send you the address to the hotel and see you in a few hours." Ava hung up the phone before Carly processed her answer.

"She's coming?" Paige looked hopeful.

"She'll be here." Ava glanced at the time on her phone. If Carly started toward Nashville in the next thirty minutes, she'd be there by nightfall. "You should call Mr. Naples. Get this thing set up. Looks like we'll be trying our hand at burglary tonight."

"Aren't those your files to begin with?"

Ava cocked her head. "Yeah, I guess they are."

"The way I see it, you're just getting back what your patients entrusted you with in the first place."

Chapter Fifty

Logan

That afternoon, Logan found himself driving down Main Street, turning toward Ava's office. His excuse? To see if any tools he might need got left behind.

When he stepped in the door, his phone rang, and a number he didn't recognize popped up. At first, he ignored the call but then decided to answer at the last second.

"Logan Carter."

"Hi, Logan. This is Carly Kirkpatrick, Ava's friend. We met at the hospital the other night."

"Yeah. I remember." *Odd that she would be calling* "What can I help you with?"

"Ava got in touch with me earlier, and she needs me to get something from her office. She said you had a key and could let me in."

Logan closed the door behind him. "Actually, I just got here. Why don't you come now?"

"Perfect. I'll be right there."

As he walked through the waiting area and stepped to the receptionist's desk, Logan grappled with feelings that again tried to surface. For several minutes, he sat in the office chair next to the desk, listening to the silence. He could imagine the room busy with the traffic of a nurse and kids, expectant mothers, and people looking for healing. He could envision Ava with her stethoscope draped around her slender neck, helping an elderly patient to an exam room. The more he pictured, the more right it seemed.

He opened the drawer where the picture of Ava with Dr. Simmons lay. It hurt just as much to look at it now as it had a few days ago, but he stared at the photo nonetheless, trying to will from it some understanding of Ava Fenn.

"Logan?"

Carly's voice startled him. He stood with the picture in hand.

"Sorry, I didn't mean to sneak up on you. I wasn't far away when I called."

"No, it's fine."

Carly looked around. "Are you here to finish the office?"

"I'm not really sure what to do." His introspection had left him weary and honest. "Ava said she was leaving town. Didn't sound like she was planning to be back anytime soon, and from the looks of things"—he set the picture on the desk— "she's not staying in Camden Grove for long."

"Oh, really?" Carly glanced at the photo as she crossed the room. She began opening boxes in search of whatever she'd come for. "That what she told you?"

"That's what Dr. Simmons told me."

Carly spun around. "I probably shouldn't be sharing this with you. Ava's pretty tight-lipped about things." She pointed toward the desk. "But nothing's going on with her and the man in that photograph, if that's what you're thinking."

Logan's eyes narrowed. "What do you mean?"

Carly moved to the next box and began to dig through it. "I mean that the time she's spent with you and your son has put a little life back into her. And that man?" She side-glanced at the photo. "He's a creep of the jerkiest kind who's trying to drag Ava into a lot of legal trouble."

"What kind of legal trouble?"

"The man's responsible for insurance fraud in the office that Ava used to share with him. She was trying to manage an honest practice, loved working in Nashville, but he started using her name and license to help run an under-the-table business of some kind. I don't know all the details. All I know is that Corbin Simmons is trying to coerce her to come back to work for him." Carly pulled a portable hard drive from the second box. "Here it is." She flipped it over in her hands.

Logan walked to the window and gazed out at a couple strolling down the street.

"You're not convinced, are you?"

"No." Logan shook his head. "No, I'm not."

"Hm, you're a hard one to crack, aren't you?" Carly crossed the room to face him. "I'm going out on a limb here and guessing that you're not interested in bringing uncertainty into your life or, especially, your son's life right now. You've been keeping guard over yourself and Toby because you know what it looks like to put your trust in somebody just to be betrayed. I get it."

"How do you know I've been betrayed?"

"Are you kidding? I could read it in your eyes if I were stone-cold blind. Not to mention we live in a small town. Word does get around." She looked out the window alongside him. "Honestly, I can't blame you. Most of us have been down that kind of road before. But I can tell you I know Ava Fenn. She's been burned too, which I'm betting is why it's been nearly impossible for the two of you to open up to the possibility of each other."

"So, you think you've got this all figured out?"

Carly looked back over her shoulder to the door. "You wait right here. I've got something to show you."

She stepped outside, and a minute later, returned holding a large, leather-bound album.

"You haven't seen these yet. Take a look." She set the album on the desk, and Logan walked closer. "Before you say anything, though, I want to tell you what I see. Chemistry. And a lot of it. What I find sad is that I see it, Jessie sees it, everybody who's looked at these shots sees it. But you and Ava are too stubborn to open your eyes and lay claim to it."

Logan slowly flipped through the album, his heart aching more with each page.

"She's in Nashville right now, clearing her name. She'll come back here to do one of two things: sell and go back to the city . . . or not. I think you should consider whether you want her to stay."

Logan closed the album and handed it to Carly, conflict brewing in his chest.

She cradled the book. "I have to go, but you should think about what I said." Heading for the door, she looked back at him. "Oh, I left you one of those photos. It's there, on the desk, in place of that horrid picture of Ava and Corbin. Some people call themselves photographers. The gall." She winked, then walked out the door. He'd never seen when she'd laid it down.

After she left, Logan first avoided looking at the photo, but then he couldn't sidestep any longer. When he finally picked it up, his chest swelled at first from the sight of her, then from the uncertainty. The photo was taken while they were playing around in the creek. Her wavey brown hair, dripping from the water, fell along her shoulders. The smile lighting up her eyes was genuine, just as true as the one he'd seen her wear the day of their peanut-butter picnic when he had watched her talk to Toby about dogs.

As he gazed at the photo, his uncertainty took a turn. He didn't feel this way the first time he fell in love. With Eliza, starting a relationship was the next logical thing he was supposed to do in life. This time around, he wasn't looking for it. He didn't even want it. Things had to be different, didn't they? His heart began to pound as he pictured the possibilities. Was it too much for him to hope for a happy life? No . . . maybe it wasn't. Maybe that was exactly what he should expect.

His breathing quickened, and a smile crossed his face as he pulled the phone from his pocket and began to dial.

"Dakota, I need help."

"Toby okay?" The concern in his friend's voice trailed through the phone.

"Yeah, man. He's good. How long do you think it would take us to finish the job if we took all the labor from the Brashear project and put it on Ava's office?"

"You mean *all* the labor?"

"Every last bit."

"Um, I don't know. There's drywall to hang in the back. Painting to do. I could have the electricity up and running in a day, day and a half at most. We've got the furniture to install."

"Yeah, but it's all here, and I can bring Dad over to start putting it together. I bet Mom would help. Wyatt and Lydia too."

"Well, with everybody on it, we could probably have it done in two days tops, but what's the rush all of a sudden?"

"I've got a deadline to meet. Can you call in all the guys for me?"

"Yeah, sure."

Logan exhaled a long, lingering breath. "Dakota . . . thanks, man. I'll see you and the team bright and early in the morning."

Logan hung up the phone, locked the office door, and left in a rush to pick up Toby. On the way, he made his second call.

"Hey brother, I need your help."

"Yeah, you bet. Everything okay?"

"Everything is just right."

He spent the rest of the ride rolling out his plan to Wyatt.

Chapter Fifty-One

Ava

Carly arrived a little later than expected, but once she settled in with Emmie, Ava and Paige left for the office. Paige had arranged for Mr. Naples to open the back door at 9 p.m.—just before he left for the evening. They parked the car down the street and reached the building just as he came out with a bag of trash.

Ava and Paige agreed to keep the custodian in the dark about the reason they needed to get into the office. If they did get caught, the fewer people involved, the better for everyone. Paige simply told him over the phone that she had to come back with Dr. Fenn to get some of her old files and that an after-hours visit would be better so as not to upset the office schedule.

When they scaled the two flights of stairs and got into the office, the real work began. Using a flashlight, they went to Corbin's personal office first. Fortunately, the door was closed but not locked. When Paige knelt beneath the desk, she came back out with a sheet of pure gold—all the office passwords beautifully organized on a neat little spreadsheet.

Ava smiled. "Now, let's get down to business."

Back at Belinda's workstation, they risked turning on a desk lamp. For forty-five minutes, Paige and Ava pulled digitized files of all the patients diagnosed with Alzheimer's that had been under Ava's care and extradited them to the hard drive Ava had hooked up to Belinda's computer. File after file had bogus claims that she had not authorized.

After a while, Ava sat back in the chair. "What are we doing? This doesn't prove a thing. It's just more of the same kind of documents Mr. Ranier already has, with my signature."

"Why don't we cross-reference these records with the date you claimed residence in Alabama?"

"But why?"

"If he filed claims after that date, maybe you could prove you were in Alabama and unable to authorize those claims in-house. If it's an ink signature, all we have to do is pull the physical file from the shelf, and he's caught."

"It's worth a try."

Paige went to work searching for files with a date after the first of June. Ava kept peeking between the blinds at the parking lot, hoping it would stay empty.

"I think I've found one. And that's all it would take to open the investigation in our favor." She pointed to the screen. "This was just after you left, and he fired me. My initials are there, too, as having entered the claim with you authorizing."

Ava turned to Paige. "Do you have a way to prove you were absent from the office by that time?"

"I applied for three other jobs and filed for unemployment. Those applications are dated and in somebody's inbox."

"Okay, upload it, and let's get out of here." She peeked out the window one more time, and her stomach lunged into her throat. Corbin stepped from his car, two floors below.

"He's here, Paige." Ava let the blind flap back into place and ran toward the desk. She scanned the room to make sure everything was as it had been. "Hurry. I'll grab the physical files from the stacks. What's the record number?"

Paige scrolled frantically. "385422-110. We're not gonna make it. If he finds us, we're both toast."

Ava scanned the files frantically. "110. 110. 110. I've got it. Shut it down and grab the hard drive. We'll have to hide in here."

Paige shut off the desk lamp and ran toward the file room. They crouched low behind the glass window as they heard the office door open. Corbin flicked on the lights that lit up the main office area. Ava grabbed Paige's hand and squeezed it. From their position, Ava could see the passwords list on the edge of Belinda's desk. She looked at Paige and pointed. Paige's jaw dropped.

They heard Corbin's footsteps disappear down the hall. Ava rose from the floor and eased toward the desk. She snatched the list and crawled back to the files room, hoping the noise of the paper hadn't alerted Corbin.

For another ten minutes, they took shallow breaths and waited for him to leave. Ava could never remember him staying late at work. She prayed he hadn't chosen now to start.

After an eternity counted in agonizing seconds, they heard shuffling down the hall. Then, a urinal flushed. Finally, the lights went out, and Corbin locked the office door behind him.

Too scared to move too soon, Ava and Paige stayed where they were until they heard the outer elevator doors open and close. Only then did they return Corbin's password list to his hiding place and exit the office down the back stairway.

Ava finally inhaled a deep breath once they were in the car and on the way back to the hotel.

By 10:30 p.m., they were back in the room with Carly who'd just surrendered her last Go-Fish hand to a wide-awake Emmie.

Paige ushered her little girl to the bathroom for a potty break, while Ava spilled all the details in answer to the half-dozen questions Carly rapid-fired at her.

"I can't believe you two had to hide in the file room." Carly stretched out across the hotel bed, propping her chin up with her hands.

"Not something I ever want to do again."

"Me, neither." Paige stepped from the bathroom, leaving Emmie to brush her teeth.

Ava bit into one of two egg rolls left over from Carly and Emmie's late-night takeout. "Let's get set up and get those files out of our hot little hands."

"I'm ready." Paige sat down to Ava's laptop. "It'll take only a few minutes to upload the files from the hard drive. Should all be there waiting on Mr. Ranier in the morning."

"Good, I'll call him first thing and let him know, and then—fingers crossed—we can go on with our lives."

Emmie came out of the bathroom and climbed into her mother's lap. "Mommy. Are we going home?" The little girl hadn't said much since they'd gotten back to the hotel.

Paige stroked the little girl's hair. "I don't—"

"Emmie, you and your mommy are coming with me." Ava raised her eyes to Paige. "That is, if you want. You can stay at my place in Alabama until the dust settles, and you can get back on your feet."

"I can't—"

"If all this pans out, you just helped us both save our careers, not to mention keeping us out of P-R-I-S-O-N." She glanced at Emmie. "I want to do this for you and your daughter."

Carly sat up on the bed. "You really should take her up on it. Camden Grove is a hidden treasure of a place. And maybe you can help me convince Ava to stick around there too."

Paige looked at her daughter. The little girl nodded, a hopeful expression in her eyes. "Maybe just for a while."

"For a while, then," Ava repeated.

Paige wrapped her arms around Emmie in a tight squeeze. "Come on. It's way past your bedtime."

"Sorry, that's my fault." Carly smirked. "You've got a card shark on your hands with this one." She winked at Emmie. "I've seriously got to up my Go-Fish game."

Paige ruffled through a suitcase until she found the little girl's gown and underwear as Emmie skipped off to the bathroom a second time. Before she followed, Paige turned to Ava and Carly. "I think I could use some good friends like you two. Thanks." Then she turned and closed the door.

Carly jumped from the bed. "This is good."

"What's good?"

"You, coming back home to Alabama. I was hoping I wouldn't have to tie you up and drag you back. You know, there's a very handsome contractor—"

"Stop right there." Ava held up her hands. "Carly, I don't think I'm ready for a relationship, and I don't think Logan is, either. Besides, I'm not in the clear until Ranier tells me it's over."

"Pshhh." Carly waved off the comment like someone's bad breath. "That's a matter of logistics. Don't evade the real issue." She stood in front of Ava. "Just lie to me and tell me you've never felt anything more than an employer-to-employee relationship with this man. Tell me you see him through a completely professional lens, and I'll keep my mouth shut. But before you do that, you should know that when I saw him earlier today, he—"

"You saw him? Today?"

"Yes, at your office. And we had a candid talk about the two of you."

"You did what?" Ava's voice rose an octave.

"I can't believe that you two are so thick-headed that you can't see what's right in front of you. You've both been burned. That's what I told him. He doesn't trust the process, and neither do you. Yet, you've both found each other—with a little ingenious intervention, if I do say so myself. Shouldn't you give it a chance?"

Ava folded her arms and turned away.

Carly laughed. "You can't say it. You can't tell me you didn't feel anything because you did. He was the same way. Now, you two just need to get on the same stinkin' page and give this a chance." She sighed. "You know what they say about pictures?" She flicked one of the Fordham Mill photos on the table. "More than a thousand words shouting from that cozy little proof, my friend."

***

The following afternoon, while Ava and Paige waited for word, Carly and Emmie went to the hotel pool for a swim. When the phone rang, Paige was showering. Ava held her breath as she looked at the screen. It was Mr. Ranier's number.

"Well, I'm still not sure how you did it, but congratulations." Ranier paused as if waiting for Ava to elaborate.

"Will that be enough evidence to clear Paige and me?"

"After I got off the phone with you this morning, I reviewed the information you sent and began the process of filing a search warrant. Dr. Fenn, you'll be glad to know that the authorities took Corbin into custody, along with his secretary Belinda, before their lunch had time to settle."

Ava put her hand to her head and took a deep breath. "I can't believe you got a warrant in place so quickly."

"I know a judge whose brother died of an overdose from prescription drugs sold on the street. He's obviously sympathetic to our cause," Ranier replied. "My guess is that with what you sent me and what we've obtained from Simmons's office, we'll have enough to put him away until his Beamer rusts in a junkyard."

Ava propped her elbows on the hotel table. "Mr. Ranier, can I go back to my life now?"

"You mean in Alabama?"

Ava paused. "Yes, in Alabama, for a while at least."

"We'll still need your testimony, and Ms. Westerfield's too. But I see no reason why you shouldn't move forward from here."

Ava stood looking out the hotel window when Paige emerged from the bathroom. The sniffles she failed to conceal drew Paige closer.

"What's wrong, Ava?"

Shaking her head, Ava turned and broke into a smile. "We're clear, Paige. Ranier called, and we're clear."

The women and Emmie celebrated that evening with a trip to the Cheesecake Factory and a Godiva chocolate cheesecake to go. Capping the night with a carriage ride through downtown Nashville, Ava chuckled at Carly's antics and relished in Emmie's delight at the size of the Clydesdales pulling them through the streets.

She couldn't deny that the city held a certain magic, but something was missing. In the middle of it all, she found herself longing for a break on a porch swing in Alabama. And this carriage ride through her beloved Nashville felt strangely like a proper goodbye.

Chapter Fifty-Two

Logan

By late evening of the day after Logan had called in the troops, Dakota had already tested the wiring, the crew had finished the drywall in the exam rooms, and Gus and a couple of other workers had most of the furniture assembled and secured in place. Margaret, Lydia, Wyatt, and Logan continued to paint while Toby played with Milo.

Knowing that everybody had worked up an appetite, Logan ordered barbecue from Wiggs's Place. Once he checked Toby's blood sugar, he talked his mother through the procedure of giving Toby his injection. Then, he joined the crew and the rest of his family on the floor along the wall of the waiting area to eat their feast from paper plates. They laughed about how much work they'd gotten done once Logan caught fire. Then they ribbed him a little about a certain doctor who may have set that fire in him in the first place.

Brushing off their good-natured teasing, he insisted, "I've got a deadline to keep, and I haven't let one slip by yet."

"Yeah, how many of those other deadlines had anything to do with a good-looking MD?" Wyatt lifted his pork-filled fork in a toast to Ava.

Toby piped up, shaking his head. "Not one."

The whole room broke out in laughter again as Logan grabbed his son in a gentle headlock.

After dinner, Logan had Lydia and his mom put the finishing touches on a chalk-painted board in the hallway of the office, just past the lobby. They bordered it with burlap ribbon and wrote in Lydia's near-perfect calligraphy, *Welcome to Dr. Fenn's Office.* Strung from one end to another in three rows were pieces of grass string with evenly-spaced, decorative clothes pins for any pamphlets or other public information Ava decided to post there.

When Logan came through, his mother stopped him. "She's going to love what you've done to this place."

Logan nodded, hopeful at the thought. "You know this isn't just me trying to get a job done, don't you?"

"Of course, I do. I could tell the first night you brought her to the house that she was something special, and I knew you felt it too."

"Mom, I'm a little uneasy about all this. You know I don't just jump in the deep end and hope to tread."

"I know that, but sometimes you have to have faith it'll all work out. Don't overthink. Just see what happens."

Logan nodded. "The guys are getting ready to load up and go. I'll check Toby again in a few minutes. Do you think he could go with you and Dad while I finish up here?"

"You bet." She looked around. "It's amazing that it all came together so quickly."

"A little bit of a miracle, I'd say."

"See? Faith, and it'll all work out." She patted Logan on his bristly cheek and went to gather things to leave.

Logan whispered to himself. "I sure hope so."

When everyone cleared out of the office, he took another pass through each room sweeping up remnants and dust and wiping down furniture. As he stepped into the hall with a filled trash bag, he set it down and looked around. The office was ready for Ava. Now, if only she were ready for it.

After one last glance, he locked the door behind him and allowed something almost foreign to enter his heart. Something that he'd pushed away far too long.

He let in his dreams.

Logan carried Toby into the house asleep that night and tucked him in on the couch. With a quick shower to wash off the dust, he went to his computer and spent two hours scrolling through information on type 1 diabetes. It had become his side gig—learning the nuances of Toby's new life. As he scrolled article after article, one popped up that caught his attention. One about a young boy with type 1 diabetes . . . who had a service dog.

Then, the conversation—that peanut-butter-picnic conversation at Ava's office—came barreling back to him with the force of a tidal wave. Why hadn't he thought of it before?

Ava had talked about a service dog.

Logan typed a line in the search bar. As he scrolled through the results, he ran up on a feature from the local news a few months back about a woman who trained service dogs—seizure response dogs, guide dogs, autism support dogs, and . . . diabetic alert dogs. And she was in Brandon Springs, an hour west of Hartley.

His fingers clicked the mouse more urgently as he pulled up the story. After playing the short clip of the newsreel, the story confirmed everything he needed to know.

He wrote down the trainer's name and, with a few more clicks, found her number. Then his search took a new turn. For another hour, he scrolled and searched, read, and made notes. Before forcing himself to the recliner at 1 a.m., he checked on Toby one last time.

Finally, as he settled under a quilt, the last thought that crossed his mind was the plan he'd begin to put in place. It had to work. This whole scheme, something he'd now dubbed Operation Peanut Butter, simply had to work, because if it did, tomorrow could be the start of something big.

Chapter Fifty-Three

Logan

"Toby," Logan said as he nudged the little boy. "Wake up, sleepyhead. We've got a busy day."

He stretched and pried his eyes open. "What's today?"

"Nana and Pops are taking you fishing today."

"You coming?"

Logan rubbed his beard. "I've got a few things to take care of, but I might have a surprise for you later."

Toby scrunched his nose. "I'm gonna catch Walter, and you'll not be there to see it."

Logan ruffled his hair. "You just might. Come on, we need to get breakfast and get you dressed."

"So, what's the surprise?"

"If I told you—"

Toby rose sluggishly from the couch. "Yeah, I know, it wouldn't be a surprise."

"Exactly."

Logan made quick work of breakfast and transporting Toby to his parents' place. On the way back into town, he took a deep breath and made a call.

"Carly. It's Logan Carter. I hope you don't mind my calling you. I found your number from where you called me about the key. Can you talk for a minute? I've been thinking about what you said . . . and I need your help."

Chapter Fifty-Four

Ava

Carly rolled her suitcase out of the hotel room and took a phone call while Ava and Paige finished packing. She peeked back in the door long enough to whisper overtop the phone that she'd be in the dining room getting breakfast.

As Ava zipped up the computer bag, she set it on the table and picked up the photo Carly had left there. One glance and the thought of Logan still caused her stomach to flutter.

Paige and Emmie put their bags near the door. "All set."

Ava shook off the feeling, slipped the photo into her purse, and hoisted the computer bag over her shoulder. "Let's go see what they have for breakfast this morning."

Emmie skipped to the elevator as the two women followed. When they found Carly in the hotel dining room, she was finishing up her call.

"Who are you talking to?" Ava mouthed.

Carly covered the phone and whispered, "Someone from one of my photoshoots." She returned to the conversation. "So, I'll check in with you later about that upcoming session I *know* you'll be booking with me. Okay, love. Bye."

Ava noticed the playful tone in Carly's voice.

"What was that all about?"

"Just business." She tossed her phone into her purse and changed the subject. "So, when I left your office yesterday, I think I may have dropped my spare set of keys somewhere inside. Could you go by and see if they're there when you get back in town? I can come by later and pick them up."

"Yeah, sure. But since when have you carried a spare set of keys?" Ava looked at the small buffet of breakfast foods as Paige and Emmie filled two cups with juice from the dispenser.

"Since I had to pay a locksmith twice to come open my door." Carly smirked. "I think I'll grab a bagel and some fruit and get on the road."

"You have someplace to be? Doing your Facetime date with Jex today?"

"That comes later tonight, but yeah, I've gotta prep my bridal fair layout. Deadlines are coming fast, and I need to fine-tune."

"I think we're almost ready to head back too. We'll follow you."

In the hotel parking lot a few minutes later, Ava hugged Carly as Paige buckled Emmie into the booster seat in back. "We couldn't have done this without you."

Carly cocked her head to the side. "I'm invaluable, I know."

Ava laughed. "Always humble, too. I do admire how you handle hard times like they're small hurdles. Someday I want to be just like you."

"You know, it's taken a while for me to come to this." Carly smiled. "Anyway, just jump high and keep running."

"We've fought some pretty tough battles together, haven't we?"

"Durable gals, right? You've dumped a jerk and cleared your name in what could have been a disastrous 10 o'clock news reel, and I've found a way to come back from personal and professional purgatory too. You know, thanks to that photoshoot you did for me, I think I've got a real stab at landing some of Hartley's biggest society weddings next season. Maybe even some Christmas accounts. I'd say things are looking up for both of us."

Ava hugged her friend again. "A promise is a promise. I hope those photos do you well."

Carly rounded her car and opened the door. "Don't forget to stop by your office."

Ava nodded. "I'll call you."

Chapter Fifty-Five

Logan

After Logan ended the call with Carly, he pulled into Ava's office parking lot. He slipped the Fordham Mill photo and a note he'd written that morning from the console and headed inside. The office smelled of fresh paint and looked like a new place. He hoped all the effort would make a difference.

With purpose, he stepped past the waiting room and into the hall where the decorative board his mom and Lydia had created greeted him. Before he talked himself out of it, he pinned the photo and the note to the board and left, praying Ava would at least consider his request.

He spun out of the parking lot knowing he had only a short time to make big things happen.

Chapter Fifty-Six

Ava

On the long drive back, Emmie played with her doll for a while, then fell asleep halfway into the trip. Even Paige dozed the last half hour. Ava spent the time alone thinking about how the last few weeks had changed her.

When she first came to Camden Grove, the emotional weight of moving to a new place, knowing almost no one, and starting a practice from scratch seemed almost too much to handle. But now, considering the nightmare she'd just avoided, coming back home to a small town seemed less daunting. She'd also come to realize that the potential for a future wasn't something to take for granted.

Images of the last few weeks, thoughts she couldn't have conceived of even a month ago after she'd first moved from the city, flashed through her mind like a slide show of best moments as she drove on. Eating mint chocolate chip at the ice cream shop with Carly. Playing in the water at Old Fordham Mill with

Logan. Making up the silly rhyme with Toby. Having peanut butter sandwiches on her office floor. Almost catching Walter at the Carters' pond. When she and Logan kissed.

That kiss.

As she connected all the images, she realized that more and more of her best moments involved Logan.

As they came into the city limits of the Grove, Emmie stirred awake in the back seat. "Mommy, I gotta go."

Paige rose from her pseudo-sleep and looked at her watch. "How far are we from your place?"

"We're almost there. A few more minutes. I promised Carly I'd run by my office, but I can drop you at my house first and get you two settled in."

Ava looked in the rearview as the little girl leaned her head against the seatbelt. Emmie reminded her of Toby, about the same age. Kids were so trusting. All Emmie had was her mother. She knew Paige would take care of her no matter what, and that was enough. And now, Toby relied on his dad to sustain his very life. Every single day. Yet, he knew Logan would move mountains if he had to, and that was enough. Something inside Ava softened when she thought of the magnitude of that responsibility, of the trust involved. She wondered if she had inside her the ability to trust like that.

A few minutes later, Ava unlocked the house and showed Paige and Emmie to the guest room where they'd be staying. "I've been using it mostly for storage, but it does have a bed with fresh sheets."

Paige scanned the room, her eyes misty with gratitude. "This is perfect, Ava. Thank you."

"And the bathroom room is right in there, Emmie."

The little girl trotted off as Paige set her bags on the floor.

"You're welcome to anything in the fridge or pantry. I'm going by the office for a bit. When I get back, we'll talk about what's next."

Paige nodded, and Ava could see gratitude in her eyes.

On her way out, before she closed the door behind her, Ava glanced at the photos on the mantel. She wondered what it would be like to have her family here in Camden Grove.

When she pulled in at the office, Ava gripped the steering wheel a little tighter as she caught sight of the front of the building. The sign company had come while she was gone. Letters in a black, fluid font spread across the brick: CGFM. A line beneath separated the letters from the words Camden Grove Family Medicine.

She never dreamed she'd have her own clinic, but then a little twinge of something—maybe it was still fear—gripped her. Maybe words on a wall were just words on a wall.

When she unlocked the door, she slowly entered taking in a sight she'd never expected. The floor lay in a perfect parquet design. Upholstered chairs framed the wall, two by two, and a dark wood table with a peace lily in a planter she'd never seen sat at the center of the room. Current magazines lined a rack that had been hung in the perfect spot.

She looked beyond the receptionist's glass into the office. Desks and chairs were assembled, walls were painted, and even smoke detectors were installed and blinking. She passed through the

office area and walked to each of the three exam rooms, to
the kitchenette, and finally, to her personal office. Each space
was finished as if someone had waved a wand and made it all
spectacularly ready for business.

As she stepped back into the hall, a bulletin board, decorated in
shabby-chic burlap and string, drew her full attention. *Welcome to
Dr. Fenn's Office.* Centered perfectly on the board, hung the photo
that was an exact copy of the one she'd placed in her purse just
hours ago. Her with Logan at Old Fordham Mill.

The look on his face drew her closer. His eyes were as
mesmerizing as the day she stood with him in the water. She traced
the edge with her finger as if touching it could somehow bring it
back.

Beside the pinned photo, the string held a folded piece of paper
by its crease. It had her name on it. She slipped the paper from
the string and, before unfolding it, held it to her heart. Logan had
done what he said he'd do. He'd kept his word, despite all his new
challenges, despite what may have coursed through his mind after
Corbin showed up. He kept his promise, and with time to spare.

She scanned her surroundings again.

This *was* her place.

Then, she unfolded the paper.

Dear Ava,

*I've never been the best with words. Will you meet me at the Mill
this afternoon? Maybe by then, I'll have found a voice.*

Logan

Ava looked at the time. She folded the letter, plucked the photo
from the board, and darted out the door, never having searched for
Carly's keys, her exit causing the peace lily to dance on the table.

Chapter Fifty-Seven

Logan

When Logan pulled into the lot at the Old Mill, his pulse raced at the memory of Ava there not long ago. "You think this is really going to work?"

"Trust me." Carly winked. She jumped from the truck with her camera strapped around her neck.

He drew in a long, deep breath and opened the door. It was time to see if his heart could stand loving someone again.

Chapter Fifty-Eight

Ava

When Ava rounded the bend in the drive, Logan's truck sat parked in the same place it had been the day she first met him. Though it was the only vehicle in the gravel lot, Logan was nowhere to be seen. As she got out of her car, she heard the water wheel spinning over the hill toward the creek, buckets of water filling and spilling from each slow round.

As she took the worn path and descended the bank, a blanket—the same one they'd sat on weeks ago—came into view, spread in a perfect square on the grass by the creek, where it had been on the day of their shoot. The basket Jessie had used as a prop now waited in the center.

Her hand rose to her chest. "Logan," she whispered.

She searched the bank behind her. The noise of the water trickling from the wheel hushed her nervousness enough that she called his name more loudly.

Her voice carried over the water and echoed back. Then she heard a sound from the basket. She knelt on the blanket as the wicker crackled and wobbled. When she lifted the lid, a small, chocolate puppy nudged his wet nose against her hand.

"Oh, my goodness." She laughed. "Where did you come from?" Lifting him from the basket, she snuggled him against her neck as he kicked his hind legs to get closer and licked at her throat in soft, wet nibbles. When she finally calmed him, she saw the tag hanging from the thin, leather collar around his neck.

Coco.

An emotion that she'd pushed down for a long time, one that left her breathless now, welled up in her heart.

Then, she saw the note hanging from the handle of the basket. "Can I be yours?"

"I'm asking for me, not the dog." Logan's low voice penetrated every ounce of resolve she had left.

When she turned around, there he stood—the man she'd first fallen for at this very place, the one she'd come to love in such a short time but had held at arm's length for too long. She set the puppy at her feet and stood.

When he came close, he touched her face, stroked her cheek. She took his hand in hers, invited him to search the small of her back, and urged his arms to pull her closer.

Then, her fingers slipped into his hair. She touched his lips with her own. Not a kiss. The butterfly on a petal. The ebb and flow. The give and take of silent promises. His touch, a commitment; hers, a determination to answer his question.

Again. And again.

And again.

Chapter Fifty-Nine

Logan

Nothing had prepared Logan for how fully he wanted to accept all that was happening. As he stood there with Ava in his arms, opening his heart with every kiss, he felt the release of all the years of resentment he held deep inside for Eliza and her abandonment. The raw hurt floated away over the rolling water as Ava healed his wounds more with every touch.

Not until the sound of tires crackling against gravel roused their attention did Logan remember they weren't alone. The arrival of his parents was the cue he'd given Carly to come close enough to start snapping distant shots.

He looked down at the puppy, scampering around their feet. "I hope you won't mind sharing this little guy with Toby."

A broad smile spread across Ava's face. "I can't imagine anything I'd love more than that. To see his face . . . oh, Logan."

He looked toward the path. "He should be here any second. I arranged for Mom and Dad to bring him to the Mill."

"Logan." Ava shook her head. "Toby's lucky to have you." She touched his face. "I have a feeling I'm lucky too."

With one last lingering kiss, part two of Operation Peanut Butter began.

Toby's voice echoed over the bank before he came into sight. The puppy at their feet barked and scampered in the grass toward the sound. Over the tall broomsedge that lined the path to the water, Toby held a jar with a red top high enough to be seen before he was. Logan had asked his mother to let Toby bring some peanut butter with him to the mill.

Just as he rounded the bend in the path, Carly reached the side of the water wheel with her telephoto lens to capture more of the magic.

Logan slipped his hand in Ava's as they walked toward Toby's surprise.

"I brought the peanut butter, just like you said," Toby yelled above the grass. When he came into full view, the puppy met him at the foot of the bank, waddling against his weight to greet his new friend.

Toby's eyes widened as he dropped to his knees. He gently pulled the dog into his lap. The longer he snuggled against the excitement of the wiggling puppy, the more his eyes teared up. He raised the pup to his cheek, the squirming animal eager to lick his tears away.

Logan smiled at Ava, then loosened his hold from her long enough to kneel beside his son. "Well, Peanut Butter, what do you think?"

The boy sniffled as he turned over the puppy's nametag in his hand. "Coco?"

"Yeah, I've been thinking about that puppy you and Ava came up with to help you with your shots. Seems to me that since you two found a good use for an imaginary puppy, maybe you'd like to share a real one. What do you think?"

Toby looked at Ava and smiled through his tears. "Does that mean you'll be coming to our house a lot?"

Ava laughed and knelt at Logan's side. "I think that's a very safe bet."

Logan then turned to Toby and rubbed the puppy behind the ears. "Hey, come look." He rose and crossed to the basket on the blanket. "I bought a dog toy today, and guess what you're supposed to put inside it for Coco." He held up the red-topped jar.

"Peanut butter!" All three of them called out in unison.

For another hour, Logan and Ava lounged on the blanket as they watched Toby play with Coco. They laughed at the puppy rolling over the top of his new toy, trying to lick out his gooey treat. They held hands and ate peanut butter sandwiches and found their new beginning at the side of Old Fordham Creek Mill.

Off in the distance, Carly continued snapping golden candids of the start of something big.

Epilogue

Four Months Later

Ava stepped out of the exam room and to the counter, arm in arm with an elderly man, her last patient of the day. "Mr. Iverson, be sure to tell your wife I asked about her." She turned to Paige. "Do you mind getting a sample of that topical cream we got from the drug rep last week? I'd like Mr. Iverson to try it."

"Of course." Paige smiled as she rose to search the sample cabinet.

"Let's do a follow-up in a month." She nodded to the man. "I want to check that spot of eczema and see if we're making any progress."

The old man pulled off his glasses and cleaned them on the edge of his sweater as Ava handed him an appointment card she'd snagged from Paige's desk. "We're sure glad you came to our neck of the woods, Dr. Fenn. I hope you stick around for a while." The old man nodded.

With a wink, Paige put the sample on the counter in front of him as Ava patted Mr. Iverson on the arm. "How could I leave when I've got patients like you?"

As he shuffled to the lobby, Mr. Iverson waved over his shoulder at the women in the office, then disappeared behind the door.

While Ava charted the visit, the back door to the clinic opened, and Carly strolled in, arms loaded with photo albums. Setting her stack on the counter beside Ava, she blew a curl out of her face and put her hands on her hips. "Can you believe this?" Her eyes widened. "Look at all these accounts."

"Are you complaining?" Ava smirked.

"Of course not. I'm singing your praises. Jessie and I might not have stayed afloat if it hadn't been for you and Logan and that first blind-date shoot. And Jex, of course, who helped me with the idea in the first place. Now it's generated enough buzz that we need to hire another backup photographer to cover all the appointments."

"You two do have a flair behind the camera." Paige stood at the counter and opened one of the albums.

Ava leafed through the book on top. Paige was right. Carly and Jessie made some serious photo magic. "Just remember, you two are mine when the time comes."

"Can't wait for that. Everybody's ready to see the next installment. Your shoots are epic. First the blind-date thing, then the puppy shoot. Sheesh."

"You know you're a sneaky woman. I didn't even know you were at the mill that day." Ava turned another page in the album.

"Yes, I'd say you were in your own world. Lucky thing I made arrangements to get back to the Grove on my own, or you two would have forgotten I existed and left me there. Anyway, I'd be lying if I didn't say it was stupidly hard to leave you two alone while you finally opened up to the idea of each other." She sighed. "I was just glad that Logan wanted Toby's introduction to Coco captured for perpetuity."

"As I remember from the proofs, you sneaked in a couple of shots before the Carters brought Toby over," Ava said. "Thus, the whole sequel to the first shoot."

Carly shrugged. "How could you blame me? Those photos are like telling your love story without ever saying a word. Good grief, my clients ate it up. I've already got the bridal fair committee asking me for a layout of your wedding shots for one of their bigger city billboard campaigns. They're ready to slide it to Wyatt, hot off the press."

"Yeah"—Ava picked up another album—"Wyatt told Logan they contacted his ad firm when they found out he was Logan's brother."

"You two can't get away from it. You're hometown celebrities."

Ava rolled her eyes. "Maybe you can turn Paige into your next celebrity. She's settled in town now and—"

"Oh, no." Paige waved her hand. "Not this girl. No time for it since night school's back on the schedule. My focus is on a nursing degree now. Not a man."

"We'll see about that. You know it only takes an hour on a Saturday." Carly winked at Ava.

Just then, the clinic's back door opened again. A rambunctious and lanky chocolate lab bounded inside. Toby, Emmie, and Logan followed.

"Hey, Coco." Ava leaned down to nuzzle the dog around the neck. As she stood again, Toby hugged her beneath Logan's kiss.

"Ladies." Logan nodded then whispered in Ava's ear, "Hey, gorgeous."

"Hello, yourself. I've missed you."

Toby slipped from beneath them to ruffle Coco's ears, and Logan squeezed her tighter. "I'm finally done with all of Brashear's projects. He completed the walkthrough today and put his stamp of approval on the expansion."

Ava soaked up his warmth. "I knew he would. I think we should celebrate tonight after dog training."

"Yeah, me too." Toby opened a cookie jar filled with pretzels stationed on the counter. "I could play with Emmie, and you could go somewhere and eat vegetables."

"And what would you eat?" Logan's smile broadened, his dimples deepening beneath the growth of his beard.

"Miss Paige, do you have peanut butter?"

"I think we could come up with a jar, along with some vegetables." Paige grinned.

"Maybe you should just go with us to training so Coco knows who he's working for." Logan ruffled the boy's hair.

"Aw, okay." His protest was short-lived.

On the other side of the desk, Paige squeezed Emmie as the little girl scooted into her lap. "How was school today?"

Emmie leaned into her mother. "Okay. I had. A good day." Her halting patterns of conversation had become a welcome sound to everybody as she'd become more talkative the last few months.

"Would you like to give Coco a treat?" Paige rolled her chair toward the desk drawer as the dog wagged his tail. After Emmie commanded him to sit, he complied, looked at her expectantly, and cocked his head.

"Immediate obedience. I like that." Paige scratched him behind the ear as Emmie fed him the treat. "Training must be going well, huh, Toby?"

The little boy climbed on the stepping stool beside the counter. "You're not gonna believe what he can do already. He's learning to sniff out my lows."

"Speaking of." Logan turned to Ava. "Are you ready to go? We've got just enough time to get to our training appointment."

Ava slipped out of his arms. "I'll grab my bag."

Carly sighed. "I've got to go too." She stacked the albums. "I just wanted to show you the power you wield before I go pack for my weekend trip."

"What?" Ava stepped from her office. "Another weekend trip? Sounds like you and Jex are getting pretty serious. When am I gonna meet this guy? It's been months, and I still haven't had a proper introduction."

"Yeah, turns out, developing his camera prototype with this new company has been more time-consuming than he thought, but I promise, soon."

"I'll expect a full weekend report." Ava slipped her sweater off the peg.

"As always. Ta-ta," Carly called over her shoulder as she exited the way she came.

"Paige, do you care to lock up?" Ava checked her watch as Toby said goodbye to Emmie, and Logan started toward the door, Coco at his heels.

Paige waved them on. "I've got it. Have a good weekend."

As the back door closed behind Ava, Paige began shutting down her computer while Emmie trotted off to the kitchenette with a tablet and headphones to wait for Paige.

When someone came through the front entry, she didn't look up at first. "Sorry, the doctor just left, and I was just about to lock—" When she raised her line of sight to the visitor, she looked directly into the eyes of the man she thought she'd never see again.

"Paige?"

Her mouth went dry, and her heart began to race. She hadn't seen him in nearly six years. She slipped from her desk and made a conscious effort to put herself between him and the photo of Emmie on her desk. The last thing she wanted him to see was that their smiles so naturally matched.

Dear Reader,

Thank you so much for spending time inside the pages of *Picture This*! Want to see more of **Logan and Ava's future?** Check out this **BONUS EPILOGUE!**

Interested in the **NEXT BOOK in the series**? Check out **WAITING FOR YOU HERE!**

Happy reading, Tessa

Acknowledgments

When I was six or seven years old, I had a healthy fear of the
dark. I'd ask my mom to come to my bedside nightly and hold
my hand until I went to sleep. One night, Dad convinced me that
I was a big girl and could do courageous things, like go to sleep
without Mom's handholding. He told me that when I got scared,
I could try thinking of something I enjoyed—maybe something
I liked to eat. That night, for whatever reason, I thought about
oranges—orange slices, orange juice, orange sherbet, baskets of
oranges, oranges on trees, grocery displays of oranges, truckloads
of oranges—until I must've fallen asleep. The next morning, I felt
like I'd won a blue ribbon in a county fair. I still love oranges,
and I still think of that story, especially when fear of some one
thing or another sets in. I was blessed to be born to a mother who
concerned herself with so much more than just allaying childhood
fears with holding my hand. She's always been the very definition
of a strong woman. I was also born under the care of a dad who
worked tirelessly and inspired not only my sense of independence,

but the courage it would take to do hard things throughout my life. It's taken all they've taught me to start this writing journey. Thanks, Mom and Dad.

I once had a teacher who wrote a marginal note at the top of my magnum opus of a senior English research paper: "Have you ever thought about writing?" Mrs. Sylvia Abell, someday I'll see you again and tell you just how many times I've reflected on that comment in the margins. It was anything but marginal.

To my six kids, you are my entire universe. You continue to amaze me with your talents, your patience, your ability to observe and learn from books, from people, from experiences. You teach me every day, and I couldn't do this without your love (and willingness to "close my door, please" and let Mom write).

To my husband, if you hadn't had faith in me, there would be no acknowledgements page. Thanks for asking, baby!

Finally, I am so grateful for my Heavenly Father who knows me and sees me and loves me despite my shortcomings. I am His.

About Author

As a child, Tessa Kinkade composed her first stories in chalk on her bedroom door. Editing was much more fun that way. Her workspace nowadays is still her bedroom, and she can often be found propped among favorite bed pillows, tapping away on a laptop with a water bottle by her side (though she continues to look for easy ways to edit). Tessa has spent much of her career in education, and in her spare time—when her children were old enough to get their own cereal bowls from the cabinet—she began writing her first novel, 15 minutes at a time.

In the past, she's worked in a rape crisis center, kept bees, organized large events, run half marathons, and traveled most of the contiguous United States, drawing upon all her career experiences and hobbies to enrich her writing. She loves to create characters who face life-altering challenges yet find a happily-ever-after through the struggle.

When she's not bingeing on research, outlining, or drafting her next novel, you'll find her dreaming about a beach vacation where she might also find a lighthouse to explore.

Connect with Tessa for a free short story, information on new releases, newsletter sign-up, and more at https://www.tessakinkade.com

Also, find her on social media:

https://instagram.com/tessakinkade

https://facebook.com/tessakinkade